PRAISE FOR WILLIAM BERNHARDT

"*Exposed* has everything I love in a thriller: intricate plot twists, an ensemble of brilliant heroines, and jaw-dropping drama both in and out of the courtroom. William Bernhardt knows how to make the law come alive."

— TESS GERRITSEN, NYT-BESTSELLING
AUTHOR OF THE RIZZOLI & ISLES
THRILLERS

"*Splitsville* is a winner—well-written, with fully developed characters and a narrative thrust that keeps you turning the pages."

— GARY BRAVER, BESTSELLING AUTHOR
OF *TUNNEL VISION*

"Bernhardt is the undisputed master of the courtroom thriller."

— *LIBRARY JOURNAL*

"William Bernhardt is a born stylist, and his writing through the years has aged like a fine wine...."

— STEVE BERRY, BESTSELLING AUTHOR OF
THE KAISER'S WEB

"Once started, it is hard to let [*The Last Chance Lawyer*] go, since the characters are inviting, engaging, and complicated....You will enjoy it."

— *CHICAGO DAILY LAW BULLETIN*

"[*Court of Killers*] is a wonderful second book in the Daniel Pike series...[A] top-notch, suspenseful crime thriller with excellent character development..."

— TIMOTHY HOOVER, FICTION AND NONFICTION AUTHOR

"I could not put *Trial by Blood* down. The plot is riveting —with a surprise after the ending, when I thought it was all over....This book is special."

— NIKKI HANNA, AUTHOR OF *CAPTURE LIFE*

"*Judge and Jury is* a fast-paced, well-crafted story that challenges each major character to adapt to escalating attacks that threaten the very existence of their unique law firm."

— RJ JOHNSON, AUTHOR OF *THE TWELVE STONES*

"*Final Verdict* is a must read with a brilliant main character and surprises and twists that keep you turning pages. One of the best novels I've read in a while."

— ALICIA DEAN, AWARD-WINNING AUTHOR OF *THE NORTHLAND CRIME CHRONICLES*

EXPOSED

EXPOSED

WILLIAM BERNHARDT

BABYLON
BOOKS

For my mother,
the wisest woman in the world.

"I raise up my voice—not so that I can shout, but so that those without a voice can be heard."

— MALALA YOUSAFZAI

PART I

THREE'S COMPANY

Chessie recalled something her grandfather told her when she won the fifty-yard dash at a middle-school track meet. "Even the fastest girl alive can't outrun all the predators out there."

She liked thinking of herself as the fastest girl alive, though it probably wasn't true. She wasn't a superhero. She hadn't been doused with radioactive chemicals or struck by lightning or anything like that. But she had been the fastest person in her high school, and now she was the captain of her college soccer team, in no small part due to her speed. Also her dazzling charisma, she liked to think. But mostly her speed.

In truth, she'd always been a bit on the shy side, and that had intensified since she lost her parents. Competing in sports was easier than making small talk on a first date or figuring out what to do at a rave. She wasn't particularly bookish and she would never qualify as a mathlete, so she was grateful for the speed. If not for her twinkletoes and Title IX, she might have nothing at all.

So what brought her to a frat party? I mean, she should know better, right? And yet, here she was. She had resolved to get out more. Although she loved her teammates, occasionally she wanted to talk about something other than the Rivelino and the Cruyff Turn.

Okay, sure, she was flattered to be asked. Not that she was homely or anything, but she didn't go in for a lot of makeup or haircare, and that plus the shyness and a physique that intimidated most Big Men on Campus, left her alone most Friday nights.

She hadn't been on a single date since she started college. Not once. Was that her fault? Did everyone assume that since she was captain of the team she must be a lesbian? That was so cliché and totally...wrong. She thought. She was pretty sure. She liked boys. Or would, if one gave her a chance.

She was totally caught off guard when the guy who sat in front of her in nutrition class invited her to a party. Was it a prank? Was he making fun of her? Was this one of those bashes where frat boys compete to nail the ugliest girl in school?

Whatevs. Bottom line—he asked and here she was.

Loud music. Loud talking, necessary to be heard over the music. Alcohol flowing from abundant portals. Herbal scents she wasn't cool enough to identify. Heavy doses of Axe, which she could identify. Lots of crazy dancing—in some cases, too crazy to be called dancing. Her grandfather once tried to teach her the Batusi. That was dignified compared to most of what she saw here at the Beta house. A few people were attempting to have actual conversations, but she suspected the chat topics were not binomial equations or the work of Caravaggio.

She made a few unsuccessful attempts at chatting, but mostly she listened. Didn't take her long to realize that, although some fraternities claimed they'd cleaned up their acts, nothing had changed much. Small wonder the Abolish Greek Life movement was gaining steam. They still made racist remarks. And sexist remarks. This group had a few token members of color, but it was still essentially a white rich boys' club. And they still treated women like meat, potential conquests. Notches on the belt. They acted as if they had the inside track, as if they knew how the world really worked, though she suspected most had privileged upbringings and hadn't worked a day in their lives.

Did she need this? Absolutely not. Especially in the middle of soccer season, and when online news outlets and campus police were focusing on all the women who had disappeared. The so-called Seattle Strangler was on the prowl and she was hanging out with a wolf pack. This was a bad idea from the get-go.

Just when she'd convinced herself to leave, the guy who'd invited her strolled up, a goofy lopsided grin on his face. What was his name? Brian. She thought. Several inches taller, perfect hair, great smile. His red eyes and loose manner suggested he'd had a few.

"You came!" He virtually shouted, with a bug-eyed expression and jazz hands fluttering overhead.

"You invited me."

"But you actually showed."

"You thought I was too stuck up?"

"I thought you were too cool."

She relaxed a bit. "I try to be open to new experiences."

"How are you doing in class? I love nutrition. Like, nutrition is my life. Call me Mr. Nutrition."

She probably wouldn't. "It's interesting enough."

"I bet it's easy for you. You're awesome."

"I am?"

"On the soccer field."

"You saw one of our games?"

"I've seen all your games. I'm like your groupie."

She had groupies? Cute groupies? "You should've said hello sooner."

"I wanted to. I sat next to you in class on purpose. But..." His voice trailed a bit. "It took me a while to work up the courage to speak to you. Aloud, I mean."

This was too much for her to handle. Her head was spinning,

and not just because of the blaring music. "I can't believe you come to our games."

"I love those games. I love the way you move." His voice dropped. "To be honest, when I watch you run across the field... I get kinda hard."

Okay, she did not need to hear that part.

"No pressure or anything, but would you like to step outside? Get some fresh air? We could probably have a deeper conversation if we got away from this electronic hook-track crap people pretend is music."

She was still fixated on his previous statement, but a chance to leave this den of iniquity was welcome. They walked through the front door—a few guys whistled and winked as they passed—and entered the yard. She admired the English country-house façade, white pillars and brown oak shutters. A balcony on the upper floor.

He motioned her to the side of the house. Dark here, she noted. Darker than she expected. She doubted anyone could see them from the street. And there was no way anyone in the house could hear them.

Maybe this was a bad idea.

"Aw, man, this is so much better," he said, pressing a hand against the side of his head. "My ears were ringing."

"They do look red," she replied. "What do you do when you're not in nutrition class?"

He shrugged. "Like everyone else in the frat. Mandatory Study Hall. Mandatory functions. Mandatory meetings."

"Do they let you pee by yourself?"

"Usually." He did a double take. "Wait, you were joking, weren't you?"

She pointed. "Nothing slips past you."

"Maybe I'm not at my best right now. I'm...well, I'm a little overwhelmed. Being here. With you. Alone."

She tried to change the subject. "You must do something other than frat stuff."

"I like music. Video games. A good burger."

"Hobbies?"

He hesitated a moment, as if weighing options. "I'm kinda into...strangulation games."

She wasn't expecting that response. "Did I hear you correctly?

"It's not dangerous. Just good fun. Have you smoked weed?"

"Once." And it made her sick. "Didn't do much for me."

"Me neither. But you can get a high six times stronger and better."

"From strangulation games?"

"Bingo. Wanna try?"

She took a step back. "I don't think that's for me."

"You never know."

"I think I do. It—"

"—could be perfect. You're an athlete, so you can't take drugs. You're in training, so you can't do alcohol. This high is stronger and leaves no traces in your bloodstream."

Another step backward. "Still a hard pass. Maybe we should go back—"

She thought she was fast, but he proved faster. His arm sprang out like a cobra. He grabbed her by the neck with surprising strength, whirled her around and slammed her against the side of the house.

Her head reeled. Bursts of light flashed before her eyes. A thousand bells thundered in her ears. She couldn't muster the strength to resist.

"Just go with it," he said, his voice breathy and urgent. "You're gonna love this."

"I...won't," she managed. "Let go."

"Trust me. I've done this before."

She tried to squirm away, but she couldn't get free. What was wrong with her? She knew she was stronger than this pampered preppie. But she couldn't get her head together.

"Don't struggle. Relax. Enjoy it."

She gritted her teeth and tried to kick him, but he was too close, pressing against her, blocking her arms and legs.

And all at once, she remembered the news stories about the disappearing women...

Oh my God. *Him?* She was going to be the next...

"If you want," he whispered, "a little arousal makes the experience even more powerful. Like an orgasm etched in rocket fuel."

"I—don't—" She twisted from side to side, but nothing seemed to work. She felt limp and uncoordinated. He counteracted her every attempt to escape, usually before she'd begun it. He had this routine down cold. Her speed wasn't going to help her. Not while she was trapped under his icy grip.

He was fumbling with the button at the front of her jeans. She felt numb, dizzy. Just a few more moments and she wouldn't notice anything...

"Hey! What's going on back there?"

Her eyes flew open. Someone was racing toward them. She couldn't make out the details, but the voice was male. As he approached, she saw that he had a cast on his left arm and a slight limp. He was older—too old to be a frat boy.

"Screw off, Grandpa," Brian said. "This doesn't concern you."

"Let go of the girl."

"Make me." Brian grinned a little. "Did you think you were going to be the knight in shining armor? Were you going to play Superman? We're just having fun. Consenting adults and all that."

The newcomer looked straight at Chessie. "Is this consensual?"

It was a struggle, but she managed to shake her head no.

"Let go of the girl. I'm counting to three."

"Look, loser, I'll call some of my buddies to des—"

Before he could finish the word, the interloper kicked Brian in the back of his knee—hard. Mr. Nutrition crumbled.

Chessie clutched her neck. He'd hurt her badly. Her skin was tender. But she could breathe again.

The newcomer hovered over Brian as he lay on the ground. "Two choices. Disappear right now and never come near this woman again. Or I call the cops and report that you're the Seattle Strangler and I just witnessed an attempted homicide."

The frat boy released a string of swear words. But in the end, he brushed himself off and skittered away.

"I don't think he'll bother you again," the man said. "Are you okay?"

She was still massaging her neck. "I'll live." She drew in a deep breath. "I thought I was toast. Thank you."

"No big deal. I live near here. I power-walk every night. Thought I heard someone struggling, though it's a miracle I could hear anything given how much noise that party is making."

Although the light was low, she got a clearer view of her rescuer. He was older than the college kids, but hardly old enough to be called Grandpa. Seemed friendly. Earnest. "Again, thanks. What happened to your arm?"

"Oh. That. Stupidest story imaginable. Fell out of a tree. How'd you get hooked up with that loser?"

"God knows. He's in one of my classes."

"And that meant he could assault you? You should probably report this. He might try the same routine on someone else. Or you might be able to sue him. I have a lawyer friend who specializes in representing women. She might be willing to help."

"I'd rather just forget about it."

"What did he want?"

She shrugged. "He talked about...strangulation games."

"What?"

"I think the idea is that you get a buzz from almost dying but not quite. Supposed to be super-powerful."

"Unless his timing is off. And then you don't get a buzz. Because you're dead."

"Right. Definitely not something I care to pursue."

He took a step back. "I should probably finish my walk. If

you're sure you're okay."

"I am. I really appreciate what you did."

"No problem. Maybe next time—screen your dates? Pass on the guys who are into living dangerously. It isn't worth it."

"Good advice."

"Plus, he was doing it completely wrong."

"Wha—?"

Before she could react, she saw his hand rise and felt her head smash against the house, this time so hard she almost lost consciousness. It took her a few moments to realize he'd thrust his knee between her legs. Pain radiated in two opposing directions.

He gripped her neck and pounded her head back several times. She started to scream, but a fist collided with the side of her face before she had a chance. Blood dripped from her nose and lip.

She summoned all her strength to resist—

And he knocked it out of her with a single blow. Her head drooped.

The fake cast fell from his arm. He pinned her back with both hands.

"This is the proper grip," he explained. "The hand has to go way back, pressed up against the throat, thumb under the hyoid. That's how you induce strangulation. Trust me, I know."

She could barely whisper. "You're—You're—"

"Not so much into the twisted orgasm thing. I've got a different endgame."

"Please." It was more air than voice. Barely audible. "Please don't—"

"Say goodnight, Gracie." His hand tightened and her lungs constricted. She struggled for air but couldn't find any. Her head was blanketed with blackness.

Her last thought was about who would captain the soccer team for the rest of the season. Because she knew it wouldn't be her.

2

K enzi had a problem. Her client, Amanda Conners, the wife in the divorce, had not performed well on the witness stand. Not that she lied or anything. But her nervousness translated to a cold unemotional delivery that had not moved Judge Barton in the slightest. Amanda's husband, David Conners, on the other hand, despite being possibly the worst excuse for a husband in the history of mankind, was warm, witty, and persuasive, scoring point after point. Though the division of marital property was supposed to be a matter of cold economics, Kenzi knew that judge sympathy could make a huge difference.

She felt desperate. This case was slipping through her fingers.

"Did you contribute to the household account?" she asked the husband, hoping to score an easy point.

"When I was working," David calmly replied.

"Which hasn't been for more than two years."

"I've been writing a novel."

"Which you haven't finished. Much less sold."

"It's a long-term investment. Amanda agreed to pay the bills for a while so I could create something that might pay the bills for many years to come."

He had a slick answer for everything. She felt perspiration beading on the sides of her head—a sure sign that she was losing. She hoped this didn't mess up her side shave—buzzed jet black hair on the left, flipped to shoulder-length on the right. Behind her, she saw Amanda struggling to maintain a poker face. She had been warned not to react, not to shake her head or put on emotive displays of disagreement that irritated judges and made you look untrustworthy. Amanda had suffered a lot of abuse at this man's hands, both physical and verbal, but she was keeping her anger in check.

"Did you help around the house?"

"Not so much. Amanda preferred to do that work herself. She's a control freak."

Another clever response—an insult to mask his marital deficiencies. This man could tap dance. But so could she. Figuratively speaking. She was wearing Sorel Ella sneakers and passing them off as court-appropriate dress shoes. Sensible footwear was an essential element of the intelligent professional woman's look. But at the moment, she was focused on tactics. She needed to turn this case around—fast. "Did you cook? Mow the lawn? Pay the bills?"

"Not so much. Writing requires a great deal of focus."

"So your contribution to this partnership was basically...nothing."

"Well, I did save Amanda's life."

A decent response. "You're referring to the convenience-store incident."

"Yes. We went in to pick up some coffee. A man pulled a gun. Amanda fainted. I stood up to the armed robber."

What happened on this dreadful day was disputed, but unfortunately, Kenzi's client had passed out and there were no security cameras, so her ability to question his account was limited. And that was a problem. A judge could forgive a great deal of uselessness for a man who had heroically faced down a huge assailant with a big gun, especially given the wave of shooting incidents that seemed to plague this nation on a daily basis. "You don't know that Amanda would've died."

"I do. Because I was there. I saw the man." David's demeanor remained calm, but his implication was apparent. *I was there, you weren't.* "Everyone else fled. I stood my ground. The creep could kill a helpless woman lying on the floor, but not a true man looking him straight in the eyes. He backed down."

Kenzi shifted to an arena that might give him less to brag about. "How about at home? Have you always kept your cool there?"

"I believe I've done an admirable job of maintaining my temper in the face of...extraordinary behavior. Amanda can be completely irrational, particularly when she doesn't get her way —which always offends a control freak—and decides to throw one of her perpetual pity parties. She needs help. I mean, psychiatric help. Which I have suggested repeatedly. But she refuses."

"You used to be a lawyer, didn't you?"

He nodded. "Got my degree from Gonzaga. Practiced for a few years. Didn't care for it. Writing suits my temperament much better."

Maybe this was a way to poke a hole in his likable facade. Bait him into insulting the judge's profession. "What was it about practicing law you disliked?"

"Frankly, the pervasive lack of ethics amongst some members of the bar." He turned his head slightly. "No disrespect to your honor intended. I'm talking more about trial lawyers, the hotshots who take cases and milk them to death for fees, over-billing clients and making conflicts worse rather than resolving them. I think it's disgraceful."

Kenzi took a handkerchief from her satchel and mopped the sides of her head. "Are you thinking of anyone in particular?"

He shrugged. "It's a well-known fact that divorce attorneys are the worst."

"Excuse me?"

"You know it's true."

"Divorce attorneys may be unpopular, since they have to deal with one of the most difficult, painful experiences in life—"

"They're shysters. Most divorces could be resolved in an afternoon. How long has this one been dragging on? Eight months?"

She batted the handkerchief against her forehead. "If you have something to say, just say it."

He smiled slightly. "Defensive much?"

"Not at all." Her voice quavered. "Because your petty little comments have nothing whatsoever to do with me."

"So you say. But I note your face is flushed and your voice is trembling. The truth hurts, doesn't it?"

She knew her voice was too loud, too accusatory. "No. No, it doesn't hurt at all. Not a bit. Because it isn't true."

"Sure."

Her voice grew even louder. "You don't know what you're talking about. You're just...a quitter. That's what you are. Someone who couldn't hack it in the law so now you're insulting those who can."

Judge Barton cut in. "Counsel...are you okay?"

"I'm fine, your honor."

"You seem a bit...upset. We could take a short break."

"I'm not letting this man off the hook." Her voice sounded uneven, desperate. "Don't you see what he's doing? He's out to get me."

The judge appeared perplexed. "Do you have a fever? You look somewhat—"

"I'm fine. Just fine. Back off already." She whirled on the witness. "It's this SOB. Trying to win his case by taking potshots at me."

"Counsel, I will not tolerate personal invective. It's not necessary and—"

"I think it *is* necessary." She ran up to the witness stand, beads of sweat flying from her face. "What right do you have to accuse me of anything? You're just a deadbeat husband."

"Better than being a divorce lawyer," he murmured.

"Is it? Is it really?" She paced around the courtroom, swerving erratically from one direction to the next. "I had a husband once too, and you're just like him. None of you can be trusted. You do anything you want and the law looks the other way. It's disgusting. You think you can get away with anything. Well, not anymore, loser. Your day of reckoning has arrived."

The witness' eyebrows knitted together. "Your honor...I believe I'm being threatened."

"I know you're being threatened," Judge Barton replied. "Counsel, you need to lie down for a few moments and—"

"And give him everything he wants?" she shouted. "Let him get away with murder? I'm sick to death of men getting away with murder!"

The judge banged his gavel. "Okay, that's it. We're taking a recess to—"

"*No!*" Kenzi's scream pierced the courtroom. "If the law won't stop bastards like him, I'll take the law into my own hands!" She reached into her satchel, grabbed something, and pointed it toward the witness stand. "I'll kill you myself!"

Someone in the gallery shrieked. David leapt out of his chair and cowered behind the judge's bench. The bailiff seemed unsure what to do. All eyes were on Kenzi.

Who was smiling.

What she had pulled out was a small black handheld hair dryer.

"What's the problem?" she asked. "Not in the mood for a blow dry?"

The courtroom slowly relaxed...in total confusion.

The witness peeked around the edge of the judge's bench.

Judge Barton's voice sounded dry and cracked. "Ms. Rivera...I need you to explain yourself."

"I should think no explanation is necessary, your honor." She pointed. "Behold the mighty hero of the 7-11. Cringing at the hem of your robe."

The witness slowly rose. "I thought...I thought..."

"Yeah," Kenzi said. "I know what you thought. What I want the court to consider is whether it seriously believes this coward stood up to an armed robber. I think he ran and hid. Just like he did today."

The judge slowly began to smile.

"And honestly," Kenzi continued, "if he's terrified by a five-foot-six, one-hundred-and-five-pound Latinx divorce lawyer, how did he handle a six-foot-two, two-hundred-and-ten-pound tattooed bodybuilder? I think he recoiled behind the beer cans."

The judge nodded. "I begin to see your point, counsel."

So did David's lawyer. "Your honor, I object. This courtroom...stunt was deceptive and highly irregular. Counsel is engaging in theatrics that are...confusing."

The judge tilted his head to one side. "Oh, I think she made her point rather clearly..."

"This was grossly improper conduct. I move for a mistrial."

"You can do that. And I would have to consider it. But you can't put the genie back in the bottle. Many people in this courtroom witnessed your client's reaction."

"Then I move for sanctions. Ms. Rivera's behavior violated the Rules of Professional Conduct."

"Which provision?"

"I don't know exactly, but..."

"Is there a provision that precludes pretending to be crackers?"

"I'm sure it never occurred to the framers that anyone would ever—"

"Right. We don't penalize lawyers for being clever." He turned to Kenzi. "And regardless of what you think of her tactics, Ms. Rivera is definitely clever. Pretty good actress, too."

She fanned her face with her hands. "Gosh. Thanks, your honor."

"You fooled everyone in the courtroom. Even my trusty bailiff."

Actually, she'd tipped off the bailiff in advance so he wouldn't interfere. But the judge didn't need to know that. "Your honor, I'm done with this witness. We're ready to submit the case and I urge the court to adopt my client's recommendations for the division of the marital estate."

"I suspected as much." Judge Barton gathered his papers and rose. "You're a divorce lawyer, Ms. Rivera, and that may cause others to give you grief. But I'll say this—you are never boring."

3

K enzi strode down the sidewalks of downtown Seattle heading for her office building, just a few blocks from the courthouse. She felt like a conquering hero and hoped that energy translated to her livestream.

"So that's how it went down, KenziKlan. A bit of amateur theatrics and justice was served. But let me note that this problem would never have occurred if my client had kept records and retained better evidence of her husband's abuse. It would be nice if there were no toxic males out there, but there are. Some good ones, too, I hear, but it seems like the good guys are harder to find every day."

She whipped around a corner, dodging passersby and clinging to the right where she was less likely to cause a collision. "Remember KenziKlan, you have value. You have worth. No one has the right to abuse you, verbally or physically, or to tell lies about you. Use that phone in your pocket and take pictures. Make contemporaneous diary entries—real ones, not self-serving Gone Girl records. Talk to friends. If he hurts you, see a doctor immediately. And then leave him. I don't care if you have children. That's not an excuse for becoming a victim. Take the kids with you. If he's abusing you now, he'll be abusing them a heartbeat later. Pack your bags and get some help."

She was almost at the front door and streaming was forbidden inside the office. This was an edict from the senior partners and a great example of a bill of attainder, since it was a rule created to restrict one person—her. She wasn't surprised when it passed. The law was absolutely horny for rules, and lawyers tended to be the same way.

"That's all for now, KenziKlan. I'll keep you up-to-date on my next adventure. Hashtag KenziKlan. Hashtag RiveraLaw. Hashtag TimesUp. Hashtag GirlPower. Hashtag LoveIs-AllWeNeed."

She glimpsed her reflection as she stood before the elevator doors. Not bad, if she did say so herself. She was trying to be less —what was her sister's word?—*flashy*, but surely that didn't mean she couldn't care about her appearance. Just maybe not obsess on it. An Alexander McQueen double-breasted blazer paired with a matching pencil skirt perfectly offset her beautiful brown skin and was bound to improve the quality of her legal work, right? If she knew anything, it was that when you looked attractive—men tended to underestimate you.

She arrived on the fourteenth floor, Ground Zero for Rivera & Perez, known around town as "Splitsville" because they'd made a fortune handling divorces. Her grandfather founded the firm and her father built it into an empire, the most successful Latinx-controlled firm in this part of the country. Her father also felt that appearances mattered, which is why the firm was bedecked with furnishings and decorations designed to impress, like the authentic mahogany furniture, some of it actual antiques, and the artwork showcased in backlit, enclosed display cases.

Speaking of her father, there stood the man himself, Alejandro Rivera, at the receptionist's desk. Just shooting the breeze with the woman he paid to look fabulous and greet clients with a high-toned British accent?

No. He was waiting for her. But it couldn't be too bad. If it was, he would've summoned her to his office. *"Buenos días, papá."*

He nodded. "Hear you scored a big victory in court today."

"Word travels fast."

"I've known Judge Barton for years. He was impressed enough to call me. Though he also warned that some of the other judges might not have been amused."

Barton cut her slack because he knew her daddy? That spoiled the whole thing. "You taught me to always know my judge. Most important thing, you said."

"Indeed. Walk with me."

She noticed it was not a request. She took her position beside him as he slowly strolled. To her surprise, they headed not toward his office, but hers. He had recently resigned his position as managing partner to her younger and unworthy brother, Gabriel, but she knew he was still running everything. What was the purpose of this little meet-and-greet?

"Everything good with Candice?" Candice was the woman her father married a few years ago, after he divorced her mother.

"Está bien. She's busy with boards and committee meetings. I rarely even see her. But I think she's happy."

"Glad to hear it."

"Kenzi, I reviewed your billables last month. They're down. Significantly."

Now we're getting to it. "Yes. After the all-consuming murder trial, I thought I should spend some time with Hailee." Surely he wouldn't disapprove of her spending time with his granddaughter.

"Wonderful girl."

"Been spending more time at the gym. Trying to get swole." She winked. "And I've been hanging out with Emma. I think we're getting to be something close to friends." Another obvious ploy. Emma was her younger sister. His youngest daughter. And he knew how reclusive and antisocial Emma could be.

"If you can break Emma out of her shell, you will have accomplished something truly extraordinary."

"I knew you'd understand."

"But." He turned abruptly and looked directly at her. "This is a business. We have bills to pay. We're here to make a profit."

"I'm the highest billing attorney in this firm."

"Were."

"You're hassling me because of one month? Isn't this an over-reaction?"

"When my highest billing attorney starts to slip, I have to investigate. We don't want Crozier catching up with us." Lou Crozier was the head partner at Crozier & Crozier, their top competition. "Got to make sure we're financially secure. It's my job."

"I thought that was Gabe's job now."

A thin smile crossed his face. "Gabriel is extremely busy. And delivering admonitions is not his strong suit. Especially not to his strong-willed big sister."

Which, in her mind, explained why the strong-willed big sister should've become managing partner. "It's an aberration. Not a pattern."

"So you say. But I have to wonder. Especially after your recent foray into..." His lips actually curled. "Criminal law. A case that consumed enormous amounts of your time but generated little profit. And you pulled Emma away from her work as well."

"My client—" She stopped herself. Daddy didn't want to hear excuses.

"I worry about you losing your focus. Becoming distracted. Like during those years you spent reading novels and interning at a psychiatric clinic."

"You mean—when I got my Masters degree?"

"You're a lawyer now. I need to know that this murder case was a one-time anomaly. And that in the future, you'll devote yourself to more profitable work."

Wasn't she a little old to be hauled out to the woodshed?

Still, he was being nice, at least by his standards, so she'd try to do the same. "I'll bring my billables back, Pops. Promise."

"There's still the matter of the deficient hours..."

"I'll make it up, trust me."

He nodded and began walking again. "I knew I could count on you. Of all my children, you're the one who's most like me."

And yet, she thought, you chose my brother to be your successor. Not because I didn't work hard, and not because I wasn't a good lawyer.

Because I didn't have a Y-chromosome.

BY THE TIME she arrived at her private office, Kenzi found the aforementioned sister, Emma, chatting up her assistant, Sharon. This was an appealing development. Emma didn't normally do divorce work and consequently officed several floors beneath them, in the so-called "basement." She rarely ventured out. But after she helped Kenzi with the case her father called "an anomaly," Emma had spent much more time upstairs.

"Hey, team," Kenzi said, strolling up to Sharon's desk. "What's shaking with my sisters?"

"Caught your livestream, girl," Sharon said. "Great stuff. Did you really pull a hair dryer on that man?"

"With devastating results. Apparently he's terrified of hot air."

"I bet the look in your eye was what sold it. I've seen you when you get fierce. I'd duck for cover, too." Sharon was African American and endlessly chic, with a curly bob cut and a blouse with more colors than the rainbow. "How did the judge take it?"

"He didn't throw me in jail, so I suppose that's a win." They all laughed. "Actually, I think he enjoyed it."

"You do know how to charm the judges. He probably thought that mean-girl look was sexy."

"Eww." Emma pulled a face. "That's a mental image I won't soon shake."

"You know, the tone of your livestreams has changed," Sharon added. "Ever since the murder case. Because you've changed."

"You may be right." She froze. "Wait. How have I changed?"

"For starters, every conversation I have with you now is a cross-examination."

"That's not true. Yesterday we were talking about breakfast cereal."

"True."

"And the day before we talked about that cute guy in the mail room. And—"

Sharon leaned in and put on her best Perry Mason voice. "And isn't it true that we once talked about cereal instead of law?"

Kenzi pursed her lips. "Okay, I hear what you're saying. I'll work on it."

Emma jumped in. "Did I see you talking with our *papi?*"

Kenzi nodded. "The usual. 'Why aren't you working night and day?'"

"At least he knows you exist. I went to Nepal and didn't bill anything for two months. I'm not sure he even noticed."

"He noticed. But he considers you an ancillary income stream. We get more divorce clients because they know you might also be able to cover any criminal offshoots. Whereas he expects me to keep the firm afloat singlehandedly."

"Shouldn't Gabe be doing the dirty work now?"

"Should be. Isn't."

"Because he's afraid of you."

"It isn't me. He's conflict averse."

"He's afraid of you," Emma insisted. "*El cobarde.* He's been afraid of you since he was four and you threatened to pull down his swimsuit and throw him in the pool."

"Sink or swim. Best way to learn, isn't it?"

Emma and Sharon both answered at once. "*No!*"

Kenzi laughed. "Emma, look at you. Talking to people, joking around. Not acting as if you hate everyone on earth or you're an alien from another planet who doesn't understand how humans think. Maybe it's time for you to move out of the basement."

"No thanks. Happy where I am."

"Might be good for you."

"Baby steps, Kenzi."

"Fine, fine."

"By the way," Sharon said, "be careful with Henry's birthday spread. The cheese quiche is about five hundred calories a bite." Her voice dropped. "Damn good, though."

"Did you take some early samples?"

"Had to."

"You're the firm praegustator?"

"Appointed to birthday duty."

"Why you?"

"As if you didn't know," Emma answered. "Women are treated differently than men in this firm. Probably every firm. Female associates are given clerical duties while male associates are given motions and contracts. Women are expected to look good and dress well to keep up the firm image, while men are allowed to dress...well, like Gabe. Women are assigned party duty and care-giving jobs and anything that involves nurturing or human compassion." She paused. "Of course, there's a reason for that last one."

"Women are paid less and expected to do more," Sharon added.

"But if women act like men, they're called mean, or ice queens, or bitches or...worse."

"We're expected to defer to men and hold our tongues, and we're punished if we don't."

"They can't hold my tongue," Kenzi replied. "I'm going to march into Gabe's office and—"

"Not now you aren't, girl." Sharon wagged her finger. "You got a client waiting in your office."

"Okay. The rant can wait. Who is it?"

"New client. Divorce."

"Rich?"

"Judging from the shoes, yes."

"That will make *Papi* happy. Anything unusual?"

Sharon's head danced back and forth. "You could say that. You got two people waiting for you in there."

"I won't represent men. And I can't represent both parties."

"I know. Both of your visitors are women."

"A same-sex couple? Okay. That's not even unusual these days."

"You're still not getting it. You got a couple waiting for you... but they both want a divorce from their husband. The same husband."

"And that's possible because...?"

"Because this divorce isn't about a couple. It's about a throuple."

4

Kenzi found two women sitting at the small round table inside her private office—although at Rivera & Perez all the offices had floor-to-ceiling glass outer walls, so the accuracy of the term "private" was debatable. The two could not have been more different physically—one was slender and petite, while the other was half a foot taller and at least thirty pounds thicker. Not heavy, but more substantial. What Kenzi's grandmother would've called "a healthy girl."

She noticed that they sat closely together. Kenzi had no idea what being a "throuple" entailed, but they did not appear to want a divorce from each other. They would've been on opposite ends of the room, not inches apart.

"Hi, I'm Kenzi Rivera. How can I help?"

The smaller of the two—the one her grandmother would've called "mousy-looking," rose halfway to her feet. She had dark hair and eyes and appeared to be Latinx. "I'm Morgan Moreno. This is Sally Beaumont." The other woman gestured in acknowledgement. "We need a divorce lawyer."

Kenzi took the vacant chair at the table. "As it happens, that's my specialty."

"Oh, I know," Morgan replied. She smiled a little. "I'm in the KenziKlan."

Kenzi couldn't help but be pleased. Her father gave her all kinds of grief for "wasting her time on the internet." And yet, those livestreams brought her client after client. "Nice to know I'm not talking to myself every morning."

"Are you kidding? Have you looked at your numbers?"

The most honest answer would be, no, she hadn't. Because her social media manager took care of all that. Her daughter, Hailee. "I've been fortunate to find an audience."

"You found an audience because you have something to say. You're kind of a hero with Latinx women. But you're saying something all women need to hear."

Kenzi would be more than happy to spend the day being praised, but she suspected that would not be the most professional way to use this time. "How can I help you? Has a divorce action been filed?"

"Yes. Our husband wants a divorce."

She cocked her head slightly. "Our?"

"Yes. There were three people in the marriage. From the start. Me and Sally and Charles. Charles Land. We never took his last name."

She tried to suppress her facial reaction while calculating the most diplomatic way of inquiring. "I wasn't aware that three-way marriages were legal in the State of Washington."

"You're just being nice. You know they aren't. Ours was...an unconventional relationship. But no less valid. No less important to us. Why does everyone have to be the same? Why do we all have to conform to the man?"

"The government tends to like conformity."

"I don't understand why the government is involved in marriage in the first place. Why do the suits get to tell us who we can and cannot love? Or how many people we can love?"

Sally reached out a hand, gently laying it on her partner's. "Morgan is a bit of a feminist."

"Nothing wrong with that."

"Maybe we should start at the beginning." Sally scooted forward slightly. "This relationship was unconventional from the get-go."

"How did the three of you meet?"

"Final Fantasy."

"That good, huh?"

"No, I'm talking about the game. Final Fantasy. Do you know anything about online gaming?"

"I have a fourteen-year-old daughter." Who almost never played video games, but never mind that.

"It's a MMORPG—massively multiplayer online roleplaying game. A series of games, actually. Very popular. Everyone assumes identities. Character names. We design avatars to represent us in the game. I was Lady Harrowgate. Morgan was the Red Knight."

"And your husband?"

"King Carroll. Of course."

"We were all in the same free company," Morgan added, as if that somehow explained something.

"You worked together?"

Morgan and Sally looked at one another. "That was the way it was supposed to be. Charles was never the best at cooperation."

"Very good at taking credit," Sally noted.

Ah. "But not so good at making valuable contributions?"

"Which doesn't mean we didn't love him. We're none of us perfect."

"Especially him," Morgan muttered. "We were all on this collaborative team and we had a friendly agreement not to harm or interfere with each other. Sally and I were trying to conquer an enemy base when out of nowhere, Charles attacked. Didn't help in the slightest. Backfired, in fact. Probably slowed us down three days. But we eventually conquered the stronghold."

"And he took all the credit for the win?" Kenzi guessed.

"You understand the situation perfectly. I roasted him in the chat box and told him to meet me on a Discord server. Sally came too. And...I don't know what to say. We hit it off."

"Even though you'd never met in person."

"I don't know what a boring date at a coffeeshop would've added to the conversation. Turned out we all three had college degrees and worked in computer programming, but we didn't talk about that much, at least not at first. We exchanged phone numbers and soon we were texting every day. We'd check in with one another each night, and that led to Zoom calls. We liked Zoom better than phone calls because we could all participate at the same time."

"Then you knew what Charles looked like. Eventually."

"Yes. And I won't lie—I liked what I saw. But I was in love with his mind. I suppose I was in love with the bold if somewhat inept King Carroll."

"You have to support your monarch, right?" Sally said.

Yeah, Kenzi thought, but you don't have to marry him. "I'm going to assume at some point you met in person. And a physical relationship developed."

Morgan nodded. "Yes. And oh my God did that work. I'd never experienced anything like it in my entire life. I mean, don't get me wrong, I had some experience. But I never had anything like this. I'd certainly never been in a throuple."

"Can you talk more about that? I have to admit, I haven't encountered this arrangement before."

"I predict you will. It's more popular than people realize. And not just in Utah. Why settle for a relationship with one person when you can have more?"

"You said you were married. But there can't be three—"

"Technically—legally—Charles and I are married," Morgan explained. "But Sally has always been part of the relationship. She stood next to me at the wedding and she recited vows, just as Charles and I did. There may be only two names on the marriage license, but there were three people in the marriage."

Why did she always get the weird ones? Kenzi wondered.

Was it possible that in this modern world, there was no longer anything else? "And I assume that means there were three people..."

"In the bedroom? Damn straight. Best sex ever. No question about it."

Sally looked embarrassed. But there was still a trace of a smile on her face.

"Before you start in," Morgan said, "let me dissuade you from any stereotypical ideas. We were not two sad, lonely women manipulated by an egotistical man. We loved him and he loved us. There's so much institutionalized misogyny in this world. People assume men want sex more than women—although there's no scientific evidence to support that proposition. Society is more permissive of men expressing sexual desires, but that doesn't mean they're the only ones who have them. Or that it's bad for women to have desires. I am not a doormat. We were all partners in a valid healthy relationship."

"A...polyamorous relationship."

"And there's nothing wrong with that. It was not Charles and I treating Sally like a human sex toy. It was not a non-stop orgy posing as a marriage. We were three people in a close loving union. At least, for a while." She paused. "And just for the record, Sally was never trying to steal Charles away from me. But that's what people believe. They think women are always trying to couple-up and shove other women out of the relationship. Because we've all been raised to believe that if you don't have a husband, you're a big failure."

Kenzi nodded. "Trust me. I don't think that way. I've been single for many moons." Since Hailee was diagnosed and her father took a powder.

"Do you get depressed every Valentine's Day because you're not with someone?"

Kenzi craned her neck. "Well..."

"Do you date more during cuffing season?"

"During...what?"

"Cuffing season. October to March. Studies show that when the weather gets cold, people are more motivated to form relationships. Because they want a warm body in their bed."

Was that true? Did people look at dating apps more frequently when the weather turned chilly? In Seattle, it was cold and rainy more or less year round...

"You know," Morgan continued, "you're not more valid with a partner than you are without. Look at yourself. Successful well-off lawyer. Huge internet following. Stylish and quite attractive. If you don't mind my saying so."

Why would she mind? Unless they were looking for a fourth... "Charles has filed for divorce against you, Morgan?"

"Correct. But he's divorcing both of us."

"I understand that's your position. But I can't promise a court will agree. Judges look for the simplest path to a decision. And unneeded complications like a third person do not make matters simpler. Much easier to say, the law does not recognize three-way marriages, Sally's name is not on the marriage license. End of story."

"What happens in a divorce?" Sally asked. Kenzi got the impression that, while tiny Morgan was the firebrand, Sally was the practical, reflective one.

"I gather there are no children of the marriage?" Both women shook their heads. "Good. Well, let me give you the basics. No one cares much about fault these days. You don't have to prove entitlement to a divorce. If you want it, you'll get it. You're all college graduates with jobs, so there's no reason to expect alimony. The court just looks for a fair way to divide up marital property." She gave Sally a concerned expression. "I don't think we can reasonably expect the court to award any marital property to you, Sally. Since your name is not on the license."

"I understand."

"Anything I get," Morgan said, "I'm splitting with Sally. Right down the middle. Fifty-fifty."

"Is there a large marital estate?" Kenzi asked.

Morgan and Sally exchanged another look. "Huge."

Kenzi blinked. Seriously? From three video-gaming computer programmers? "How huge?"

"Almost a billion bucks," Morgan explained. "We have a company called DigiDynamics. And the last annual report put its value at just under one billion."

Kenzi whistled. She wouldn't have trouble justifying this case to her father. "Is this a...computer programming business?"

"Let me explain," Sally said. "The bulk of that wealth comes from a program called Face2Face. Basically a facial recognition program, but by far the best, simplest, and most exhaustive the world has ever seen. Input a photo—even a poor one—and within minutes the program can produce a list of every photo of that person found anywhere on the internet. On social media, YouTube, wherever. The idea was to help people find their loved ones. Help them locate old friends, catch up with people they haven't seen since high school."

Sally took a deep breath, then continued. "That was Morgan's start-up idea. This was originally part of an earlier program, the Love Library, that was supposed to use the facial recognition app to fund a nonprofit focused on providing laptops to underprivileged children all around the world." She paused. "That's how Charles got Morgan to work on Face2Face. By making it look like something it wasn't. But he secretly let the Love Library go bankrupt and turned Face2Face into a for-profit enterprise."

"I wrote most of the code," Morgan added.

"And Charles...?"

"Is CEO of the company. And just like when he played Final Fantasy, he takes all the credit. Reaps most of the rewards. And owns most of the stock. But does precious little of the actual work."

Kenzi understood their problem. Proving entitlement to the proceeds of a program someone else owned legally could be challenging. But not impossible. "May I ask what caused the marriage to fall apart? You made it sound like such a perfect arrangement."

"Charles has always been insecure," Morgan explained. "Perhaps he realized how much of his success he owed to women he kept in the background. He became physically and verbally abusive. Called us hideous names I won't repeat. Especially me. And he hit us both, on some occasions at the same time. Hit me more than Sally. But we both got it."

Kenzi felt her teeth clench. She understood that sometimes marriages didn't last, but there was no excuse for physical violence. As far as she was concerned, men who hit women should be thrown into a black hole and never released. "How often did this happen?"

"I'll make a list," Sally murmured.

"Please do. And assemble any evidence you may have. Photographs. Videos. Contemporaneous records."

"I'll try. But there won't be much."

She frowned, then made a note on her phone. "Was there anything else that contributed to the divorce?"

"Charles was unfaithful. He cheated."

As if she didn't dislike the man enough already. Two women weren't enough for him? "He was messing around?"

Morgan blinked. "Like, sex? Oh, no. I don't know that he ever did that. I think we were okay sexually. I'm talking about Face2Face. He sold us out. In secret. Behind our backs."

"Can you explain..."

"We made an agreement when we founded the company. We would not work for the man. Especially the pigs. No defense contracts. No law enforcement contracts. We wouldn't take money from fascist bastards who kill people in cold blood because they have darker skin. But Charles betrayed our trust. He sold Face2Face to a law enforcement consortium for a huge sum without telling me or Sally. Quadrupled our net worth with a single deal, but now all the worst people have our program—

the FBI, the CIA, the cops. A program that was supposed to bring families together is now being used to tear families apart."

"He didn't have the right," Sally insisted. "That program was Morgan's idea. We formed the company together. We had an understanding. And he broke it."

So he lied to them, cheated on them, and battered them. Yeah, Kenzi was all in on this one. She looked forward to draining the man dry. "Look, we're going to have evidentiary problems. But I think we can make it work. I see both of you getting a large sum of money from this divorce and partial ownership of the company. Or the program. Or the cash equivalent. Whatever you want. We should be able to wrap this up quickly. Morgan, you'll be our key witness, since you're the legal wife. You can—"

"About that," Morgan said, cutting her off. "There's something I haven't mentioned yet."

Kenzi sighed. There always was. "What would that be?"

"I see monsters," Morgan replied, with the flattest, most matter-of-fact expression imaginable. "Flying monsters. Dragons, sometimes. Flying cheese toast, too. And a ten-foot-tall clown who wants to kill me."

5

The soccer girl was a mistake.

He had acted on impulse, and at this point in his journey, he should know that impulsive actions could be disastrous. His specialty was methodical planning, careful selection of victims, prudent consideration of risks, and skillful manipulation. That was how he'd remained active so long, evading law enforcement even after they called in the FBI and launched a major manhunt for the Seattle Strangler.

He had to grin. That label made him sound so important. He was famous, in his own way.

And despite all their efforts, they hadn't caught him. They hadn't even come close.

He was too smart for them.

But that would end if he made more imprudent choices like the soccer girl. Chessie.

He normally targeted women who were isolated and alone, with no immediate family, no roommates, no one who would miss them. At least not immediately. Women on the fringes of society. Until the frat house...

It had just seemed too perfect. He was in his new costume, with the fake cast and the dopey eyeglasses, but he was just trying it on for size. His keen night vision glimpsed an opportunity to rush in and play the conquering hero. And then collect another victim.

So he did. And it worked.

Turned out Chessie was the granddaughter of a state senator. Now the story was in the news every day, with the senator and his politico friends demanding action. He doubted they were accomplishing much. But if they poured in enough manpower and money...it was just a matter of time before someone got lucky.

He didn't believe they would ever get smart. Certainly not anywhere near smart enough to catch him. But they might get lucky. And even he couldn't stop dumb luck.

Damn that soccer girl anyway!

The smartest precaution would be to lay low. Wait until the heat was off. Wait until the next celeb crime or mass shooting. That shouldn't take long.

Except he couldn't. There were some things he could do and some he could not...and this was one he could not.

The chain could not be broken. The chain *must* not be broken. Because if it ever was...

Better not to think about.

This morning's escapade represented a return to form. No more risk-taking. Meticulous planning. That was why he'd come to Discovery Park.

He'd been watching Jess Heller for some time. She had a low-paying job at the front desk of a low-rent flophouse three days a week. She lived alone and rarely went out. No social media presence. She wouldn't be missed until Monday, if then.

And to think that he had a phone app to thank for finding her. He'd snapped her photo surreptitiously as she jogged by a few days ago. In less than a minute, the program found several photos of her on the internet. She might not have a Facebook page, but others at the flophouse did, and she'd been caught in the background during a birthday party. She was in the audience at a free park concert Bruno Mars gave a few years ago. And she was just barely visible in the background of someone's video of a celebratory cupcake taken at the bakery.

Marvelous little program. Worth everything he'd had to do to get it.

Jess might live on the fringes, but at least she took care of herself. She started each day with a jog, even on rainy days, which here in Seattle, was about half of them. She ran before her daily breakfast of a hardboiled egg with a low-fat milk chaser. It paid off. With a little effort, maybe some makeup and the occasional use of a hairbrush, she could be attractive.

One thing at a time.

He'd spotted her as she entered the park today, so he knew it would only be a few moments before she arrived at the underpass. He'd chosen this spot because it was impossible to see it from above and few people came to this section of the park. They were almost guaranteed privacy long enough for him to do what needed to be done...

The chain could not be broken.

He heard the crunching of leaves not far away. That would be Jess. Time to get into position...

He sat down on the ground, extended his left leg, and massaged his ankle. The appearance of helplessness was crucial.

A few moments later, Jess jogged into view.

She slowed as she approached. He knew what she was thinking. Should she be leery? She'd undoubtedly heard all the babble about the Seattle Strangler. Still, he looked harmless...

She slowed but still maintained a safe distance. "You ok?"

He turned toward her and grimaced. "Twisted my ankle."

"Oh. Wow. I did that once. Gotta watch out for the rocks and twigs."

"Exactly. And I didn't." He rubbed the ankle more vigorously. "Hurts like hell."

"I know." She glanced down the path as if she were going to

move on. But then, poor thing, her conscience got to her. "Do you...have anyone else out here?"

"No. I jog alone. My girlfriend hates running."

"Too bad." Girlfriend. He wasn't a creeper, right? Just a nice normal man who wasn't threatening in the slightest. "You live nearby?"

"A few blocks away on Portland. But if I can make it to the street, I can catch a cab or call an Uber."

"The street's over there." She pointed.

"I know, but..." He paused. "You see a large branch? Something I could use as a crutch?"

"Not really." She thought for another moment. Deliberated. "Look, I'll be your crutch. The street isn't far. It should only take a few minutes."

"I don't want to impose."

"It's no problem. We runners have to stick together, right?"

He laughed. "Okay. Thanks."

"Can you get up by yourself?"

"I can try." He grunted and groaned and winced, doing his best to sell the twisted ankle bit. He hobbled and bobbled on his "good foot," finally resting one hand against the stone arch of the underpass. "I think I'm steady."

"Great. Now wrap one arm around my shoulder..."

He did.

And a second later, once she was unsuspecting and vulnerable, he shoved her backward. Her head crashed back against the stone underpass so hard it left a streak of blood. Her eyes flew wide open, then closed. The shock rattled through her body. She would've crumbled to the ground, but he caught her, with one hand under her right arm and the other hand around her throat.

She made a gurgling noise. She was trying to pull it together, trying to speak. But he wasn't interested in hearing anything she had to say.

He inched his hand upward, pressing hard against her larynx. "Say goodbye, my jogging princess."

To her credit, she struggled, but it was useless. He had her firmly under his control. Soon they would both be gone, with nary a trace of what had happened here.

He smiled, pleased. This was a welcome return to form. The Strangler had struck again!

But most importantly...the chain would not be broken.

6

K enzi's many years toiling in the divorce courts had earned her an almost unshakable poker face, but this remark cracked it. "Flying cheese toast?" "And ten-foot clowns. Murderous clowns." Sure, everyone was afraid of clowns. But toast? If her potential client had mental problems, the case would be more complicated. And everything the woman told her was in question. "How long has this been going on?"

"About three years." Kenzi could see this was a difficult subject for Morgan, but her attorney needed to know. "Came out of nowhere. One day I had a normal life. And then the monsters came. A sudden burst of eye floaters, sparkles, and jagged lines that took insane shapes. My legs appeared to expand to elephantine size. Hideous creatures arose, like demented Disney characters, zooming through my field of vision. I felt physically ill. Nausea, stomach cramps, spotty vision. I was suddenly exhausted, and that didn't go away, even when the visions stopped. Temporarily."

Sounded nightmarish—literally. Kenzi knew a nasty divorce attorney could use this to make Morgan look unbalanced. "Did you seek help?"

"Eventually. I tried to ignore it for a long time, but the attacks were so debilitating that others began to notice. Sally was the first. She insisted that I see a doctor." Sally's hand snaked out and rested gently on Morgan's shoulder. "Thank God we'd made some cash, because given how our American health care system works, without a fortune I would never have been able to afford this long series of specialists and headshrinkers, most of whom contributed absolutely nothing."

"What did they say?"

"The first doc thought I had migraines. But I don't, and even if I did, why would that cause such vivid hallucinations? I tried head scans, MRIs, biofeedback procedures, and a wide variety of mind-altering medications. Nothing helped. They sent me to an epilepsy lab. Spent about a year there, without the slightest progress or improvement. Even I began to wonder if I was bonkers."

"The visions were tearing her apart," Sally said. "And there was nothing I could do to help."

"Eventually I found a doctor who'd actually seen something like this before. He diagnosed me with a rare condition called Todd's syndrome, or more commonly, Alice in Wonderland syndrome. It causes people to see things that aren't there or to see things that are there through a distorted lens, like they're bigger or smaller, closer or farther away than they actually are."

"Like Alice," Kenzi said, nodding. *Alice's Adventures in Wonderland* was one of her favorite books.

"Exactly. Some people believe Lewis Carroll suffered from it, which might explain where he got the idea for some of Alice's experiences. Doctors call this macropsia—believing things are much bigger than they are, and micropsia—believing they're smaller. Carroll's diaries mention that he suffered from extreme head pain and often didn't feel quite himself. He might've understated the magnitude of what he experienced. Or his relatives might've expurgated all discussion of wacky visions from his diaries after he died."

"Okay," Kenzi said, "so someone managed to put a name on it. Is there anything they can do about it?"

"I get regular Botox shots. Not to improve my face. Because it deadens the pain. I also take Maxalt, riboflavin, and magnesium. They help, but they haven't made the hallucinations disappear. I'll probably be living with it all my life. Which worries me. If this case goes to court, what happens if I suddenly get sick? Or see a yodeling Mr. Potato Head divebombing me?"

"We may have to apprise the judge of your situation," Kenzi said. "If the court understands that you have an ongoing medical condition, it'll be more sympathetic when I ask for a break or if you have an inexplicable reaction. We don't want to give anyone any reason to think you're an unreliable witness."

"Like the police did," Sally added softly. "When she reported that someone killed our dog."

Kenzi's eyes bulged. "What?"

Morgan nodded. "About three days ago, we reached a breaking point. Charles was drinking, and he always becomes loud and violent when he has a little alcohol in his system. I accused him of betraying our trust. I vented anger that had been building for a long time, ever since I learned he used our creation to support fascist America. Sally was smart enough to stay out of it."

"Except when he tried to hit you," Sally said.

"Yeah. I told him I was going to the Board of Directors to move that we disable the facial recognition software so no one would ever be able to use it again. Even if we had to give all the money back. I don't care. I don't want this on my conscience. I want to reclaim the soul of our baby. Even if that means burying it." She looked down. "Charles did not take this news well."

"I would imagine not."

"He's had several surgeries in the past year, and I think it's affected his personality. If Sally hadn't been there with her phone videoing him, he probably would've taken my head off. As it was, he moved out of the apartment and we haven't seen him since."

She covered her face. Her voice shook. "But yesterday I came home and found my little beagle, Baxter, stabbed to death with a garden trowel."

Kenzi pressed her hand against her mouth. "And you think Charles did it?"

"Who else? I told the cops, but they said I didn't have any evidence. It didn't help that I kept seeing airborne geometric shapes attacking me while I gave my report."

Probably not. "Any other dangerous events?"

"I don't want to make too much of it..." Morgan began.

"You have to tell her the truth." Sally leaned forward. "Someone attacked her on the way home last night."

Kenzi felt the short hairs rise on the back of her neck. "Tell me what happened."

"I was walking home from a gaming shop in Columbia Center that I like. Someone grabbed me by the neck and slung me into an alley. Slammed me against a brick wall, hand around my throat. I was stunned and couldn't think straight. At first, I thought it was another hallucination. But the assailant wasn't flying and didn't change shape. I couldn't see him at all. I say 'him' because I assume it was a man, but I can't even say that for certain."

"Did this person say anything?"

"Only once, and it was in such a growl I couldn't tell you anything about what that voice might be like normally. It was just three words. 'Let it go.'"

Curiouser and curiouser. "Was it Charles?"

Morgan shrugged. "I don't think so."

"Charles hired a thug," Sally said. "He was warning you to stop interfering with his high-dollar sale."

Perhaps. If someone was trying to scare her off, they should've been more specific. "Did you tell the cops about this?"

"After the way they treated me? No way."

"You should."

"That ship has sailed. And Charles has filed for divorce."

"I'll get a protective order, just the same. Did you bring a copy of the petition?"

"Of course."

Kenzi gave it a quick scan. Charles' divorce attorney was Lou Crozier, her firm's archnemesis. Yes, they had good reason to be worried.

This case had more weird parameters than she was currently able to process. But she wasn't backing off. It looked like this was a chance to help some women who needed it. And maybe to stop someone who needed stopping.

"I'll be more than happy to take your case. But let me make a few things clear up front. I can't represent both of you. I'm sure you feel like you're on the same side, but from a legal standpoint, you're not. You're two different people with different interests potentially vying for the same pile of cash. I can take one or the other of you."

"Take Morgan," Sally said, before her partner had a chance to argue. "She needs you. And she's the one who's legally married and getting divorced."

"As far as that goes, Sally, I think your lawyer could make a strong argument that you were in something like a common-law marriage with Charles. The fact that he was legally married to someone else complicates the matter, but some judges would be sympathetic to your situation. The world is changing. My assistant Sharon can give you a list of good lawyers. I appreciate you making this easy."

"I appreciate you helping Morgan. I would do anything for her. She's the best thing in my life. She's my rock."

"I'll file a response and enter my appearance on behalf of Morgan. Sorry, Sally, but you and I won't be able to talk privately about the case anymore, since you're theoretically an opposing party. Morgan, I charge a flat fee and it isn't cheap. If we settle early, I come off well, so you know I'll be pushing for it, and that benefits you as well. Lets you get on with your life. But even if the case drags on for years, you'll never pay me a penny more than the flat fee."

"Sounds fair. And incredibly reasonable."

"I'll set up a settlement conference as quickly as possible. I know Charles' attorney. He's not the easiest to work with, but I've reached early settlements with him before and with luck I might do it again. I will not compound the case with motions and discovery requests. I will not make this more difficult than it needs to be." She meant it. She still remembered what it was like when her parents divorced. She remembered the pain of her own divorce. She would never protract that kind of misery. "Sound good?"

They both nodded. She was beginning to see a light in Morgan's eyes that had not been there before. Which told her it was time to deliver the "Harsh Reality" speech.

"Even with me at the helm doing my best to minimize the agony, this is still a divorce case and there is absolutely nothing pleasant about that. This is not an outpatient procedure. It's more like open-heart surgery without benefit of anesthesia. You'll feel like your guts have been ripped out, like you've been taken apart piece by piece, and even after you reassemble yourself, you won't be the same. Boundaries have to be remapped. Longtime friends will stop calling you. It will break your heart, but some will remain loyal to Charles for business or personal reasons. I will be at your side doing everything possible to alleviate the stress. But it won't be painless."

The sober expressions on both faces told her the message was getting through. This was one of those things people never fully understood until they experienced it. But at least she'd given them a taste of reality.

"One more thing, Morgan. If you're going to be my client, you must tell me the truth. The whole truth and nothing but the truth. If you hold back something important, it will come back to haunt you. Believe me. I've seen it happen. And if I find out you lied to me, I will drop you in a heartbeat. I have a reputation in this community and with the courts. I won't have that tarnished. So don't do it."

"I won't. I promise."

"Thank you for being straight with us," Sally said. "Does Morgan need to sign something?"

"Sharon will have the paperwork ready for her. And please— start being more careful. Don't walk the streets alone. Think about hiring a bodyguard."

Morgan waved a hand in the air. "I'll be all right."

"No, I want you to take this seriously. Some people behave irrationally during a divorce. You have to protect yourself."

"I will. I promise."

"Good. Stay safe. I'll let you know when I've got the settlement conference scheduled. You let me know if anything unusual or threatening occurs."

Morgan smiled slightly. "Like an attack of flying cheese toast?"

"Or a killer clown." Especially one who looked like her husband.

7

"Flying cheese toast? You're making this up."

Kenzi shook her head. "I couldn't make that up if I tried. I'm not that creative."

After work, Kenzi and Sharon had retreated to Sherman's Ferry, their favorite watering hole, not far from the office. It was a recurring Friday night ritual. Kenzi made a point of taking a streetcar to work so she wouldn't need to drive home. The Ferry was pleasantly upscale but not snooty and was frequented by members of the local bar. Many a time she'd closed a deal here. Lawyers tended to be so much more reasonable when they had a margarita or two inside them.

Since they worked together and Sharon usually handled the research (something Kenzi despised), it was important that she stayed informed about new cases. "It's bizarre, granted, but I don't think it will impact the divorce much."

"Girl, you have a knack for attracting the outrageous."

"It's a gift."

"The husband will say she's bonkers. Hallucinating. Joan of Arc and then some."

"Which could alienate the judge. Hard to like someone who takes advantage of his wife's illness."

"He'll argue that you can't believe anything his wife says, since she claims to see flying cheese toast."

Kenzi shrugged. "He said, she said. Story of every divorce. Judges tend to ignore it. Just divide the estate. But we will need to document the physical and verbal abuse."

"And the mutt murder. Who would do that?"

"When this kind of money is on the table, extreme behavior emerges."

"I don't get why that program made them so rich. Doesn't seem all that revolutionary. Facial recognition software has been around a long time."

"This must be the best iteration yet, if law enforcement is paying a billion bucks."

"That business with the dead dog and the stalker worries me. Maybe you should've invited Emma to join us."

"I did. Coming to a popular bar was way too social for her. But she said she'll help if she can."

Sharon made a note on her phone. "I'll see what I can learn about Charles Land."

"And while you're at it, see what you can dig up about Face2-Face. And DigiDynamics."

"On it." She pointed over Kenzi's shoulder. "Heads up. Opposing counsel just entered the bar. He may be headed our way."

Kenzi craned her neck. Lou Crozier, senior partner at Crozier & Crozier. He was about her father's age, middleweight, bearded, and ultraconservative. Even when he wasn't wearing his MAGA cap he seemed to be wearing his MAGA cap. He admitted to being on the Capitol steps the day the building was invaded. QAnon was his Bible.

She hadn't seen him since their last case together. He'd offered her a job back then, when she was still angry about Gabe being promoted to managing partner. She'd never given him a definitive answer.

"Kenzi," Crozier said, with open arms and apparent

bonhomie. If you didn't know better, you'd think he liked her. "How are you?"

"Hanging in there." Crozier bent over and kissed her cheek. *My, my, aren't we pretending to be friendly?* "And you?"

"Fine, just fine. Please give my best to your father. I have so much respect for that man. And what he's accomplished."

Sure. So much respect that you'd like to seize everything he's built. And raid his best lawyers. "I'll tell him."

"Looks like we have another case together."

"Yup. Any idea who's representing Sally?"

"Uh...Sally?"

"The third member of the throuple."

He blinked. She got the impression he'd never heard the word before. "Oh, the woman who lived with them. My client says she was more like a house guest than anything else."

Why would he say that? So no one would expect him to pay her anything? "That's not what my client says."

"Whatever. She wasn't a party to the marriage, so I don't see that it matters much. I'm hoping we can settle this quickly."

"Nothing would please us more. But there's a large estate to divide."

"My client is willing to be reasonable. There's enough money for everyone, and he feels no ill will toward your client. He just wants to get this behind them so they can all move forward with their lives. They've been through a lot together and he's hoping they can remain friends."

Sounded good, but she was skeptical. Crozier always talked a good talk, but the proof of the pudding would be how he behaved at the settlement conference. "That sounds good to me. Let's set a date and hash this out."

"Great plan. I'll check my calendar and get back to you."

"Hey—didn't you tell me you were going to phase out your legal work?"

Crozier sighed. "That's what I wanted. But you know how it goes. The best laid plans of mice and men..."

"I'm sure they need you at your firm."

"Too much." He glanced at Sharon, as if judging whether he could speak in front of her. He lowered his voice. "My offer still stands, Kenzi. That last case didn't change anything. In fact, it only increased my admiration. I'd love to have you in my shop."

"You mean, you'd love to have someone named Rivera defect and join your shop."

"No. I want you. You've got what it takes, and you're insufficiently appreciated where you are. Join the Crozier team and you'll be a top-level partner on Day One. You'll get the same salary I do. Maybe not all the perks, but that will come in time."

"Where would I go from there?"

"When I retire, you'll become managing partner. Guaranteed."

"That could be a long wait."

He shook his head. "You'll be running a major firm before you turn forty. Which I believe will be a first for a woman in this town."

The worst part of this was, she believed him. He'd told her about some prophecy he received from a bizarre dark-web source. Crazy as it sounded, he was convinced he was going to be appointed to the Supreme Court soon. That being the case, he might want to diminish his legal entanglements.

"Think about it," Crozier said. "Maybe when we get together for the settlement conference, we can close two deals at once." He nodded toward Sharon. "Nice seeing you both."

Sharon waited until he was far away before she spoke. "Okay, just to be clear on this, if you go to that man's firm, I am not going with you."

Kenzi mock-pouted. "I thought you'd follow me anywhere."

"Not to that man's snake pit. Who knows what might happen? A month in his firm and I might be babbling about voter fraud or telling people to drink bleach."

"I don't think your mind is that malleable. I know mine isn't."

"I don't care. I'm not going near him. And given the color of my skin, I seriously doubt he'd want me."

"Don't jump to conclusions. Every conservative is not a bigot."

"True. But he is. I can feel it every time I come near him. I can sense it every time he looks at me."

In other circumstances, Kenzi might be tempted to argue, but not this time. "I should get home to Hailee."

"You're going to leave me here alone? Without my wing-gal?"

"I'm your wing-gal?"

"Why else would I hang with such a well-dressed cutie?"

"I thought there was something deeper..."

"You're a lightning rod. And I need one. I haven't been on a date for almost a year."

Kenzi hadn't been on a date for almost two, but she wasn't about to admit it. "Okay, tell me what you're looking for. What kind of guy turns you on?"

Sharon looked away. "I'll...tell you if I see someone. Actually, this might not be the best bar for me."

"We don't have to come here every Friday. Is there someplace else you like better?"

Sharon didn't answer immediately. "I don't know. I should probably head home myself. It's been a day."

"Wanna come back with me? Hailee would love to see you. You know she calls you her big sister."

"Aww. That's tots adorbs. You don't mind, do you?"

"Why would I? She's not likely to get a sister the usual way."

"You couldn't improve on Hailee. She's the real deal. You've done a great job with her."

Kenzi fluttered her eyelids. "Thanks." She pushed away from the chair. "I'm off."

Sharon also rose. "Let's walk to the streetcar together."

"That's not necessary. I—"

Sharon cut her off with a look. "Don't argue with me, Little

Miss Gorgeous. The Seattle Strangler is still out there. We girls need to stick together."

"I think I could take some creep hunting for helpless women to strangle."

"That's what all his victims thought. That's why they were alone. When he got them."

"I suppose you can't be too careful."

"Right. So I'll come with you. To protect you from toxic men." Sharon paused. "And if necessary, flying cheese toast."

8

K enzi stood outside her apartment door and inhaled deeply for several seconds. The sudden inrush of air was supposed to sober you up, right? Not that she was that bad off. She'd stopped after the third vodka gimlet. Or was it the fourth? Or had she completely lost track?

In any case, she needed to put on an adult façade, if only for the sake of the fourteen-year-old girl on the other side of the door. She managed to get the key into the lock and pushed the door open...

She was assaulted by music. Of a sort. Sounded like the soundtrack from *Mad Men*.

Her daughter Hailee swiveled around. "Hey, Mom! Did you have fun tonight?"

She squinted, trying to focus. "Is that...Dean Martin?"

Hailee smiled. "You're developing a good ear. Under my tutelage." Her eyes narrowed. "Maybe you should sit down."

That was a good idea. She slid into the nearest available chair at the kitchen table. Felt good to take a load off. "I did listen to music before you came along, you know."

"That wasn't music. That was corporate claptrap manufactured to sell downloads to children."

Ouch. Her adolescent music snob. "Are you hungry? Should we order a pizza?"

Hailee rolled her eyes, then wheeled into the kitchen. "I fixed you scrambled eggs. With mushroom and diced tomatoes and a few other goodies."

Eggs? Her stomach churned. "I'm not sure..."

"Best thing for you, after all that alcohol. Eggs are rich in cysteine, the amino acid your body uses to make glutathione. That's an antioxidant you need. Especially in your current condition."

Now wait a minute... "I haven't had that much to drink. Just a gimlet or two..."

"Or five." Hailee scraped the eggs onto a plate. "Sharon texted me. So I could get the eggs started." She slid the plate in front of her mother. "Eat."

Sharon ratted her out? "I feel betrayed."

"You should feel loved. Because you are. Is something bothering you?"

"No. Well, just the usual." She took a bite. Not bad, actually. "Um, thanks for dinner."

"No problem. It's in my job description. Social media manager, chef, legal consultant, and loving daughter."

Kenzi had to smile. Hailee had been helpful during a recent case. Consultant might be pushing it. But if it made her feel useful...great.

For years now, Hailee had suffered from a chronic illness called ME—myalgic encephalomyelitis. Some people called it Chronic Fatigue Syndrome, but she avoided any labels that suggested it was a matter of energy. Hailee had boundless enthusiasm. But she became physically tired much more quickly than others. She could walk, but not for long, so the wheelchair was always close at hand. She was homeschooled but still managed to stay in touch with friends. Kenzi couldn't be prouder of her. But the disease was a lurking specter. There was little chance it would get better and a great possibility it would worsen. Some people with ME ended up bedridden or eating through a tube.

She wanted Hailee to remain active and to feel she had purpose, which was one reason Kenzi agreed to let the girl become her social media manager. As it turned out, that had worked to her benefit. Hailee was good at it and in a matter of months her internet following, the "KenziKlan," had swelled to five-digit numbers. She was now a top influencer, and one of the few who was also a lawyer. It was great PR for both her and her firm, which was one of the reasons she'd been Rivera & Rivera's top-billing attorney for several years running.

Except, according to her father, not last month.

Hailee let her get halfway through the eggs before she started with the questions. "I hear you have a new case?"

Apparently she needed to have a discussion with Sharon about boundaries. But whatever. She was lucky to have a daughter who was interested in her work. She told Hailee everything she could about the case without violating any privilege— basically what was set forth in the Petition and Response and now a part of the public record.

"He killed her dog?" Hailee was practically bug-eyed. "That's completely psychotic."

"We don't know that it was the husband."

"Who else would it be?"

Kenzi shrugged. "I doubt he's the one who attacked her on the street."

"I thought she couldn't identify the assailant."

"She couldn't. But you gotta think she would've recognized the man she's been sleeping with for years. Even if he disguised his voice."

"OMG. She could be mixed up with a violent ex or the Seattle Strangler." She paused. "Or maybe he *is* the Seattle Strangler."

"Calm down, let's not go completely off the rails." Morgan

said her husband was violent. But surely not that violent. "You surf the internet more than I do. Have you heard of this Face2-Face thing?"

"How could I not? It's all over Reddit. People are calling it the end of personal privacy. Big Brother has arrived, etcetera."

"It doesn't seem that revolutionary to me."

"Then you haven't put two and two together. Imagine being able to assemble an exhaustive social media portfolio about someone in a matter of minutes. In a world where everyone has a miniature computer with a camera in their pockets, even the most reclusive soul on earth will be on social media eventually. Give that to the cops and the government and personal freedom becomes a complete fiction."

"I think you're exaggerating."

"I'm not. Defending this awful program has become Charles Land's full-time occupation."

"You've heard of him?"

"Mom, if you're going to represent these high-flyers, you should do a little research."

"What do you know about him?"

"He likes to be in the limelight. He wants everyone to think he invented Face2Face singlehandedly, although apparently he can't even write code."

"I think Morgan did some of that."

"He likes to think of himself as a techie bumblebee. Flits from one worker to the next, pollinating. I don't know that he does anything himself, but he orchestrates the incubator. When he puts on his sales shows, you never see anyone else on the stage. Just the Bumblebee. He thinks he's Steve Jobs. Or at least Tim Cook."

Violent *and* self-absorbed. "See what else you can dig up on him, would you? Look for hints of violent explosions, temper tantrums, anything along those lines."

"Then I'm on the case?" Her eyes brightened. "I'm your partner?"

"In an...unofficial way."

"Why unofficial?"

"Because you're underage and you haven't passed the bar." In fact, Hailee talked about going to medical school. Given her condition, Kenzi had no idea if that was a realistic aspiration. But she wasn't about to discourage the girl. "And monitor my social media. If this guy is as prominent as you think, there may be some blowback."

"If people think you're taking that blowhard down, it could only boost your ratings."

"If he has an office filled with computer geeks, he might be able to manipulate online opinion. He probably has more internet trolls on the payroll than Russia."

"I'll keep an eye on it." Hailee scooted closer. "Are you free this weekend?"

"So far as I know. Bainbridge Island?"

"I was thinking Pike Place Market. We haven't had tea and crumpets lately."

And her favorite place for it was smack in the middle of the famous seaside market. "And maybe pick up some fresh salmon?"

"Oh ick." Hailee, of course, did not eat meat, including fish. "Maybe we could ride the Great Wheel at Pier 57. You keep saying you'd like to do it if you could find the time."

"True." Her stomach seemed to have settled. Maybe Hailee's cooking had done its job. "Any chance of getting some more scrambled eggs?"

Hailee beamed. "Give me five minutes." She rolled into the kitchen.

Kenzi rested her head on the table. Her eyelids began to close...

Until the buzzing of her cellphone rocketed them open.

Whose idea was it to put a phone in everyone's pocket?

"Hello?"

"Kenzi? It's Morgan Moreno. Your new client."

"I know. I was just—"

"I'm sorry to bother you at night, but something horrible has happened."

Kenzi sat up straight. "Are you safe? Are you hurt?"

"I'm...not hurt. Not in the way you mean."

"Are you alone?"

"No. Sally's with me."

"What happened?"

Morgan's voice trembled. Kenzi got the definite impression she'd been crying. "There are...pictures of me. On the internet."

Her forehead wrinkled. "You mean like...a Face2Face search?"

"No." Morgan drew in her breath. Something between a cry and a moan escaped. "Like...sexy pictures. Nude pictures."

Kenzi's pulse quickened. "Are they deepfakes?"

Several seconds passed before Morgan replied. "No."

"Then—?"

"It was supposed to be private. We were just fooling around. Having fun. But now they're everywhere. Even on—" A sudden intake of breath. "—porn sites. People can see my...everything."

"I don't understand how this could happen." Hailee wheeled beside her and pressed an ear to the other side of her phone.

"Apparently there's been a hack. A data breach at a website called Taylor Petrie."

That name sounded familiar, but she couldn't quite place it. Where had she heard that before...?

She looked at Hailee. Her daughter held up her phone. The screen showed a website...

Oh hell. The site was like Ashley Madison. It catered to married people who wanted to have discreet trysts with someone other than their spouse.

"Is this something Charles made happen?"

"I don't know," Morgan replied. Her voice was barely understandable. "Don't you see what this means? No one will take me seriously anymore. I can't go to work without knowing everyone there has seen me...seen me...like that."

"I'm sure it will blow over."

"It won't. First my dog. Then the guy in the alley. Now this. Someone is out to get me. And they're not going to stop until I'm completely destroyed. One way or the other."

9

While Kenzi talked, Hailee used her phone to scan the internet, periodically holding it up to show her mother what she'd learned. Taylor Petrie had suffered a data breach and many famous names had been exposed, including Hollywood celebrities, tech titans, and politicians—even the current mayor of Seattle. Charles Land was prominent enough that the photos of his wife received plenty of media play.

"I could go to court for an injunction," Kenzi said, "or a cease-and-desist order, but I'm not sure what it would accomplish."

"It's too late," Morgan said, choking. "The genie is out of the lamp. I'm probably on a million teenage boys' desktops now. And in the Saved Photos file of everyone who works at our company. Can you imagine trying to deal with banks and investors after this? Everyone will be sniggering behind my back."

"Don't assume the worst. Not everyone is evil."

"Someone is." She took another long, deep breath. "Charles is."

"Charles took the photos?"

"No. An old boyfriend. But Charles leaked them. I'm certain of it."

"If we can prove that," Kenzi said, "it might work to our advantage. The judge will not like it and Washington has revenge-porn laws that—"

"It doesn't matter anymore." Morgan's voice dropped, barely more than a murmur. "Nothing matters anymore."

"Listen to me, Morgan. Don't become despondent. This will blow over. The press and the internet will move on to something else. But I need to ask you a question. And I apologize in advance, but if you've been having an affair—"

"I was not cheating on Charles. Or Sally. I would never—"

"But the photos—"

"Were from a long time ago. We were a little high and someone decided we should pose for pictures. I never posted them anywhere and I never went to that website looking for an affair." Pause. "And if I did want an affair, I wouldn't need that website. DigiDynamics is full of men constantly hitting on me."

"Morgan, I told you this before. If I don't have all the relevant information, I can't represent you properly."

"I'm telling you the truth. Promise."

"Okay. Keep it that way."

While they talked, Hailee found some of the photos. She didn't approve of her daughter visiting those kinds of websites, but she supposed this was in the line of duty.

They were even worse than Kenzi'd imagined. Much worse. Vivid, sexual, vulgar. Posing like a porn actress in a wide variety of come-and-get-me positions. And not a stitch of clothing. Just Morgan's naked body and the occasional sex toy. And a big smile that suggested she was enjoying every minute of this.

Hailee pointed a finger into her mouth and made a gagging face.

"Morgan, I'll call opposing counsel and make a formal request that Charles stop releasing photos. Of course, they won't admit that he's behind this. But we can make the request. If we can trace this back to him, he'll have to answer to the judge."

"He's already done his worst." Morgan sounded as if she were drifting. "I'm ruined. Crushed. He swore he'd get even with me... and he has. The bastard managed to think of something even worse than killing my dog." Morgan sounded as if she were in mortal pain. "He killed me."

———

Kenzi felt massive mother-guilt, but she canceled the proposed crumpets venture. She needed to spend the weekend mitigating the damage and prepping for the settlement conference. Now more than ever, this case was best resolved as quickly as possible.

Hailee did not complain. In fact, she helped. Once the case took on an internet dimension, with hackers and celebrities and sexting, it was squarely within a teenager's wheelhouse. She spent several hours doomscrolling the internet—only to realize that Morgan's worst fears were realities. Those photos went viral, in the worst possible way.

Monday morning Kenzi hit the office bright and early. She did her usual KenziKlan livestream but decided not to go into many details about her current case. She didn't want to do anything that negatively impacted the chances of settlement. Instead, she focused on the clear takeaways...

"Do you hear what I'm saying, KenziKlan?" She held the phone close to her face to make sure they knew she was serious. Don't look at the fabulous outfit. Look at her. "Never let anyone photograph you in compromising poses. I don't care how old or young you are. I don't care how much you love or trust the person. Don't do it. If every relationship lasted forever, I wouldn't have a job. I don't care how much he begs you. Say no."

She dodged pedestrians as she walked. "If you can't resist the temptation, make sure you're the only person who has copies.

Make him use your phone. And never *ever* post compromising materials on an internet website. Especially ones that specialize in creepy cheating losers who want sex with someone new but don't have the game to find a partner on their own..."

She wrapped up the stream and strolled into the elevator. She arrived at the fourteenth floor at eight on the dot. To her surprise, Morgan was already there, waiting in the lobby.

Judging by her face, she'd been crying all weekend.

Kenzi reached out and gave her client a hug. "How you holding up?"

Her voice caught several times before she managed to speak. "Not—not well. Haven't slept at all."

Kenzi examined her carefully. Dark circles around both eyes. Morgan didn't appear to wear much makeup, but what little she wore this morning had been applied with a shaky hand. Divorce was always unpleasant. But the release of those photos was shaking her to the core.

She hoped she hadn't spent the weekend alone. "Did Sally come with you?"

"No. She had some meetings. Said she'd come by later. She's been busy all weekend, while I've been mostly crying into a big bowl of ice cream. She's much better at holding it together. I may look like I'm the level-headed one—but I'm not. She's my rock."

How fortunate. Everyone should have a rock. Especially during times like these. "Sorry to bring this up, but I need to know as much as possible before we go into the meeting. Can you give me some information about who took those photos?"

Morgan reached out, steadying herself against a wall. "His name was Brent. Brent Coleman. We were a thing for about two years. Back when I lived in Canada. He was an amateur photographer. Didn't use digital. Preferred to develop his own stuff."

That made sense. You probably couldn't take this film to the local drugstore. "Do you have copies?"

"I don't think I ever did. What would I do with them?"

"But Brent kept them."

"Apparently."

"I gather you broke up with Brent at some point."

"Of course. He was even more abusive than Charles. And a womanizer. Never met a female he didn't try to screw. After a while, I'd had enough."

Morgan appeared to have a pattern of forming relationships with abusive men—and staying in them far too long. Well, she wasn't the only woman in the world guilty of that. "Any idea what Brent is doing these days?"

"Yes. He works for Charles."

Kenzi tried not to show her astonishment. "Seriously? He works at DigiDynamics?"

"Not exactly. He works for Charles personally. Sort of an assistant, gofer, right-hand-man situation."

"How long has this been going on?"

"Not long, actually. I didn't know anything about it until I bumped into Brent at the office one morning. Shocked the hell out of me. But there was nothing I could do about it. Charles doesn't make his decisions based upon what I think. Obviously."

Hell of a coincidence, though. "So it's possible Charles knew about the photos, got access, posted them on Taylor Petrie, then engineered a data breach to release them."

"Who else would have the resources? He may not be able to hack, but he has hundreds of employees who do. He didn't want my photos to be traced back to him, so he engineered a data breach. With hundreds of thousands of photos. Which gives him a lot of cover."

That part was true. Kenzi had read articles about this all weekend. Many celebs were mentioned, as well as known internet blackmailers like DarkSide. But no one was blaming Charles.

"I'm sorry this had to happen. But technically, it bears little relevance to the divorce. Our biggest problem will be dividing a massive marital estate. If we can get a grip on that, there's no reason why we shouldn't have a successful conference today."

"Please." Morgan grabbed her hand and squeezed tightly. "Make this misery end."

Kenzi returned the squeeze. "I'll do my best."

10

Kenzi parked Morgan in her office, then checked in with Sharon. "Is Crozier here?"

Sharon nodded. "I put him in the corner conference room."

"Were you nice about it?"

"I didn't spit in his coffee."

"That's your definition of being nice?"

"For that fascist, racist, gun-loving conspiracy nut, yes. Let me reiterate—if you take Satan up on his job offer, I will not join you on your descent into hell."

"Understood. But I better go talk to Satan and get this—"

"He's not alone."

"He brought an associate?"

"No. Over the weekend, Sally appears to have obtained counsel."

Is that what Sally was busy with over the weekend? Was Morgan aware? "Do I know her lawyer?"

"All too well. Wreck-It Rhonda."

Kenzi's heart dropped. Rhonda Stanley, solo practitioner, divorce specialist. She was effective, without question, but a pain in the butt to work with. The kind of courtroom bully who made you fight for everything and ultimately extracted concessions just because you were sick of the struggle. Kenzi tended not to give an inch without a good reason, so the two of them on opposite sides of a case did not increase the likelihood of settlement.

"Lovely. Is she in the conference room?"

"Yes. I thought I'd let her get started on the first round of angry arguing with Crozier."

"Sound thinking. Maybe they've already reached a settlement and all I'll have to do is sign the papers."

"Sure. That could happen."

The two women looked at one another...and a second later burst out laughing.

"And for that matter," Sharon said, "it's possible Crozier's heart could grow three sizes today and he could learn the true meaning of Christmas."

When the giggling subsided, they looked at one another and spoke in unison.

"But I doubt it."

———

ONCE ALL THE parties were present, Kenzi put the three litigants in separate rooms. You could never be certain, but she thought it might be useful if the lawyers talked amongst themselves first. When clients were in the room, lawyers tended to put on a show, trying to score points with name-calling and angry histrionics. Might make the clients feel good, but didn't advance the settlement. If they could speak among themselves, they might be able to establish some ground rules. Maybe carve out a path for resolving this three-way mess.

When she re-entered the conference room, Crozier rose to his feet. Always the gentleman. Wreck-It Rhonda Stanley did not rise. She sat at the table with a stack of papers in her lap and her feet propped up on the table.

Stanley peered at Kenzi through her cheaters. "And here's our hostess. Long time no see, Kenzi."

Stanley was a relatively large woman, at least compared to Kenzi. Broader shoulders and several inches taller. "I gather you're representing Sally."

"Someone needs to. Since you declined."

"Sally needed independent counsel. She and Morgan may have conflicting interests."

"You can say that again." She and Crozier exchanged a look.

"Something I need to know?"

Stanley smiled. "Kenzi, dahling. I thought you already knew everything."

"Far from it."

"That's what they believe in the KenziKlan. Isn't it?"

What was this? Internet envy? "I've seen your Twitter page. You've got thousands of followers yourself."

Stanley's voice suddenly rose. "Tell him I want it tomorrow morning. Or I'll have his ass dragged into court. In handcuffs!"

Kenzi blinked. "Now...what?"

Stanley waved her hands in the air. She mouthed, "Not you."

Kenzi took a closer look. Stanley wore an earpiece on the left side. She was taking a phone call at the same time she was in this settlement conference. Of all the arrogant...

"No! No extensions. No exceptions. Do it now or explain to the judge why he shouldn't be held in contempt." Stanley looked up and lowered her voice. "Sorry. Juggling so many cases I can barely keep track of them all. You know how it is. Sometimes you have to be the hardass."

"That's not really my—"

"Especially when you're dealing with a very male opposing counsel." She glanced at Crozier. "No offense."

Crozier settled back into his chair, hands behind his head. "None taken."

"Maybe it's my imagination, but I think women are more

reasonable. Matrimonial law works best when there's no testos-terone in the mix."

Did Stanley really think female lawyers were more reasonable —or did she think they were easier to manipulate? So hard to tell with Wreck-It Rhonda—part Nancy Grace, part Cruella de Vil. "I prefer to think we can all get along. All genders. Or no genders."

Stanley made a snorting noise. "Are you kidding? Men fear us. They know women are smarter and stronger. That's why they kept us down so long. Isn't that right, Lou?"

Crozier was too smart to get into the thick of it. "I love women. Always have. We have complete gender parity at my firm."

Another snort. "Sure you do. But someone has to make the coffee in the morning, right?"

Crozier shook his head. "Women have come a long way."

"Since *Bradwell v Illinois?*"

Was this Final Jeopardy? The case name seemed vaguely familiar...

"Infamous case," Stanley explained. "It should be etched on your overachieving brain, Kenzi. The court declared that women were unfit to be lawyers, because of the, and I quote, 'natural and proper timidity and delicacy which belongs to the female sex.'"

Crozier laughed. "That was another era."

"The truth is," Stanley continued, "women make better lawyers. Law school doesn't teach people how to deal with emotions or clients. We're taught to become thinking machines, rational automatons living in a vacuum where all that matters is the logical application of the law. Applying the so-called 'reason-able *man*' standard. Women instinctively bring emotional reality to a situation, while men live in this pseudo-logical fantasy that bears no relationship to real life."

Crozier put his papers aside. "Perhaps it would be best if we talked about this case. Anything we need to discuss before we bring the clients in? Any speed bumps we can smooth?"

"There you go," Stanley said. "Being Mr. Rational. Trying to avoid emotions."

"It usually works best that way."

"In fact, it never works best that way. That's why early settlement is such an elusive goal. Clients are upset and lawyers do nothing to alter that. Look what we have in this case. A bizarre three-way marriage. A program that could mean the end of personal privacy. A data breach that's spilled vile photos all over the internet. Pretend there are no emotions in this and you have no chance of settling anything." She turned her head. "Kenzi, dahling, tell him I'm right."

She thought before speaking. "I would like to know if Mr. Crozier's client was behind the leak. Because if he was, he owes my client a great deal more than the standard marital settlement. We could be looking at a civil suit for invasion of privacy. Or defamation of character."

"Do you really want to go there?" Crozier asked. "Your client allowed those photos to be taken. Drawing more attention to them could not possibly benefit her."

"Is that what your client is counting on? She'll be so embarrassed she'll let him walk all over her? Maybe even accept a crappy settlement, just to make it all go away?"

"Divorce is a messy business. No two ways about that. But this meeting will be more productive if we all stay calm and don't escalate. Law is best handled in a calm and rational manner."

Kenzi rolled her eyes. "Says the man who participated in the January 6 insurrection."

Crozier shook his head, unfazed. "I was there. I did not participate. I did not enter the Capitol building."

"You support the people who did."

"They have a right to express their dissatisfaction with their government. Someone has to. The news media is not doing its job. They're hopelessly biased."

"They do the best they can. Most legitimate journalists try to be fair."

Crozier laughed out loud. "Tell it to Richard Jewell."

"Those Capitol rioters were the danger, not the media. Extreme-right crazies who—"

"The real danger is the far-left Antifa, which the mainstream media barely admits exists, working in cahoots with the FBI. They orchestrated the trouble on January 6."

"You wouldn't know reality if it kicked you in the—"

"Whoa, whoa, whoa!" Stanley cut in. "We have definitely gotten off track here."

Crozier pursed his lips. "You wanted more emotion. You got it."

"We don't need to get into personal politics. There's no cheese down that mousehole."

Yeah, especially not with a lunatic in the room. But Stanley was right. Back to the case.

AFTER SEVERAL MORE MINUTES OF fruitless discussion about various settlement issues, they brought in the clients. Kenzi escorted Sally, then Charles, who was not at all what she'd imagined. Judging by appearance, he seemed harmless. Slight and somewhat shambling. She had a hard time imagining him threatening anyone, or running a major tech company, for that matter.

She collected Morgan last because she wanted to make sure she was stable. To her dismay, she found Morgan staring at her phone, obviously scanning the internet. Why torture herself? Nothing good could possibly come from that.

"It's showtime."

Morgan nodded. She rose and wordlessly followed Kenzi.

When they entered the conference room, Kenzi was startled to see the other parties, Sally and Charles plus lawyers, sitting on the same side of the table.

Granted, there were two sides, not three. But wouldn't Sally prefer to sit with Morgan?

"I think we may need to rearrange the seating assignments..."

Stanley shook her head. "You're behind the times, Kenzi, dahling."

"Meaning...?"

"Our clients have been talking over the weekend, with our full knowledge and consent. They've reached an agreement."

Morgan's eyes widened with evident horror. "No..."

"You've...settled?"

"We still need to work out the details," Stanley explained. "But my client has decided to join forces with Charles. She supports him and denies your client's claims of violence and abuse."

"And you didn't mention this during our previous discussion."

Crozier hid a smirk. "Didn't seem relevant. Till now."

He was playing her, making a fool of her the whole time. They both were.

Morgan tentatively reached out a hand. "Sally?"

Sally averted her eyes.

Stanley continued. "Both Sally and Charles deny your claims and further state that your client is suffering from extreme mental illness. She hallucinates. Sees things that aren't real. Which could explain her absurd claims. And could also explain the...well, the sexually charged and rather disgusting photographs that have come to light."

"Sally," Morgan said. "She's—she's lying. Isn't she? You wouldn't—"

Kenzi tugged at Morgan's arm, urging her back, but she continued. "Sally? Speak to me. You wouldn't turn against me. Would you?"

Sally didn't look at her and didn't say a word.

"We may have to sue for slander," Crozier continued, "given some of the claims your client made while engaging in numerous extramarital affairs and behaving...well, exactly as you might expect from someone who would pose for those photos. Your client doesn't have a leg to stand on, Kenzi. No one to back her outrageous story. The best thing you could do is accept the proposed settlement Rhonda and I have drafted. It will leave your client enough to live and to get the psychological help she so desperately needs. You have no right to expect anything more."

Kenzi's jaw clenched. This wasn't a settlement conference. It was an ambush. "There's no way in hell I'm agreeing to—"

Stanley cut in. "I can't force you to be reasonable, dahling. But it will be best for your client if you are. She's dangerous. A danger to herself and others. She could be locked up in some horrible institution. For the rest of her life."

Stanley peered through her reading glasses. "So tell me what you want, Kenzi. She can get a little money and seek voluntary aid for her problems. Or she can fight us. And spend the rest of her life drugged up in a maximum-security mental hospital. Your choice."

11

The Strangler felt the heat. In every direction. From every possible avenue.

Judging by news media reports, everyone was looking for him.

Some degree of attention was inevitable. He'd taken more than two dozen victims, and even though he favored women on the fringes, women unlikely to be missed, at some point the numbers alone guaranteed he would attract notice.

Nothing he could do about that. If he could stop, he would. But he couldn't. The chain could not be broken. So the numbers kept climbing...

The soccer girl's grandparents were still on the evening news, begging for information about their beloved Chessie, hoping she was still alive. Embarrassing, really, this constant begging, offering reward money, as if Americans could only find their consciences if someone waved dollar bills in their faces. If they really wanted to learn something, why weren't they investigating themselves? No doubt the FBI discouraged that. But toeing the fed line was another way of guaranteeing nothing would be accomplished.

When he peered into that grandmother's eyes, red and

hollow, he could see the truth. She knew she'd never lay eyes on her granddaughter again. She cherished no hope of reunion. She wanted vengeance.

Who didn't, when you came right down to it?

They would never catch him. He was far too clever, far too smart, far too methodical. They had a better chance of catching the Loch Ness monster. They hadn't even publicly acknowledged half his victims. They probably didn't know about all of them.

Just as they might never know about today's target, Cynthia Porter. Mail clerk for a large law firm, practically invisible. Barely on social media. But his exhaustive research revealed that she'd been fired, apparently for drinking on the job. Those high-class attorneys couldn't permit that. How could anyone sort the mail if they were in a jolly mood? Two weeks without a job had left Cynthia unable to pay the rent, which was why her landlord kicked her out. She'd come back to the firm today to beg for reinstatement, but judging from her demeanor, it hadn't worked. She would be descending this long flight of stairs for the last time. She knew that.

What she didn't know—yet—was that this would be the last time she walked down any flight of stairs. Anywhere.

Fortunately, most of the firm used the elevator. Even the power-walkers who took the stairs to "get in their steps" took the front flight. Only Cynthia habitually took the rear flight intended for service workers.

Why would Cynthia choose the path that guaranteed she would never be seen by her colleagues?

Because she didn't want to be seen. She wanted to be invisible. Like so many others in this great society of ours...

That would work to his advantage.

He heard the door slam three floors above him. She was on her way down.

Time to make his way up. Slowly. He wore glasses and a shaggy bowl cut and a striped shirt, all chosen to subtly suggest he was harmless.

He let her set eyes on him first. She was obviously surprised to find someone else in the stairwell, but he scooted to the other side of the stairs. The least threatening move possible.

They were almost parallel to one another when he turned abruptly. "Cindy?"

She stopped, slowly making a quarter-turn. He could see the deliberation in her eyes. Stop and talk? Or run like hell?

"Cindy? It's Bobby. Bobby Johnson. I—" He laughed. "I think we went to school together. At Ridgecrest."

He knew where she went to grade school. He even adopted the name of someone in her class. If she didn't remember Bobby, that was probably just as well. His story would have plenty of verisimilitude without inspiring deliberation about whether he looked like a grown-up Bobby.

She took another step downward...then stopped. "Bobby? From Ridgecrest? Oh wow. That's been a while."

He laughed. "No kidding. You haven't changed much though. I recognized you right away."

"Seriously? My hair is a different color and I wear contacts."

"The face is the same. I'd recognize it anywhere. I...well. I always kinda liked you." He held up his hands. "Not in a creepy way. But I did."

"Well..." Small talk was obviously not her forte. "What brings you to this building?"

"Applying for a job. I'm embarrassed to say I'm currently between situations."

"Hard times, right? COVID and all. So much job turnover. Hard to keep your feet on the ground."

"Amen to that." This was the point where, if he really were Bobby, he'd suggest they get together for coffee. And given how repressed and reclusive she was, she'd probably make an excuse to avoid the invitation. He wasn't going to do anything that might scare her away. "Well, it was great bumping into you like this."

"Yeah." Her head bobbed. "Super cool. Maybe we could...do it again."

Aha. She was going to invite *him*. Much better.

"Wanna meet tonight? Maybe grab some coffee? Pizza?"

"I love coffee."

"Let me put it on my calendar." He pulled out his phone.

"I'll do the same."

And the instant she looked away and had her hands inside her purse, he grabbed her by the neck. Her lips parted wordlessly. He threw her against the wall.

Her head slammed back and made a hideous clanging noise. Her eyelids fluttered. Her eyes rolled up.

"No need for panic," he whispered. "It will all be over quickly. Before you know it." He dropped his phone into his pocket so he could grip her neck with both hands. He brought them under her chin, then compressed her windpipe. "No time at all."

Her face was turning purple, but there was still some life left in her. She started to struggle, squirm. He pressed hard, restricting her movements, but she continued to fight, even as she should be losing consciousness. Despite all the bad news she'd had of late, she was not ready to quit. Apparently she still thought she had something to live for.

How wrong this foolish girl was.

She shifted from side-to-side, making it hard to maintain his grip. He lost balance for an instant and she took full advantage.

She brought her knee up into his stomach. It hurt. His grip loosened.

Okay, this struggle had been cute at first, admirable even, but now it was becoming a problem. He needed to end this. He brought a fist around to club her on the side of the head...

And missed. Because she ducked.

Her hand dipped into her purse and emerged with pepper spray. She pushed the button.

He turned but not fast enough. He didn't get the full dose

but enough to sting. His eyes watered. He felt dizzy and disoriented.

She fled down the stairs.

And she'd seen his face.

If she escaped, his adventure was over. And he hadn't reached the climax yet.

He could not allow that to happen.

Stumbling and half blind, he raced after her. She was ahead by at least a flight, maybe more. Only six floors to ground level.

He would not catch up to her like this.

Could he possibly jump flights? Leap into the empty space between flights? He'd seen that in movies. Seemed dubious, but he had no other ideas and no time to find any. He grabbed the banister and leapt over the rail.

He managed to skip a floor, not enough to close the distance between them, but it helped. And made a thunderous noise. Would anyone hear? He hoped not, but there was nothing he could do about it now.

She saw him coming and screamed, but not nearly as loud as she needed to attract attention. She looked backward over her shoulder and that was a fatal error. She tripped, and like some pathetic cheerleader in a teen horror film, she fell flat on her face.

A moment later he was on top of her.

"Sorry, Cindy," he murmured. "Can't screw around any longer." He raised her head by the neck and banged it against the metal floor. He did it again and again until she was unconscious, leaving a bloody stain beneath her.

He needed to get out of here. Someone might've heard the commotion.

Fortunately he'd left his SUV just outside the building. It was equipped with duct tape and zip-ties and everything else he might need. It would be pleasure delayed, not denied.

That had been close, he thought, as he threw her limp body over his shoulder, fireman-style. Errors of judgment like that could bring this operation to a sudden and disastrous end. The chain would be broken. Permanently.

He loved his work and he still had much to accomplish. He needed to return to form, get back to basics, recoup his confidence.

Cindy had put everything he worked so hard for in jeopardy. But it was just an aberration. Not an omen.

He would not let this prevent him from achieving his end. He had so much left to do. And so little time to do it.

12

Kenzi felt like she needed to say something, but had no idea what it should be. She'd never felt so blindsided in her entire life. Morgan looked as if she were about to crumple into a heap on the floor of the conference room.

"You could have told me this in advance, Rhonda," Kenzi said through gritted teeth. "Instead you decided to play tactical games. So our chances of settling anything today are nil."

Stanley craned her neck. "Don't mean to tell you how to do your job, Kenzi, but shouldn't you ask your client about that? Maybe speak to her before you reject an offer? I think that's the way the Rules of Professional Conduct say it's supposed to go. It's just possible your client may not savor the possibility of spending the rest of her life in a straitjacket being felt up by disgusting men in white scrubs."

"You dirty little—"

"Tut, tut, Kenzi, dahling, let's not descend to that. Here's a written copy of our offer. Look it over, talk to your client, and let's see if we can get this unpleasant matter resolved as quickly and quietly as possible."

"You're in on this railroad too, Crozier?"

He simply smiled.

"You know your client beat Morgan. Physically abused her."

"He denies all such claims. And the other woman in the relationship, Sally, says it never happened. Was all part of your client's hallucinations."

"He's the one who leaked those photos."

"He denies that as well. Sadly, he didn't know those photos existed. If he had, he likely would never have entered into the marriage. I mean, honestly. Who would?" He paused. "Consider this. If your client has secrets of this magnitude, and is foolish enough to post these photos on the internet...what else might be revealed in time?"

"Is that a threat?" Which it obviously was.

"Mere speculation. People like your client are, in my client's opinion, eating away at the moral fabric of this nation."

"That sounds more like something you'd say."

"But then, you know nothing about my client, because as usual, you haven't done your homework, much less any strategic planning. You're talented, Kenzi, but you lack the discipline a truly great lawyer needs. That might be...one more reason for you to consider a change of venue."

She couldn't stop herself. "Go to hell."

"Hell is the current state of the world. Unless and until true Americans start taking action."

True Americans? She felt her lips thinning. She should probably keep her mouth shut. It was unlikely she was going to say anything that would help Morgan, and highly likely she would tell Crozier and Stanley exactly what she thought of them, which would probably end with her in front of a Bar Disciplinary Committee.

Kenzi glared bullets at Sally. "And you're going to sit there and go along with this? Let them screw over your lover? And wife?"

Sally continued to look away.

Stanley jumped in. "If I may remind you, Kenzi, Sally is represented by counsel, so it's completely inappropriate for you to communicate with her directly. Talk to me."

"I wouldn't waste my breath."

Morgan teetered, clutching her stomach, staring at Sally. "You said—you said—" The words caught in her throat. She gasped for air in short, quick bites. "We had something wonderful."

Sally's voice was barely audible. "And now it's over. Time to move on."

Morgan wailed, loud and keening, like a bereaved banshee. Her pain was almost tangible. Kenzi could feel it in her teeth, in every syllable that escaped Morgan's lips.

She took Morgan by the arm, then stopped to speak to Stanley in hushed tones. "It was terrible when judges declared women too weak to be lawyers. But that was better than women getting ahead by acting like the worst of men."

———

KENZI TRIED to comfort Morgan in her private office.

"At the end of the day," Kenzi explained, "Sally was in a bad situation. She wasn't a party to the marriage. Charles would surely push her out of the company. She saw a chance to walk away with a large sum of money and she took it."

"By betraying me! I told her I'd split everything I got."

"True. But she took the bird in the hand."

Morgan covered her face. "I thought she loved me."

Kenzi didn't know what to say. Love was a wonderful thing when it worked. And a devastating thing when it failed.

After Morgan left, Kenzi assembled her teammates for a tactical huddle. Sharon and Emma protested that they already had too much work to do, but Kenzi ignored them. Crozier was right about one thing—she hadn't prepared for the conference like she should've done. If they were headed for trial, Kenzi needed to know more about all the parties involved. She needed to know everything.

Emma sat at the round table in Kenzi's office, looking pale and Goth as usual, dressed entirely in black. "Just as a reminder, I don't do divorce."

"I know. But you're our expert on computers, and specifically on hacking."

"It's a gift. I can think like a computer."

Probably because she liked computers more than she did people. "I want you to find out everything you can about this Taylor Petrie hack. Who did it? How was it done? Was Charles behind it? How did Morgan's photos get in there?"

"The obvious explanation—"

"Is not always the correct one," Kenzi said firmly. "Find me the correct one."

Emma tilted her head to one side, obviously unconvinced. But compliant. "Whatever my big sis needs."

"Hacking is illegal, as is disseminating nude photos of people without their permission. This case might well spawn criminal charges."

"Settle the divorce and everything else will go away."

"Find me the ammo I need to get a decent settlement."

"I'll do my best."

Kenzi turned her head. "Sharon."

"I don't know anything about computers."

"But you're an expert on ex-boyfriends."

"That's getting a little personal."

Kenzi raised her palms. "I can't ask you to interview Charles. He's represented by counsel. But I would like you to find this ex who took the photos. And now works for Charles."

"Like that's not suspicious."

"Just get his story and report back."

"Looks like all roads lead to Charles."

Kenzi nodded. "Looks that way to me too. There's more to this CEO than appears on his wimpy surface. I think he has secrets. Major secrets." She reached out and gave both team-mates an arm squeeze. "And I want to know what they are."

13

Sharon approached the motel as cautiously as she could. To be sure, dumps, dives, and slums were nothing new to her. She'd grown up poor, in nasty neighborhoods in the worst parts of L.A., so there was not much that could shock or surprise her. Rats scurrying under the floorboards? Check. Carpet that looked as if it hadn't been cleaned in thirty years? Check. Hoods on the street corner so obviously peddling drugs that they might as well use a lemonade-stand? Check.

But this joint was bad. Seriously bad. Not what she would expect for the home of anyone Morgan once dated. And certainly not what she would expect for the home of anyone Charles Land currently employed.

She had to wonder why he wanted to meet her here. He presumably had an office they could've used. For that matter, there were any number of public places, parks, beaches, jogging trails, where they could stay away from prying eyes. But he wanted to meet here...

Her seventh sense tingled. She was getting messed up in something she didn't want and would probably regret.

She stopped in the lobby for directions. Did every motel have a skeezy old guy sitting in the lobby drooling over a porno mag? A neon VACANCY sign with one of the letters fried? A glowing clock that didn't keep time? A placard about towel-rationing? The guy looked up long enough to point the way, then leered at her with the same undisguised interest he'd given the magazine. "Undressing her with his eyes" didn't cover it. He'd consummated and sired several children with his eyes. She couldn't get away fast enough.

She found room 242 and knocked. The door felt thin and hollow, like she could put her fist through it without scraping a knuckle.

She heard someone stirring inside. How long could it take to get from one end of this room to the other? After a few moments passed, she heard footsteps. And after a few more protracted moments, someone answered.

Brent Coleman was almost the definition of undistin-guished. If the dictionary needed an illustration to go with the word, his mugshot would do nicely. Maybe five foot seven, stocky, curly dust-brown hair. Wore a flannel shirt with the sleeves unbuttoned. Sweatpants. Hadn't shaved for at least two days. And it was a Monday. Why wasn't he at work?

"You the lady from the law firm?" He had a bit of an accent, but she couldn't place it. Canadian, maybe?

"That's me."

He gave her a quick once-over, his eyes lingering in places where a gentleman wouldn't stare. "I didn't know you were gonna be..." His voice trailed off.

"Shockingly beautiful?" The word he was searching for was "Black," of course. "Is that going to be a problem?"

"Live and let live, these days. We're all colorblind and sex-blind and whatever feels good, do it. Right?"

She suspected that a debate over gender politics or LGBTQ issues would not be the best way to kick off the interview. "May I come in?" Not that she wanted to cross the threshold. But he probably wouldn't say much in the hallway.

He closed the door behind her, which sent a shudder up her spine. Not rational, but...still.

The room was exactly what she thought it would be and less. One twin bed with a ratty spread, something her poorest grandmother would've burned as a health hazard. No windows. A door that presumably led to a bathroom. An exposed rack with two shirts hanging from it. Could that be his entire wardrobe?

"I'd offer you a seat," he said, "but as you can see, there aren't any. You can sit on the bed if you want."

That was never going to happen.

"What was it you wanted to ask me?" He glanced at his cell phone. "I don't got all day. Have to start work."

He didn't appear to be anywhere close to working. "Do you take the train to DigiDynamics?"

"Sometimes. I work from home, mostly."

"Here?" She had a hard time imagining anyone calling this dump "home."

He pointed to a brown bag shaped like a laptop. That item alone doubled the value of this room. "I work remotely. Have ever since the lockdown."

He wasn't alone there. She knew many people who had once gone to an office, but during the lockdown learned they could work just as well and more efficiently without the daily commute —so they never went back. "What kind of work do you do?"

"I'm Charles Land's personal assistant."

"Did you work on Face2Face?"

He awkwardly shifted his weight. Was that his idea of a swagger? "I helped with the negotiations."

She was having a hard time positioning herself. She finally managed to lean sideways, one hand on the clothes rack, though Brent was still too close for comfort. "I understand you've known Morgan a long time?"

"That's right."

"How did you meet her?"

"In school. In Montreal. McGill. We had classes together. We were both regularly at the top of our classes and in all the geek clubs."

"And you dated?"

"We lived together for two years. Never went out that much, though. We tended to stay home with our books and computers. And sex. Lots of sex. Constant sex. She was insatiable."

Sharon winced. "You must've been close."

"I thought so. I thought we were going to be together for a long time. Like maybe forever."

For the first time, she saw a glint of regret in his eyes. "You said you were at the top of your class. Are you good at hacking?"

He tucked his chin modestly. "I can hold my own. But the one who's really good is Morgan. She's an absolute genius. It was instinctive, like she couldn't really explain how she did what she did. She just did it. Like she and the internet were one."

Very Zen. "Did you two play a lot of computer games?"

"No. I was never much into that. Didn't see the point. Which was what ultimately doomed the relationship, right?"

She'd come back to that later. "What else did you and Morgan do?"

"I let her set the schedule, if you know what I mean. I was content to follow her lead. We did what she liked."

"And what did she like?"

Brent shrugged. "Hot fudge sundaes. Making music. Strangulation games."

He dropped that last item as if it were of no more interest than the other two. "Can you explain that?"

"Sure. I play keyboard and she plays a little guitar. We talked about forming—"

"Not the music. The strangulation thing."

"Oh, she was super-into that. Have you done it?"

"I don't even know what you're talking about."

"It's very popular these days. Especially with kids. Morgan told me she'd been doing it since she was twelve."

Sharon's eyes fairly bulged. "What are we talking about here?"

He spread his hands. "Blackout. Funky chicken. Flatliner. Suffocation roulette."

"Still lost."

"It's a way to get a healthy, non-drug-induced high."

"By strangling yourself?"

"Usually someone else handles the strangling, you use a rope or a belt or a plastic bag. You cut off oxygen to the brain till you almost pass out, then release the pressure. Makes your whole upper body get an intense tingling sensation. A state of euphoria that lasts...oh, at least ten or fifteen seconds. A major-league high."

"Is this...sexual?"

"It can be. Increases sexual pleasure like you wouldn't believe."

She couldn't believe any of this. "And you say Morgan enjoyed this?"

"Still does, I'd be willing to bet."

"Sounds dangerous."

"If you're not careful, sure. But Morgan's a pro. She knows what she's doing. I know others who tried and totally botched it. Ended up with brain damage. Or a coma. Or seizures. But Morgan had been doing it forever. She said it was a thing at her middle school. She and the other girls used to do it in the locker room, till they got caught on a security camera. She was almost expelled, but she didn't stop. She was hooked."

Could this be true? Or was he helping his boss build a case against Morgan? Your honor, in addition to being insane and delusional, she's also a bizarre sex pervert... "Give me an example. When you two were together."

"One time we were at an airport. She was doing it in the ladies room. With a towel dispenser."

Sharon's eyes narrowed. "Excuse me?"

"Has to be one of those old-fashioned machines with an

actual cloth towel attached at both ends. You wrap the towel around your throat, lift your legs, and hang from the dispenser. Works better than you might imagine. You can have a nice buzz before anyone intrudes. Especially if you're flying late at night."

"How did you know Morgan was...buzzing in the bathroom?"

He explained matter-of-factly. "Marks on her neck. Red eyes. Headache complaints. The buzz doesn't last forever, unfortunately, and the brain tends to complain about being oxygen-deprived."

This description was stirring mental images she did not need in her life. "Did you help her do this?"

"I tightened the ropes for her sometimes. And made sure it ended before she suffered any permanent harm."

"I suppose this must've brought you two...closer together."

"I guess. I just wish I'd joined her online gaming community. That's how I lost her."

"You knew that she was forming an online threesome?"

"Not till she told me. When she said she was moving to the United States to live with two other people."

"That must've hurt."

"Like you wouldn't believe. I'm still not over it."

"And yet, you seem to have followed her here to Rain City."

"On Charles Land's invitation."

Sharon arched an eyebrow. "Really."

"Believe me, no one was more surprised than me. I knew he was one of the people Morgan dumped me for."

"What did he say?"

"He needed help. He'd had his eye on me for some time. Like ever since McGill. He invited me to move to Seattle. So I did."

"Does he pay you?"

"Generously."

"Then why....?" She gestured around the flea-bitten motel room.

"You think like too many people today. Having money doesn't mean you have to spend it. I don't plan to be a wage slave my entire life. In fact, I plan to retire before I hit fifty. So I minimize my expenses. Live here. No car. Don't go out to eat. Invest my money in high-profile tech stocks and watch the portfolio grow. That's the smart ticket."

She supposed that did make sense. If you wanted to waste your entire youth. "One more thing I have to ask you about. Those photos of Morgan that leaked onto the internet. You took them, didn't you?"

"Yes. But I did not leak them."

"Why did you take them?"

"Because the love of my life asked me to. Morgan thrived on that sort of thing. Not so much porn as make-your-own porn."

"Did this relate to the strangling?"

"Several of those pics were taken while she was in the afterglow of a strangulation high. She was always a little frisky afterward. If you get my drift."

No elucidation required. "If you didn't release the photos—who did?"

"I have no idea."

"Who had access?"

"So far as I know, only me and Morgan. But I did digitize them, so they'd be easy to copy. I suppose someone could've taken them from Morgan's computer, or mine, without us knowing about it."

"I'm gonna ask you point blank. Did Charles put you up to this?"

"Up to what?"

"Don't play dumb. He gave you a job to get friendly, then he asked for the pics. He knew they'd be useful in the divorce he was planning. So you gave them to him. Or planted them on the Taylor Petrie site."

"You're completely off base. I never did any of that. I loved Morgan. I've been kinda hoping that, now that Charles doesn't seem to want her anymore..."

Seriously? "You'd take her back? After all this?"

He kicked the shag carpet with the side of his foot. "I know. I'm pathetic. But weird as it was sometimes, those days with Morgan, just the two of us, were the happiest days of my life. Now I've got money in the bank, a decent job...but no one to share my life with." He looked up abruptly. "If you see Morgan, you might tell her...I'm interested." He stopped, swallowed, then continued. "Now that she's done hitching her star to a guy who never appreciated her and never will...call me. I'll appreciate her. Always."

14

Emma decided that her assumed persona for this interview would be nervous—and that wouldn't require much in the way of acting skills. This was not her first infiltration. She'd engaged in this sort of escapade for Kenzi during their last case, and for that matter, had done it before she started working with Kenzi. But she much preferred hacking into computers from a remote location. Safer, simpler, no face time required.

She'd tried to hack into DigiDynamics. But she couldn't do it. Count on techies to have an impenetrable firewall. They knew better than anyone how vulnerable computer records could be. Her first thought had been to arrive on some pretext, extract a hard drive and make a copy, but the amount of information this company stored was huge. They had their own server farm. There was no reason to believe any single desktop computer contained all the information she needed. She'd have to hack at a level far beyond her abilities. Probably beyond anyone's abilities, outside of the NSA.

But if she had a password, she could get anything she wanted, anytime she wanted. Morgan said she didn't have the passwords because she didn't do that kind of work, but there must be plenty of people in the IT department who did. She just had to find one stupid enough to give it to her. So here she was, supposedly interviewing for a job, but in reality cozying up to the gullible.

Kenzi might call her "antisocial," but there was much more to it than that. She wasn't exactly sure where she fell on the spectrum, but she had no doubt that she was on it somewhere. She was awkward in social gatherings, often failed to understand humor, didn't grasp the niceties of conversation. It wasn't true that she disliked people and preferred to be alone, but knowing how bad she was at personal interactions left her insecure. She liked people, but she wasn't good with them.

Yet here she was, putting on a show and trying to hack into people's heads. The irony was intense.

In an effort to blend, she had actually worn colors other than black this morning—though still earth tones. Ironically, the escort from Reception was dressed head-to-toe in black. He looked like an unpleasant blotch on the airport-lounge beige of the building.

Is that what she looked like at the law firm?

"Mr. Batista will be conducting your interview," the man explained. He hesitated outside a closed door. "I'll show you to his office."

"Thanks so much."

The man opened the door—to shouting.

"*Don't give me don't,*" someone shouted. "I don't want to hear *don't*. See this dictionary? It doesn't contain the word 'don't.' And neither should you!"

To her astonishment, the man threw a thick dictionary at someone's head.

Her escort cleared his throat. "That is Mr. Batista. Would you like riot gear?"

Emma almost grinned. "No, thank you. I can handle a dictionary."

"Mmm." The man turned away. "I've seen him throw computer monitors."

She entered the office just as the dictionary target skittered away. She didn't know what this man was attempting to communicate, but he had done it effectively.

He spoke first. "Who's this teen tootsie?"

Emma licked her lips. "I'm thirty-two. I'm applying for—"

"I don't want any more babies. I don't have time to explain what a computer is."

"I can assure you I'm not—"

"You look young to me."

"I moisturize."

He grinned. "Okay, score one for you. Sit with me. Call me Miguel."

He gestured toward what was apparently his office, a double-size cubicle with low walls. They let this guy be completely visible—and within throwing range—of the other workers? Seemed like they'd want him behind bulletproof glass.

He took the chair in front of a computer monitor. She took the only other chair, which was rigid and uncomfortable, like something you might find at a low-rent swimming pool. A deliberate choice? Maybe he didn't want visitors getting comfy.

"You want to work in our department? Why?"

Emma spoke with precision. "Money."

"Direct and economical. I like that. But there must be more."

"Health insurance."

"God knows we all need that these days. America ranks in the mid-thirties globally in terms of healthcare quality, but a stratospheric Number One in terms of cost. The American Dream."

He was a big man, with a beard and mustache, hairy arms, hairy everything. If he was gay, the LGBTQ world would call him a bear. He had spiky black tresses, the same color as his eyes. He wore an oversized hockey jersey, balloon pants, and a baseball cap turned backwards.

"Betty Lauren," she replied. "I've applied for—"

"I know why you're here. And I've read your resume. Impressive."

Should be. Since she made it all up. "I would love to be part of this department."

"Then you are a crazy person. This joint sucks."

Wasn't expecting that...

"But let's face it. All work sucks. We give up precious sunshine so we can buy stuff. Stupidest way to live life imaginable. Have you had lunch?"

"Well...no."

"Good. I ordered for you."

As if on cue, a skinny young man entered with two white bags. "Lunch for Mr. Batista."

"I'll take that." He opened one bag, glanced inside—then screamed. "*This is not what I ordered!*"

The kid glanced at his list and stammered. "It—it says right here—salmon—"

"Salmon prepared the right way, not the disgustingly wrong way!"

The kid trembled—but Emma got the distinct impression this had happened before. Come to think of it, the kid was trembling as he walked in.

"Do you understand that I'm on a diet? Do you have any idea how hard it is for someone like me to be on a diet? I love food. You get me? I looooooooove food!"

Most people do, Emma thought, but most didn't behave like this. Note to self: since the man wasn't married, didn't have children, and so far as she knew wasn't dating anyone—it seemed highly likely that his password revolved around food.

"I keep a running record of my calorie intake on this phone app, which also talks to my Fitbit. I've already recorded this meal. If I have to go back and erase everything it screws up the whole program. Do you have any idea how hard you're making this for me?"

The kid clearly did not, but then, how could he? "If—if you'd like me to get you something else..."

"I don't want something else. I want what I ordered."

"I have you down for the salmon."

"Of course I ordered the salmon. With no oil. No butter. No potatoes. What am I going to do with potatoes? What are they, six hundred calories a bite? All I wanted was the salmon. Just the salmon."

"I'll take it back and see what they can do."

"The hell you will!" He pulled the bag close to him. "I'm starving."

The kid slowly backed out of the cubicle. "If there's nothing else..."

"There is something else. I want you to look up the word 'calorie' in the dictionary. Because apparently you don't know what it means!" A second later he had another dictionary in hand and flung it across the cubicle. The kid ducked and skittered.

Did this man keep an infinite supply of dictionaries around to use as weapons?

He passed Emma the other bag. "I got you the shrimp scampi."

Ok, so he ordered the diet salmon, and got his guest the most buttery, high-calorie item on the menu. Was he eating vicariously through the people he interviewed?

"The worst of it," he explained, "is now I'm going to be sorely tempted to skip dessert. And I already had it calculated. If I ate the salmon plain, I could have five bites of ice cream."

"You're dieting, but you eat ice cream?"

"What else is worth living for? Ben & Jerry's Chunky Monkey. Or Phish Food. Dole Whip. Salt & Straw Hazelnut Praline S'mores..."

"I like that one."

He closed his eyes, as if astral projecting to a happier place. "The food of the gods."

She took the shrimp but did not open it. "Perhaps you could tell me more about the position?"

"Pretty simple. We're in charge of the administrative systems that keep this giant bloodsucking corporation running. When the execs screw up their computers, as they do on a daily basis, we fix them. We make sure the systems are secure."

"We create firewalls?"

"And then some. Under my direction. Everything runs through me."

Which meant if she could just get inside his computer, she would have the run of DigiDynamics. "That's a lot of responsibility."

"I imagine you can handle it. It's not like we're dealing with the Great Secrets of the Western World. Just a bunch of techie rich kids making more money for themselves."

Emma nodded. "I read that Face2Face has been crazy popular."

"Very true, kiddo. One more reason we need to keep the systems secure. Every company in the city would love to get access to our code. A few pages of gobbledygook end up being worth more than Tesla, Spotify, and Nvidia combined."

Emma released a fake shudder. "I'm not sure I can handle that much responsibility."

"Don't worry about it. All you'll do for the first five years is staff the help line." He took a nibble of his salmon. "Damn that's good." He looked up. "But deadly."

Before he could speak again, another man entered the cubicle. This guy was tall, thin, and well-dressed—the complete Mutt to Miguel's Jeff. "Hey, Boss."

He looked up. "Speak of the devil. Harvey Vasquez."

"You were talking about me?"

"We were talking about Face2Face, which is the same thing."

He glanced back at Emma. "Meet the brains who made that program a reality."

Emma smiled at the newcomer. "You must be very proud. But I thought Charles Land made that program happen."

Both men laughed out loud. Miguel explained. "There's a difference between taking credit for everything and actually doing the work."

"A big diff," Vasquez added.

"Didn't Morgan Moreno write some of the code?"

"Morgan does at least know how to write code," Vasquez said, "but her problems interfere with her productivity."

"Take my word for it," Miguel said, leaning forward conspiratorially. "Harvey is the man who made that program happen. He may not get invited to trade shows and shareholder presentations, but he's the reason they exist. All Land did was sell the program to markets we supposedly opposed on philosophical grounds. And collect the dough. Lots of it."

"I myself received a lovely plant," Vasquez said. "Cute little fern. It's in my office."

Emma tried to take it all in. The true creator of the program got a fern—while Charles got a zillion bucks. Hard to imagine that didn't create some anger somewhere.

"I would be willing to share credit with Morgan," Vasquez explained. "She was the visionary. And she set many of the basic parameters. The structure. The binary architecture. But my team wrote most of the lines. Then Charles sold it to law enforcement. Which I considered a betrayal. We were supposedly a socially responsible company, not a pawn for the military-industrial complex." He pressed his hands together. "But Charles didn't ask what I thought."

"And Charles didn't acknowledge your contributions?"

"Never once. Bad for business, he explained. The company thrives on the cult of personality. And he's the personality. I'm just the worker bee."

"And you have a fern to prove it," Miguel said, chortling as he ate. "Maybe if you write something that makes a trillion bucks, you could get an entire tree."

"No. All I'm ever going to get is this." Vasquez whipped out an official-looking document.

"What would that be?"

"A summons. I guess Charles' lawyer wants to talk to me."

Emma arched an eyebrow. Crozier wanted this guy on his team? Why?

She played dumb. "Is someone suing the company?"

"No. Charles is getting divorced."

"Oh. Why?"

"Who knows? He's rich, he's in reasonably good shape. Probably wants to play the field a little. Before it's too late."

"Morgan was fine when he was young and poor," Miguel explained. "But at this point, he's earned an upgrade."

"Has he found one?"

Another conspiratorial glance. "Big time. Lola in Marketing. Super fox."

"He's dating her?"

"They've been doing the dirty deed. Since long before Charles filed." He grinned. "See? Don't you want to come work here now? Never a dull moment."

Vasquez agreed. "Just a little Peyton Place. Sex, lies, and facial recognition."

She looked at Miguel. "What about you? Have you been contacted by the lawyers?"

"Me?" He pressed a slightly greasy hand against his jersey. "I don't know anything."

"Sounds like you know everything."

"Well." He giggled. "True."

"Would you be willing to talk to lawyers?" she asked as casually as possible. "If they asked. If someone needed insight into what's been going down?"

He paused reflectively. "I don't know. I like working here. I wouldn't want to do anything that would get me in trouble. I've got a plan. Put in my twenty and save enough to retire. Spend the rest of my life sipping cocktails on a beach somewhere." He paused reflectively. "Still. I could shake up the waters but good. And what fun that would be. I know where all the bodies are buried."

"I assume you're speaking metaphorically."

"Assume all you want, little girl. But let me tell you. This company wasn't built by a bunch of nerds playing nicey-nice."

"You're saying Charles has secrets he doesn't want exposed?"

"He's not the only party to this divorce. Actually, this case has more than the usual number of parties."

"And you'd be willing to cooperate?"

"With which side?"

She paused. This man was too smart to give away the password, but she thought she'd already picked up some useful clues. And she was beginning to think Miguel could be more valuable to Kenzi in a different capacity. "With Morgan's side."

"Against my boss?"

"Unless of course the divorce makes her the new boss. And she promotes people who supported her at a critical juncture."

Miguel's eyes narrowed. "I thought you were applying for a job."

"Well...truth is...I already have a job. But I could use your help. What do you say?"

Miguel thought for a long moment, then shrugged. "Can I bring my dictionaries?"

15

Kenzi felt certain she was not the only woman on earth who didn't relish visiting the doctor. Was it written in the Hippocratic Oath that doctors' offices had to all look alike, equally cold and sterile? Seemed even worse these days, when solo practitioners were a thing of the past and most doctors were employees of large health-care groups or the government. All semblance of personality had evaporated.

Therefore, although she was initially thrown by the suggestion, she was not unhappy when Dr. Harcourt Quinn suggested they meet at Mister Blisters, a local coffeeshop not far from her office and a frequent stop when she wanted an espresso with a real kick. Here in the Coffee Capital of the World, coffeeshop meetings rivaled church attendance.

She scanned the lobby but didn't see anyone who could pass for a sixtyish neurologist. She took a seat and waited.

Was her heart racing just a bit? Even before she sipped her coffee? Was she that anxious about meeting the doctor? No, why would she be? After a moment's reflection, she realized her excitement was about getting out of the office. She'd been cloistered for several days. After that disastrous settlement meeting, she realized she needed to knuckle down. She felt like an underdog—because she was. Crozier and Stanley were ganging up on her, just as Charles and Sally were ganging up on Morgan.

If she didn't want to be buried, if she didn't want Morgan to get steamrollered by the onslaught of her loved ones, she needed to prepare. So that's what she'd been doing, while Emma and Sharon conducted the investigations.

She felt like she needed to take this one herself, though, and not just for the coffee. Charles was planning to claim his wife was insane. He'd tipped his hand at the settlement meeting, not that she was surprised. Given the magnitude and frequency of Morgan's hallucinations, it was an obvious move for an ugly, bullying narcissist. She needed to make sure she understood everything about this condition so she could defend Morgan properly. She might even call the doctor to the witness stand.

Kenzi was alerted by the tinkle of the bell over the front door. Harcourt Quinn wore a Hawaiian shirt and loose-fitting cargo pants. Sandals. Long gray hair pulled back in a ponytail.

She waved. He ordered some coffee and brought it to her table. "Nice to meet you."

"Thank you for coming. As I think you know, I'm Morgan's lawyer in this divorce her husband filed. I should tell you that Morgan has waived all physician-patient privilege. So you're free to tell me about her situation."

Dr. Quinn nodded. "Morgan called and said the same. And completed the necessary paperwork. You should know that I adore Morgan and would do anything to help her. What do you want to know about?"

"Let me put my cards on the table. At a settlement meeting, Charles and his lawyer indicated that Morgan was insane. Crackers. Delusional."

Quinn pursed his lips. "About what I would expect from Charles."

"You know him?"

Quinn took a few moments, inhaled deeply. "I've seen the bruises on Morgan's arms and chest when she came to my office.

Which she always wrote off to some unfortunate accident. Walked into a door or something absurd like that."

"You didn't buy it?"

"I'm a doctor. Not an idiot."

"Did you take any photos? Make any records?"

"Sorry, no. I don't have the right to ignore my patients' wishes, except in a few narrowly prescribed situations. But I can tell you this with absolute certainty. Morgan is not crazy. She's as sane as they come, and holding up well under incredibly difficult circumstances. She does not have a mental illness of any kind. She has a very real physiological and neurological condition."

"Alice in Wonderland syndrome."

"The official name is Todd's syndrome, but the Alice moniker does a better job of explaining what life is like for people who have it. At any moment, your day could be interrupted by flying playing cards, monsters threatening to kill you, geometric shapes attacking you. Honestly, it's a miracle Morgan has kept her head together as well as she has. Do you know that, as a software developer, she sometimes spends as much as ten hours a day sitting in a chair, staring at a screen? Now imagine doing that kind of work, which requires intense focus, while monsters are zooming in and out of your vision."

Kenzi grimaced. "Can it be treated?"

"Yes, but not well, since we don't know what causes it. Experts speculate about proteins forming in the brain—the same explanation often given for Alzheimer's. But no one really knows. Mostly we treat the symptoms, try to minimize the impact. Maxalt seems to help Morgan. She takes it regularly."

"She also mentioned Botox."

"Right. Not to smooth out wrinkles. For pain. Which I'd imagine is about three times worse these days. Going through a divorce makes everything worse."

"I assume you're familiar with Morgan's living arrangement. I mean, prior to Charles moving out."

"I am. She was very proud of it. Not in the closet at all.

Called it a throuple. Said she and Sally and Charles were a close-knit loving family unit."

"Could Morgan's medical problems be exacerbated by her lifestyle?"

"You mean, is she having delusions because she has two partners rather than one? That's preposterous."

"I'm just trying to head the opposition off at the pass. Anticipate their moves."

"If they try that line of reasoning, I will personally laugh in their face."

"And testify?"

Quinn sighed. "If Morgan wants me to. I've been on the witness stand three times and hated every minute of it. Being pummeled by questions from lawyers who didn't go to medical school and probably couldn't hack it if they tried. Please. But these days, it's practically part of the job. No doctor can stay clear of the courts forever." He leaned across the table. "You know, polyamory is not that rare. Not as rare as people think. And not just in Utah, either."

That's what she'd discovered from her own research. An estimated sixty-thousand Americans were in polyamorous relationships, including Hmong Americans, many Muslim ethnicities, and Pan-African Ausar Auset Society members. They had to deal with all kinds of problems stemming from intolerance, but legal challenges were the worst. Marriage, divorce, parenting rights, inheritance, hospital visits—you name it. Unmarried partners were always left by the wayside, trapped in a legal netherworld.

"Do you have other patients who are throuples?"

"More than you might imagine. One leads to another, once word gets out that you're not judgy and don't expect every other person on earth to look just like you. It seems to have become my niche."

"Are there that many polygamous relationships in Seattle?"

The doctor raised a finger. "Polyamorous. Not polygamous. There's a difference. Some overlap, but not the same. In my experience—" He corrected himself. "In my professional experience, polygamy is usually religiously motivated and involves a guy who has multiple female sex partners—but those partners don't normally have sex with one another. Polyamorous relationships usually involve people in erotic relationships with all their partners and have not religious but utopian philosophies about sexual freedom and diversity."

"Like Morgan's throuple."

"Precisely. Hence her profound feeling of betrayal now. There are political differences as well. Polygamists, at least stereotypically, are right-wing misogynists. Polyamorists are stereotypically left-wing anarchists, decadent rule breakers eating away at the American way of life."

"Is there still an American way of life?"

Quinn chuckled. "If there is, I'd be hard-pressed to define it."

"But it doesn't include polyamory?"

"Is this any further from the mainstream than same-sex marriages? Doesn't seem so to me. But same-sex marriages are legal in every state. And polyamorous marriages are legal nowhere."

Kenzi knew this to be true. The US Supreme Court's ruling in *Obergefell v Hodges* made same-sex marriage a constitutional right, but that ruling didn't extend to other marital permutations. Chief Justice John Roberts noted in his dissent that if it was unconstitutional to prevent same-sex couples from marrying, they couldn't "disrespect and subordinate people who find fulfillment in polyamorous relationships." He questioned why "the two-person element of the core definition of marriage may be preserved while the man-woman element may not." Kenzi had to admit he had a point. Historically, polyamory was fairly common, far more so than same-sex marriage.

Even if the Supreme Court hadn't embraced polyamory, other legislatures were beginning to fill the gap. If Crozier tried to argue that this throuple was immoral or illegal everywhere, she was prepared to cite chapter and verse on Utah's new

"Bigamy Bill" passed in 2020, which decriminalized polygamy from a felony to a misdemeanor. Both Somerville and Cambridge Massachusetts passed ordinances allowing groups of three or more who "consider themselves to be a family" to be legally recognized as domestic partners.

Even though initially she'd been surprised by the idea of a throuple, she was beginning to see the logic. On the other hand, they had drawn an older, male, conservative judge, and she didn't think he was likely to promote a major paradigm shift. He was much more likely to think the world was changing too fast and didn't need to change any faster.

"I blame the dictionaries," Quinn said, sipping his latte.

Kenzi blinked. "Beg your pardon?"

"Any time you want to see which way the wind is blowing, what people find acceptable and what they do not, look at the dictionary. Here's a fun fact: in 2006, both the Oxford English Dictionary—the world's greatest—and Merriam-Webster—America's greatest—added the word "polyamory." In fact, today you can type that into Microsoft Word and you don't get red squiggles. If the word is accepted—how long can it be before the situation it defines is?"

"I have no idea," Kenzi said. "But I doubt it will happen fast enough to help Morgan."

———

THAT NIGHT AFTER DINNER, Kenzi consulted her daughter. Hailee might be young and inexperienced, but hours studying online and cruising the internet left her far more knowledgeable than most about the world around her. Not that Kenzi particularly wanted to have an in-depth discussion about polyamory with her teenage daughter. But she needed insight on how to approach the court on this delicate subject.

Hailee was crocheting—a new hobby she'd taught herself by watching YouTube videos—and listening to Nat King Cole.

"Hailee, do you have friends who have more than two parents?"

Hailee did not look up from her yarn. "You mean people like your new client?"

"Exactly."

Hailee shrugged. She set down the knitting and wheeled closer to her mom. "I know far more kids who have only one parent."

No doubt. "But you do know some with...three?"

"My friend Staci. The track star. She has two moms. And a dad, apparently, though I've never seen him."

"Does that seem all right to you?"

She shrugged. "I don't see why I should care. If it works for them and it isn't hurting anybody, who am I to judge? Honestly, Mom, I've never understood why the government should be involved in people's personal lives anyway. What gives a judge or a politician the right to decide what constitutes a marriage? Or a family? We don't all have to be the same, you know?"

"I hear you."

"I mean, I don't want to wreck your life. I know you've made a ton of money off the current system, where people can't get married without the government stamp of approval, and can't get un-married without undergoing a hellacious legal process. But sometimes I think we'd be better off if the government stuck to national defense and highways and stuff we actually need them for—and stopped trying to govern our private lives."

Spoken like the sweet little libertarian she was. But she had a point. "Do you think the KenziKlan will be dismayed? If word gets out that I'm repping a polyamorist?"

"Newsflash, Mom. The word is out. If anything, your stock is rising because it shows how hip and progressive you are."

"They don't care?"

"Not about that. Now those sexy photos from the cheaters' website are a problem. But I'm sure you have an answer for that."

"She didn't post those."

"I believe you. I mean, who would? Just remind everyone that she was young and foolish when they were taken and Charles arranged for their release because he's a vicious vindictive person. She's never committed adultery but apparently Charles has. This could turn into something that helps you."

"What else do people online care about?"

"Same as people who aren't online. Same as people everywhere. They care about stopping wifebeaters. And cheaters. And tech magnates who steal other people's ideas to make themselves rich. If you stick to the right themes, I think you'll win the court of public opinion. And maybe the real court, too."

"You think I can win this mess?"

"I know so."

"How?"

"'Cause you're my mom."

"Aww—"

"Plus, you have me on your team. So how could you lose?"

She gave her daughter a big squeeze, her eyes feeling watery. Occasionally, being a mother was worth the trouble.

16

C hessie awoke to darkness.

The last moment she'd been fully conscious, she was certain she was dying. So being awake and alive was a surprise—but a welcome one.

Why was everything so dark? How could she be certain this wasn't some altered reality? Purgatory. Waiting to transition to... whatever the future held.

She could tell she was seated. She could feel some kind of floor beneath her feet. But she had no idea where she was or how she got here. She had a sense that time had passed, but couldn't be certain how long.

She felt helpless. And terrified. She might prefer being dead to the ominous feeling that death was right around the corner. And not a quick, painless death like strangulation. Something far worse. She didn't know why, but she felt it, felt it in every inch of her flesh.

How many soccer games had she missed? It seemed stupid, worrying about college sports while she sat in darkness. But she couldn't help herself. She was the captain. She was supposed to be in charge.

She supposed by now someone else had been made captain.

Probably Audrey. She was the best and the other girls liked her. She'd do fine. Might even be an improvement.

For the first time since she'd awakened, tears came to her eyes. She loved those girls so much. She loved the team. She loved playing and thought this might be the year they went all the way. And now that had been taken away—at least from her—because she made the stupid mistake of going to that frat—

That was it. The memories started flooding back, clarifying in her head. She'd gone to the party. Mr. Nutrition asked her to go outside. He'd tried to strangle her, saying she was going to get some fantastic high.

And then the other man came to her rescue. Or so she believed. The cast that fell from his arm when he started choking her. She fought as hard as she could but she was still weak and he was strong and experienced and she couldn't get it together...

And then the darkness.

She heard a noise. A creaking sound. Someone was opening a door. A heavy metallic door. A few moments later, she heard footsteps. Echoing. Where was she?

She heard a whooshing sound, then felt something brush against her face. All at once, she was bathed in light.

Bright white-hot light. More than she could bear. So much it hurt. She squeezed her eyes shut, trying to block it out.

"Good morning, Chessie. Nice to see you again."

It was him. She recognized his voice. He was standing before her, over her. Him.

"You've been out a long time. But you'll be happy to know you're still well and in one piece. Keeping you asleep made the transportation easier."

She slowly opened one eye, letting the light creep in bit by bit. He was holding some kind of black hood.

She looked around.

She was pinned down. No. Chained. She was chained to the floor. That was why she could barely move.

"You have not reached your ultimate destination," he explained, "but you're getting closer. Normally I would've taken you out of Seattle long ago. But it's getting a bit hot outside right now. Mostly because of you."

Slowly her eyes adjusted well enough to see more. She was in a large space, poorly lit. Basement? Warehouse? Storage container? She couldn't be sure.

But she could see him. The strangler. And he had another man beside him, shorter, thicker, scowling. A salt-and-pepper mustache. Watching.

"Your grandparents have moved heaven and earth trying to find you," he said, continuing his monologue. "Must be nice to have a senator in the family. But they have not been successful. And they will not be successful."

The man beside him grunted. His voice was deep and lightly accented. "Make her talk."

"You're the boss, Kingsley." The first man stepped toward her. "Chessie, could you please say something? He wants to hear you speak."

She did not immediately oblige. Why should she? Though after a moment passed, she realized she did have some questions...

Her throat still ached but she managed to form words. "Where am I?"

The two men glanced at one another. She could talk. She was still functional.

"You don't need to know where you are. It would do you no good. You won't be here long. And you can't escape." He paused. "Your life is about to change."

She glanced down at herself. She had no mirror, but examining her clothes and skin told her she was disgusting. Had she wet herself? How many times? She was still in the clothes she'd worn to that damned party. Her skin looked dirty and bruised. Even torn and cut in places. The so-called transportation had been hard on her, it seemed.

"Where are you taking me?"

"Another question I won't answer," her captor replied. "But what difference would it make? It wouldn't change anything. You'll know when you arrive."

"And then will you let me go free?"

The two men glanced at one another again. A few moments passed before her captor responded. "That will never happen."

She tried to leap up, tried to struggle, but it was useless. She was a bug in a science exhibit, pinned down and virtually immobile. She shook from side to side but it got her nowhere. Soccer had given her strong thighs, but it didn't help. She strained as hard as she could, but she couldn't break her bonds.

In the midst of her struggle, the other man began to laugh. "She's a strong one, no? I like that."

"She's healthy, that's for sure."

"Given the proper instruction, she could be worth a great deal of money."

Chessie's heart sank. She found it hard to catch her breath.

"I will never cooperate," she spat out. "No matter what. I will never give you what you want."

Her captor looked completely undisturbed. "Never is a long time."

"What does that mean? What are you going to do? Beat me till I give you what you want?"

He shook his head. "Beating would mar your features."

"Hunger is a great persuader," the other man suggested.

"And so is pain."

Her captor placed the black hood over her head. She plunged back into darkness.

She felt desperate, terrified. Amazing how a few moments of limited vision could make you fear darkness.

"I'll let you think about it," he continued. "Pleasure...or pain. A full stomach or an empty one. You decide."

All at once, she felt his hand clutching her throat. "I can give you pleasure like you've never felt before. Or I can make you miserable. It's your choice."

His hand tightened. "But in the end, the path you follow to arrive at your destination will not matter. You will give us what we want. One way or the other."

17

E mma entered the offices of Taylor Petrie inside Columbia Center, the tallest building in the state, wondering if it was possible she had underestimated her sister.

For years now, and especially since she joined their father's firm, she'd felt as if she existed in Kenzi's shadow. She supposed to some extent she existed in everyone's shadow, since she dwelt in the basement of the firm and for the most part liked it there. But she never thought Kenzi's divorce practice amounted to much. What did she do, really? She helped women who hadn't worked for years get enough money to ensure they would never have to work at all. Woot, woot, right? While Emma toiled in the fields of criminal law, exonerating the innocent, going undercover and potentially risking personal danger to learn the truth.

But after working with Kenzi, first on the Breville case and now on this one, she was beginning to see divorce law in a new light. Morgan deserved half of DigiDynamics. Arguably, she deserved all of it. And this case wasn't just about money. It was about the future of American privacy. It was about a husband so malicious he would leave his wife completely exposed, trotting out private pictures just to gain a bargaining tool. Many of the clients she'd helped were forced into criminal acts by unavoidable circumstances, like poverty or love. Charles was hurting Morgan for money, and because he was a violent, ugly, human being. That was the definition of evil, as far as she was concerned. if Kenzi could stop a man like that, then her work was more important than Emma had realized.

After her meeting with Miguel Batista, he'd agreed to help, but she suspected that wouldn't extend to revealing computer passwords, so she handled that herself. It didn't take a genius to realize that his ice cream obsession would fuel his password selection. He went with Chunky Monkey. Sure, he added a bunch of numbers and punctuation marks, but once she had the key words, it didn't take her code generator long to produce the correct assortment. She'd managed to break into the DigiDynamics records and access everything there.

Everything. Too much, actually. It would take weeks to go through it all, even with computer programs scanning for important words and phrases. She hoped to have something useful before trial.

And now Kenzi wanted her to investigate the source of the leaked photos. Her computer skills made her by far the most qualified person to handle the assignment.

This time she decided to pose as a journalist. It seemed credible, given how intense the coverage of the Taylor Petrie leak had been. She also thought it would make Pete Taylor—yes, the company name was a rearrangement of his own name—more likely to be helpful. He needed some positive PR.

She wanted inside his office. Near his CPU. She knew she'd never have a chance to steal his hard drive, so she invested in a high-dollar wireless digital duplicator. Something the NSA developed. The specs were complicated but the bottom line was not. If she could get near his hard drive, she could copy the data on it, even without knowing his password. She'd designed a protocol that targeted anything related to Morgan and her photos. Or her husband. Or her disgusting ex-boyfriend. She hoped there wouldn't be that much and it wouldn't take too long.

A receptionist escorted her to Taylor's private workspace, an unexceptional, isolated room that would've made her feel lonely. And she worked in "the basement."

Taylor kept her waiting for more than ten minutes. Fine. That gave her time to activate the device in her shoulder bag. She found the Wi-Fi network, targeted the hard drive, and started the search. Once the device found all the files it wanted, it would initiate the download. She couldn't be sure how long it would take since she didn't know how many files would be copied. But she was prepared to keep Taylor talking for a good long while if necessary.

Eventually, Taylor rushed in. "Sorry, sorry, sorry. Didn't mean to keep you waiting."

"It's okay."

"Yeah, people say that, and then I get trashed because someone had to drum their fingers for a few minutes."

"I can assure you—"

"Never mind. Again, sorry. I just got in. Been approving designs for our new Vancouver headquarters. Lot of tax perks over there. Much cheaper than Seattle. Of course, what isn't?"

Emma smiled. Taylor was a skinny guy with wire-rimmed glasses and an awkward manner. Someone who would fit right in on Tech Alley. He appeared to use Bill Gates' barber, and to share his fondness for off-the-rack clothes.

Taylor perched on the edge of his desk. "How can I help you?"

Emma drew herself up. Time to get official. Give him her best Lois Lane impression. "You issued a press release indicating that you were investigating the hack of your database. What have you learned?"

"We've found no reason to believe the hackers were out to get a particular individual."

"How can you be certain?"

"I'm sure you're familiar with the recent waves of internet terrorism. People who lock agencies, governments, and energy suppliers out of their computer files, then demand ransom, usually paid to anonymous cryptocurrency wallets."

"Given the high profile of some of your clients, it seems like a blackmailer could've made a great deal of money."

"Exactly. But they didn't." He picked up a file on his desk. "I've actually reached out to some of our most famous clients to make sure they weren't blackmailed. The hacker wasn't after money."

"Then what?"

Taylor scooted forward slightly. "I think they were after us."

"And by us, you mean..."

"Taylor Petrie. The company. The whole organization."

"Why would anyone do that?"

He gave her an incredulous look. "You know what we do for a living, don't you?"

"You provide a...dating service."

He laughed. "Yeah, we started that way. And got nowhere. We were too late to the party. Match.com. OkCupid. eHarmony. Tinder. Grindr. They had the dating franchise locked up. If we were going to carve out a niche, we needed to become specialists. I noticed there were dating services that targeted smaller groups. Jewish guys who wanted Jewish wives. People looking for partners of a specific race, creed, religion, color, or political persuasion. But you know what niche was underserved?"

Emma chose her words carefully. "Married people who wanted to have an affair?"

"Precisely. We weren't the only ones in that category, but there was less competition, and we tried to take some of the sleaze factor out of it. Targeting people trapped in unhappy, loveless marriages but lacking the economic power to get out."

She had to keep him talking. "Do you have any moral compunctions about what you do?"

"Helping people find love?"

"Helping cheaters cheat."

He pointed a finger. "You used the word 'cheat.' As if you're talking about people playing a game. Which, let's face it, is all marriage is these days."

"That's a rather cynical view."

"Let me ask you something. Have you ever been married?"

"Once. Briefly."

"Didn't work?"

"He turned out to be a big bucket of lies."

"But it still cost you a bundle to get out of it, right?"

True enough. Even with a family full of divorce lawyers. "What's your point?"

"I would've thought that was obvious. Marriage is a farce. Maybe not originally but it certainly is now. Once upon a time, civilization was structured around families. Someone had to raise the young. We needed a mechanism to transfer the wealth and property of the previous generation."

"Not anymore?"

"No. It's an antiquated concept and we'd all be better off if we buried it in a crypt and forgot about it. Half of all marriages end in divorce, and why should that surprise us? We only have one life. Why waste it? Love rarely survives, especially when sex is involved. Eventually one partner gets tired of the other, and who are we to say they should waste the rest of their one and only life on a loveless relationship? It's human nature to want to try new things."

"It's easy to try new things," Emma replied. "It takes hard work to make a marriage last."

He waved a hand in the air dismissively. "Even the ones who hang on rarely do so because of abiding love. They stick together because they're lazy, or for appearances, or for the children, or because they fear making their way in the world alone. That's not a loving relationship. That's a prison sentence."

"And yet, people keep getting married."

"But fewer every year. People under thirty are waiting. Only marrying if and when they want children, which can be better managed today thanks to birth control. How long before we admit it's possible for two people to raise children in a strong loving relationship without being married? Or even living together? It's time for us to shatter these millennia-old templates and start making new ones. We need to restructure society so it reflects our reality, not the sexist patriarchal desires of people who died a long time ago."

Emma tried to maintain an objective reporter's poker face. "So this is how you justify what you do? Marriages are farces, so we're going to help destroy them?"

"I don't believe we break anything that isn't already broken. If people decide they want an affair, they're going to have an affair. At least we sift the wheat from the chaff. Provide options. Allow people to find someone without going to creepy singles bars."

She supposed that much was true. She casually glanced into her shoulder bag, pretending to search for a pen. The duplicator had found all the files and the download was in progress. Just a few more minutes and the deed would be done. "But who specifically would target your company? Who wants to bring you down?"

"Religious extremists."

"If you're classifying everyone who still believes in marriage as an extremist, then—"

"We found a few fingerprints in the hack. Traced them upstream. We don't know enough yet to bring charges, but we strongly believe the hack may have been engineered by a group called the National Unity Center. Have you heard of them?"

She certainly had. That group played a role in the Breville case. They sent threatening letters to a science lab they believed used embryonic stem cells in their research, employing the cover name Christians for the Sanctity of Human Life. "You think this group hacked your files because you're a threat to marriage?"

"Something like that."

"But some of the photos that were released...I mean, they're all but porn."

"I know. Isn't it ironic? Christians releasing porn into cyberspace." He adopted an airy tone. "'O brave new world that has such people in it.'"

She felt a brief vibration. The download was complete. She had what she needed. "Thank you for your cooperation. And please inform me if you learn anything new."

"Happy to help the fourth estate. Would you...like to give me your phone number?" He had an odd expression on his face.

"Um, sure."

"Great. I'll let you know if anything breaks. You know, we could continue this conversation over a drink."

She squinted. Was this guy coming on to her? "Thanks. I've got more appointments today. Then I need to write up the story..."

"Dinner then. The Skyliners Club? I'm a member."

"Sorry, I hate heights."

"Or we could just play video games."

She held up a hand. "Take a hint. Not interested."

"Oh. Fine. Sorry." He wandered behind his desk. "I guess you're not into guys."

She felt her steam rising. She turned him down, so she must be a lesbian? And he considered himself so progressive. "I like guys just fine. What I don't like are assholes. Next time you ask a woman out, treat her with respect. Not like a future one-night stand to pass the time till you troll the internet for your next one-night stand. But I guess you think that's okay, because after all, committed relationships are a farce."

She left the office and slammed the door behind her. It wasn't even her office, much less her door. But it still felt good.

18

"Hello, KenziKlan. Today's the big day. Okay, not *the* big day, as in the actual trial date, but today we're going to work through the preliminary issues to grease the judicial wheels and get our ducks in an opposition-busting row. I have several matters to discuss with the judge. I won't go into the details, but rest assured I will be in the arena fighting hard to make sure my client gets the respect and attention she deserves. Girls get the job done, right?"

Kenzi was streaming earlier than usual, but she had a big day ahead. The air was still misty and sprayed her face as she walked and talked her way through downtown Seattle. She didn't mind. The dimmer light probably didn't show her face and clothes to their best advantage, but sometimes she enjoyed a little chill. This being Seattle, it might be pouring later.

"Let me talk about something more serious, people. I know some of you were dismayed when those awful photos of my client hit cyberspace. Let me tell you what I will be telling the judge. Those photos were taken years ago in private by two people who loved one another and were having some fun. We can't prove who leaked them—but it sure is coincidental that they're being released just as this divorce case approaches trial, isn't it?"

Kenzi tried to be careful what she said—hard as that was for her. But she knew the judge disliked people trying to win their cases in the court of public opinion, and he equally disliked people making allegations they couldn't support. Nonetheless, she had a reason for raising this and she wanted to make sure her audience got it.

"Look, KenziKlan, do I need to say it again? Don't sext anyone. For that matter, don't write love emails that might come back to haunt you. Don't think you can go out and avoid digital eyes. We live in a world where the exchange of data is easy and virtually instantaneous. What's been posted can never be taken back. I hate to be the bearer of bad tidings, but relationships do not always last forever. So don't give your future ex ammunition."

Would anyone listen? Who knows? But Hailee told her a sizable portion of her audience was young, so if she could prevent them from ruining their lives—so much the better.

She slid her phone back into her satchel and headed inside the office building.

————

"Don't get comfy," Sharon said, as she saw Kenzi approach. "You've been summoned by the boss."

Kenzi tried to suppress her smirk. "Big Boss or Little Boss?" Meaning her father or her brother, the erstwhile managing partner.

"Hard to say. I note that you're meeting in Gabe's office, but the call came from Marjorie."

Her father's ice-queen assistant, who clearly did not like or appreciate Kenzi. She was so attached to her boss that at times Kenzi wondered if there might be something going on between them. Not that she would gossip or anything.

"I have a hearing this morning."

"I rather suspect that's why they want a meeting."

"What's the gripe this time? I'm keeping my hours up. Morgan has tons of money—or will, once this divorce is completed."

"As your trusty assistant, I wear many hats, girl. But a mind reader's turban is not one of them."

"Fine, fine. I'll endure it. The sacrifices I make to keep this practice going."

"Sacrifices? You're saying that to the woman you sent to Skid Row to chat with Morgan's revolting ex-boyfriend?"

Point taken.

"And your sacrifice is occasionally spending time with your super-rich relatives?"

Kenzi checked the time on her phone. "That's exactly right. On my way."

————

THIS WAS Kenzi's first time in her brother's office since he'd been anointed managing partner by their father. It had changed. He obviously laid down some major cash to give his private workspace the rich-and-successful lawyer look. What he'd ended up with, though, was an unpersuasive copy of their father's office. Original art by Latinx artists—Angel Otero, Glendalys Medina. Carpeting and wallpaper that set it apart from the rest of the firm—but some of it was just tacky. Reminded her of the Mexican pavilion at Disney World more than it did Mexico.

And even though this was supposedly Gabe's office, her father sat behind the desk.

Alejandro Rivera sat up when she entered the office. "Kenzi, *querida hija*. Thank you so much for coming."

"Anything for you, *Papi*." She considered taking the vacant chair beside Gabe, then decided she'd rather stand. "But I don't have much time. I have the first setting on Judge Pritchard's docket this morning."

"I know. That's what we wanted to talk to you about."

Sharon was right. "Got some strategy suggestions? Killer cases to win the pivotal arguments?"

He smiled faintly. He knew he was being ribbed. He probably hadn't set foot in a courtroom in twenty years and hadn't been inside a law library for much longer. "No. We're speaking in Gabe's capacity as managing partner and my capacity as—"

"Firm busybody?"

Again the faint smile. "Manager emeritus. We have concerns about this most recent case of yours. Don't we?"

Gabe straightened, looking like nothing so much as a schoolboy who unexpectedly found himself called on by the teacher. "Yes. That's right. We do."

Kenzi decided to take the offensive. "I don't see the problem. You were concerned about my hours. You were concerned that I don't represent rich people. Morgan's a millionaire. May become a billionaire."

"Yes," her father said, folding his hands in his lap. "But her husband is already a billionaire."

Now they were getting to it. "Unfortunately, he did not come to my office asking for help."

"Would you have taken his case if he had?"

Why not put all her cards on the table? "No. I don't do men."

"So I've heard. But isn't that a little...sexist?"

Pretty ironic, coming from him. "Maybe. But I don't think that billionaire scumbag needs my help. Morgan does."

"You might be wrong about that." Her father glanced across the desk. "Tell her about your phone call."

Gabe cleared his throat. He sounded nervous, but Kenzi knew that wasn't because he was speaking to her. It was because their disapproving father was in the room. "I got a phone call from the HR manager at DigiDynamics. They were inquiring about whether our firm would be available to handle matrimonial matters for them on an ongoing basis."

Her brow wrinkled. "Crozier is representing Morgan's

husband."

"I know. And wouldn't it be sweet if we could steal that business from him?"

"We can't. I'm representing Morgan. That's a conflict of interest. You have to turn this down."

"I don't think you understand," her father continued. "We aren't being offered one case. We're being offered an extremely lucrative retainer. By the corporation. To handle any matters that might arise in the future." He leaned forward, as if to emphasize the obvious. "This could be worth millions to us."

"It's a bribe," Kenzi said flatly. "He's trying to buy us off. He's trying to buy me off. To get rid of me. Force Morgan to find another lawyer at the last minute. Surely you can see that."

For once, her father offered a smile that was completely genuine. "I do see that. And I'm okay with it."

"You're okay with taking a bribe to get your daughter removed from a case?"

"Sweetheart...this is one of the benefits of having a reputation for being a great lawyer. Especially in the divorce arena. People have confidential meetings with you, not because they want you to represent them, but because they don't want you to be able to represent their spouse. People give you retainers to make sure you can never represent their opponents. It's one of the perks of being the best."

"It's revolting."

"It's a compliment. One you richly deserve. And one I think we should embrace."

"I will not abandon my client."

Her father made a dismissive noise. "There are many good lawyers in this town. She'll find someone else."

"I repeat. I will not do it."

"Kenzi—"

To her surprise, Gabe cut in. "You don't speak for the firm, Kenzi. I do. This is a decision for the managing partner. This is one of the reasons we have managing partners. Someone who can see the big picture and make decisions for the good of the entire firm. And I've decided we should accept this retainer." He shrugged. "I mean, it's a no-brainer."

Her father extended his hand. "And there you have it. From the boss."

"Yes," Kenzi said, leaning over the desk. "I heard what your little sock monkey said. But I won't do it. And you can't make me."

Gabe looked extremely uncomfortable. "Technically, I can."

She whirled on him. "Really? You gonna fire me? Is that it?"

"Your partner status does not make you immune from dismissal."

"You need a vote of the partners."

"That won't be difficult. We stand to make millions of dollars here."

Would her partners really betray her for a single retainer? Sadly, she had to admit that would probably depend on how much money it would put in their pockets. "You do what you have to do, Gabe. I won't fire my client. I'm going to represent her in court today, and I'm going to win."

"Kenzi..."

"While you two Scrooges count your gold pieces, I'll do what lawyers are supposed to do. Represent my client. And win!"

She stomped out of the office, not giving either of them a chance to argue with her.

Did she handle that intelligently? Probably not. But it certainly felt good. And she knew her father wouldn't allow her to be fired. She was too profitable, and it would cause too much public embarrassment. If they wanted to sign a retainer agreement after Morgan's case was over, fine, though she suspected the deal wouldn't be offered at that point. No great loss—she didn't trust Charles anyway. He'd probably renege on the deal as soon as he no longer needed Rivera & Perez under his thumb.

But she didn't have time to worry about that. She was due in court.

19

K enzi arrived at the courthouse ten minutes early, but Morgan still beat her there. She seemed uneasy. Clients tended to be nervous at hearings when their future was at stake. And no one liked being in the same room with their soon-to-be ex. But Kenzi had a nagging feeling there was something more going on. She just didn't know what it was.

"Did you take a taxi?"

"No," Morgan answered, "I drove. It was fine."

Kenzi glared at her. "Morgan, what did I tell you? Be safe. I know you're used to being strong and independent, but the fact is, someone may have targeted you. You can't be too careful. Plus we have this crazy Seattle Strangler running around disappearing women. You need to be careful."

"I was."

"Next time, I'll call the taxi. All you have to do is get in it."

Morgan did not appear to be paying much attention. Her eyes scanned the courtroom. "Do you think Sally will be here?"

"I don't know. Crozier hasn't mentioned it to me. But I'd be surprised if she weren't. They may need her to testify."

"I still can't believe she threw me over. Abandoned me for that toad."

Kenzi laid a hand on her shoulder. "Divorces are hard on everyone. I warned you about that. It instigates this painful process of people picking sides. Deciding whose basketball team they're going to play for."

"But Sally and I were close. I mean...really close."

"All three of you were close at one time, weren't you?"

"Yes. But Sally and I...that was different. Special. And what she did..." Morgan turned her eyes downward. "I just can't believe it. I can't get over it."

"You're going to have to. I need you at your best. We're both going to have to be tough to get through this. And who knows? If we put on a good enough show, maybe we can reignite the settlement talks and save everyone a lot of time and misery."

Morgan nodded, but she was obviously riddled with unhappiness.

Crozier entered the courtroom and sure enough, he had an associate and both Charles and Sally trailing behind him, as if they were all players on the same team. The associate was Kent Raymond, a tall blond man who she instinctively distrusted because he looked more like a romance-novel model than a lawyer.

Crozier stopped, allowing his entourage to pass beside him. "Ready to give in and give us everything we want?"

"You wish. You know you're going to lose these motions."

"I've known Judge Pritchard for decades. We've always gotten along well."

"You're counting on the old-boy network to help you even though the law doesn't?"

"It never hurts to have friends. Judge Pritchard and I have much in common."

"You're saying he's also an extreme-right conspiracy nut?"

His smile faded. "You know, politics are not my only interest. Judge Pritchard and I both collect classic cars."

That tracked. Collecting expensive old cars you never drive. Because you can. "You know I'm going to ask for the production of all documents relating to whatever deal it is you've made with Sally to get her to turn on my client."

Crozier bowed his head slightly. "You are welcome to try. I'll ask for full production of your client's dirty pictures. And they'll be admitted into evidence."

"Those are not relevant to the divorce. Why would the judge allow that?"

Crozier chuckled. "Because he'll want to see them."

"Is Wreck-It Rhonda coming today?"

"No, she thought I could handle this on my own. She doesn't get along with Pritchard as well as I do." He started to turn away, then stopped. "Have you given any more thought to my offer?"

"I am not going to work for you."

"Are you sure? I hear things may be getting hot for you in your shop."

How the hell did he know that? "You need to stop listening to gossip."

"I know about the offer DigiDynamics made to your firm. And I know it hasn't been accepted, despite its extreme generosity. I can imagine how well that's sitting with your dear old daddy."

"We won't be accepting your client's bribe."

"And you won't be accepting my offer?"

"Also a bribe. No."

He shrugged, then started toward his table.

She settled into her chair and continued trying to calm Morgan—without much success. While they talked, Emma informed her that Miguel Batista was in the courtroom. He looked much as Emma had described him. He was still wearing a hockey shirt, but had somehow wrapped a necktie around it. He was as hairy as anyone she'd ever seen and had black spiky locks that must require significant quantities of product. He waved, all smiles. Emma waved back.

"I assume you know him," Kenzi said to Morgan.

"Miguel? From IT? Of course. Sally and I used to play Hearts with him during the lunch hour. One of the most flamboyant guys at DigiDynamics. And one of the few I actually like."

"I guess he's never thrown a dictionary at your head."

"Several times, actually. It's how he shows affection."

"Interesting." She glanced behind her. "Is that Harvey Vasquez?"

Morgan nodded. "They tend to travel together."

"Couple? Throuple?"

"Not sure. But definitely friendly."

A few minutes later, Judge Pritchard entered the courtroom. He was a twenty-plus-year veteran of divorce court, which was unusual. Most judges moved on to calmer, more prestigious assignments after a few years. The fact that Pritchard was still here indicated that he liked it—or perhaps, that no one thought he was capable of handling anything else. He was in his late fifties, very white, and apparently very conservative.

"Before we begin," the judge said, "let me save you all a lot of trouble. First, I'm not granting anyone's motion for attorneys' fees. It appears to me that both parties are quite well off financially, so they can pay their own way. Second, as to the motions for discovery—consider them granted. This will be a bench trial, not a jury trial, and I'm capable of assessing what's relevant and what's not. I'm also capable of restricting access to sensitive documents and, if necessary, viewing evidence in camera." He paused. "And yes, that includes the nude photographs."

He drew in his breath. "The one possible exception is Ms. Rivera's request for the production of documents relating to whatever arrangement may exist between the petitioner and the third person in this relationship, Sally Beaumont. Usually, private arrangements of this nature are just that, private, and it's improper for the Court to interfere. We don't want to do anything that might discourage people from reaching private settlements. In this case, though, there's the possibility of some sort of financial arrangement that could bear on the veracity of the testimony of certain parties. Just to be clear, I'm not in any way suggesting that this has happened. I'm just saying that I can see the possibility. So I'll hear what you have to say and then make a decision. I've read the pretrial orders and briefs and they're fine. As far as I'm concerned, this one evidentiary dispute is the only matter we have to resolve before trial."

He glanced across the bench. "Ms. Rivera, I believe this is your motion. How would you like to proceed?"

Kenzi rose. "I suggest we get right to it, your honor. We call Sally Beaumont to the witness stand."

20

Kenzi had no idea what to expect from Sally at this point. She seemed like an almost entirely different person than the woman who had come into her office promising to support Morgan any way she could. Would she be a sympathetic witness? A hostile witness?

"Could you explain to the court how you first became involved in this...to use your word...throuple?"

Sally did not appear embarrassed or reluctant. "We were all participants in an online roleplaying game. I lived in Canada at the time. We formed a team, played together, became fond of one another. In time, we agreed to meet in person." She shrugged. "What can I say? We hit it off. One thing led to another."

"And you decided to form a threesome?"

"We were deeply in love and decided to make a commitment. Three people who cared about one another."

"But all things were not equal, right? Morgan married Charles. You were left out."

"I don't see it that way at all." Despite Kenzi's questioning, Sally was keeping her head together. She'd either practiced a lot or had a knack for maintaining her equilibrium. "As you are perfectly well aware, the State of Washington does not permit marriages with three members."

"But Charles married Morgan. That must have made you feel neglected. Perhaps hurt."

"Not in the slightest. I was technically still married at the time, so Charles couldn't marry me. And I do wish you'd stop trying to graft your soap-opera clichés onto our real-life relationship."

"But—"

"Here's the reality. I couldn't marry Charles. Morgan could. So she made us official. But it made no difference. I lived in the same house. We shared expenses. And we shared love. Equally. For the first four or five years, we were insanely happy. I think of those years as the happiest of my life."

"And yet, Charles filed for divorce. What happened?"

"Now this is where you can trot out your tired clichés. Success is what happened. As I think you know, we formed a company that took off. DigiDynamics. We all worked together and with a brain trust like that, it should come as no surprise that the company was a success. When Charles made the deal to franchise Face2Face, we became a billion-dollar company."

Kenzi raised a hand. "Before we proceed, let's clear up a few details. Face2Face was actually Morgan's idea, wasn't it?"

"True."

"And she wrote much of the code?"

"Also true."

"Charles can't code, correct?"

"Neither could Steve Jobs."

"Please answer the question."

"No, he can't. But he was our leader. You can't expect coders to run a company. That takes a special leadership ability, which frankly, Morgan and I do not have. But Charles did."

"And Charles also sold Face2Face to law enforcement. Without you and Morgan knowing about it."

For the first time, Sally hesitated before answering. "That's... not entirely true."

"Which part isn't true?"

Sally inhaled deeply, her eyes darting toward Morgan. "I knew about it. He confided in me."

"But he didn't tell Morgan?"

"He knew how she would react. He was afraid she'd do something to block the deal." Her expression was plain, matter-of-fact, but there was some regret there, too. "I understood Charles was trying to make some money, real money, which is theoretically the point of a company. I love Morgan, but she tends to have...tunnel vision."

"Eventually you had to tell Morgan."

"And she reacted just as dramatically as I expected."

"So far, most of the profits have gone back into the company, right? Which is the main reason we're having a divorce trial. To determine how the company will be divided."

"That's true."

"Are you bringing any claims against Charles?"

"No. We've reached a private settlement. And Morgan was angry about that, too." Sally paused. "I want everyone to understand that what I'm about to say comes from a place of love. I love Morgan. But she can be quite...strident."

Kenzi felt hairs stand up on the back of her neck. In her experience, that was a word men only used to describe women.

"Can you explain what you mean by that?"

"Morgan is headstrong. Loud. Temperamental. More and more, Charles and I found ourselves enduring rants and tantrums. Eventually it got to be too much. She needs help. When she gets angry, she totally loses control. I'm not sure there's anything she wouldn't do."

This was going south in a hurry. She needed to repair the damage but fast. "You know, when you first came to my office with Morgan, I didn't get that vibe at all. You two seemed close, and you both made disparaging remarks about Charles."

Sally craned her neck. "I was trying to be supportive..."

"Were you supporting Morgan? Or setting her up."

"That's...ridiculous..."

"And now you've abandoned Morgan. And cozied up to Charles. The man holding the purse strings."

Crozier rose. "Your honor, I object. I don't know what the point of this examination is, but trashing the witness does not address any relevant issue."

"If I may," Kenzi said, speaking to the judge, "my worthy opponent is deliberately missing the point. This witness has been bought off. There's no other explanation for her change of heart. And we're entitled to receive the documents that will provide insight into what she received for this betrayal. It goes to her credibility as a witness."

Crozier feigned bafflement. "Betrayal? Where is this coming from? She hasn't even asked about that."

"I can remedy that quickly enough." Kenzi swung back to the witness. "You appear to have switched from a loyal attachment to Morgan against Charles to a loyal attachment to Charles against Morgan. Have you and Charles reached some kind of accommodation?"

"I'm not sure what you mean."

"Have you made a deal? Have you been bought and paid for?"

Crozier shot up. "Your honor!"

Kenzi waved her hands in the air. "I'm sorry. Ms. Beaumont, have you made any kind of deal with Charles Land?"

Crozier answered for the witness. "As I have already informed Ms. Rivera, I reached a private accommodation with Ms. Beaumont's attorney."

"There you have it, your honor. They admit they've made a deal. We want all documents pertaining to the deal. We want to know exactly what was promised."

Judge Pritchard's head flipped back and forth like he was watching a tennis match.

"In the first place," Crozier said, "there was no payment for testimony. We recognized that Ms. Beaumont had tenable claims for a portion of the company stock, so we resolved those claims. The settlement is confidential, as most settlements are. I request that the court respect the wish of the parties to not have their private matters exposed in opposing counsel's daily livestream."

"He's trying to change the subject. These documents are relevant and they need to produce them. We have a right to know."

Judge Pritchard cleared his throat. "I'm not sure you do."

Kenzi glared at him. How could he say that?

"I could see the point if they were denying they'd buried the hatchet, but since they're admitting it, why do you need to know the details? I hope someday your client settles too, and if she does, would she want the details all over the internet? I suspect not. You're free to argue that this witness' testimony might be influenced by the fact that she has made a financial accommodation with the petitioner. As the judge, I will take that into account and give it whatever weight it deserves. But the Court finds that the right of a party to enter into confidential agreements, which promote settlement and ease the burden on the courts, outweighs your need to know the details. Your motion is denied."

Kenzi couldn't believe what she heard. "Your honor, this witness has completely sold out her—"

"I've ruled, counsel."

"But your honor—"

"I've *ruled*, counsel. Which is a nice way of saying it's time for you to shut up." He slammed his gavel, then left the courtroom.

Morgan looked stricken. "What—what does it mean?"

"It's no big deal," Kenzi said, which was a total lie. "I mean, I hate to lose, but the judge is right. We don't need to know the amount Sally was paid. We'll argue that she's a biased witness. The judge will take that into account. He may be conservative but he isn't stupid."

She turned, and to her surprise, found Sally standing behind her. "I wanted to speak to Morgan for a moment."

"I don't think that's a good idea." Kenzi could see Crozier watching, looking concerned, but since he didn't represent Sally, he couldn't tell her what to do.

"Please." Without waiting for a response, Sally pushed forward. "Morgan, honey, please understand—"

"Get away from me!" Morgan flung her hands forward, and a second later, the two were entangled, arms entwined, struggling, wrestling. Fighting.

"You filthy liar!" Morgan screamed, clenching her fists. "You said you loved me!"

"I did!" Sally grabbed Morgan's hands. "I mean, I do. I never meant—"

Kenzi tried to get between them. "Okay, stop this! Now!"

"You're nothing but a whore!" Morgan screamed. "You took Charles' money and screwed *me* over! I'll make you pay!"

"Break it up!" Kenzi bellowed. She could see the bailiff eying them. In another second they could all be in jail. "We are not doing this. Not now. Not ever, I hope. Sally...please go away."

Sally appeared on the verge of tears. "I just wanted to talk—"

"You had a chance to talk at the settlement conference. You chose not to, which is why we're in a courtroom now. Leave!"

Sally reluctantly slunk away, giving Morgan one last look before she disappeared behind the doors.

Thank God. Fight Club in the courtroom. Her life got weirder by the moment...

Morgan braced herself against the table for support. "I can't believe Sally would do this. I can't believe she'd betray me like this."

"I'm sure she doesn't see it that way..."

"We spent so many years together. We slept in the same bed. We loved one another. And now she's sold me out for...what? A few million bucks? Stock shares? Thirty pieces of silver?"

"I'll talk to Emma—"

"Don't bother. It's clear. I'm on my own now." Her eyes

seemed to harden. "Sally doesn't want anything to do with me. Fine. She wants to be my enemy? Fine."

Kenzi felt a shiver creep up her spine. What was happening? Morgan's eyes seemed to drift to a distant place. "Sally told me she loved me. But it was all a lie. A filthy lie."

"Divorces are always difficult, Morgan. People don't act normally. Give it some time and she—"

"Give her time for what? To hurt me again? I don't think so." She turned, her jaw set. "She wants to stab me in the back? She can try. But I won't sit here and take it. I'll strike first. Hard."

21

S ally left the train station and headed toward the apartment she'd rented downtown, walking as quickly as she could. The swiftness in her step was not due to the chill in the air, or her hunger, or even the fact that the cops still hadn't caught the damned Seattle Strangler. She rushed because she felt sick and she wasn't sure she could make it home before she vomited all over the street.

Today had been a nightmare, far worse that she could possibly have imagined. She knew it would be bad...but nothing like this. As she stared down from the witness stand, peering at Morgan, the woman she once loved—the woman she still loved, would always love—she imagined she could feel her heart ripping into pieces. Why did life have to be so hard? Why did everything have to be so complicated?

Yes, she tried to tell herself, Morgan was not a completely innocent victim. Some of this she'd brought on herself, with her constant demands, her refusal to just let it be. She could be a difficult person to live with and there had been moments when she thought she'd reached the end of her tether.

But those eyes. Those piercing, plaintive eyes...

And that's why she was sick and alone, rushing toward a

crappy, temporary apartment. Charles was doing his thing, Morgan was doing hers. She had no idea what she wanted to do with the rest of her life. She felt ruined, spoiled, washed up. Exposed.

Charles was pleased with her, for the time being, but that wouldn't last. He would take and take until there was nothing left to—

She stopped. Did she hear something? Ahead of her? Behind her? She couldn't be sure...

She clutched her stomach. Now she felt worse. Why, why, *why?* One thing compounded another. It was too much. Just too damn much...

She quickened her pace, which only exacerbated the stabbing pain in her gut. Was she being followed? And if so, why? Sadly, she could think of many people who hated her enough to want her removed from the face of the earth...

She ran faster. Only three more blocks to go. Was she being stalked? Was she imagining this? Had the courtroom trauma made her paranoid? She didn't actually hear anything anymore. But she kept running just the same.

She crossed the street at a brisk pace and kept moving. When she reached the next corner, she started to relax. Almost there. She could slam the door behind her, triple-lock it, turn on the television and mindlessly binge-watch something. Just to take her mind off...reality. Morgan. Charles. Face2Face. Money. Dark shadows from the past.

She crossed the last street. Barely two hundred feet to go, cross the alleyway, soar up the steps, punch the security button...

The blow came out of nowhere. She didn't see who delivered it. All she knew was that one moment she was racing down the sidewalk and the next she was spiraling into an alley, out of control, her head slammed back against a brick wall.

She blinked several times. "What...happened?"

She didn't so much see the figure as realize that the illumination of the streetlamps had been blotted out. It was a total eclipse, but instead of being round, the silhouette was human-shaped.

Was the silhouette wearing some kind of hood?

"Who...are you? What do you want?"

No answer. She felt her strength ebbing. She struggled, but something pinned her firmly against the wall.

She started to scream, but the figure grabbed her head and smashed it back against the wall. She felt her skull crack. She felt blood smear.

The assailant did it again and again until she was barely conscious, unable to speak, much less scream.

A hand slid under her throat.

She tried to make some kind of noise, but couldn't. Every time she tried, the hand slid further forward, cutting off her windpipe.

Her lungs fought for air. She was becoming light-headed. The light was dimming. She rocked her lower body, but her assailant had her firmly under control.

She knew she had a few more seconds at best.

She summoned all her strength and twisted away as hard as she could. The figure seemed startled by this last bit of resistance.

The hand slipped. She brought her hand up and knocked back the hood.

And gasped.

"No!" She was so stunned she couldn't think straight. "Not...*you!*"

The moment was lost. The hand gripped her throat once more, this time tighter and with a steely grip she had no chance of breaking.

She knew she was lost. As the darkness gathered, her brain was clouded with confusion...and despair...and regret.

How could it possibly be you?

22

Kenzi reluctantly agreed to let Hailee teach her how to crochet. She had no actual interest in crocheting and little confidence she would ever be competent. But it seemed to make her daughter happy. Kenzi had never been much interested in the domestic arts. She'd never learned to sew. She could barely do the laundry. She couldn't cook (though she could prepare a meal, she insisted). And home decorating wasn't her forte either. So...crocheting? I mean why? You could buy a shawl at Macy's for ten bucks...

They sat at the kitchen table, side-by-side.

"Mom, I don't think you're grasping the mechanics of the hook. Now watch. Copy what I do."

"I'm doing exactly the same thing you're doing. It just doesn't turn out the same way."

"Catch the yarn from behind with the hook pointing upwards, then pull gently...."

"I think I'm not holding the hook right."

"It isn't hard."

"Easy for you to say."

"You're not concentrating."

That was entirely possible. Even though she tried to put this day behind her, it was difficult. The hearing had not gone as she'd hoped. Not only did she lose a critical motion, Sally had planted a lot of negative seeds she knew would come back to haunt them later. And Morgan's reaction...and some of the things she said...were deeply concerning.

What she needed was a good shopping expedition. Was Sassafras closed? Yes. But online shopping was always a possibility...

Hailee gave her a stern look. "You're thinking about buying clothes, aren't you?"

"What makes you think that?"

"I recognize that look in your eyes. The same glassy-eyed gaze heroin addicts get when they fantasize about their next hit."

"I am not a...clothes addict."

"You're in denial."

"I don't even think that's a thing."

"It is. And you're the proof. I'll call Aunt Emma and start an intervention."

"It's important for a female attorney to maintain a professional appearance."

"You've got enough clothes to go to court every day for the next year without wearing the same outfit twice."

"That's an exaggeration."

Hailee gave her mother a playful jab. "Maybe. But wouldn't it be cooler if you could crochet your own accessories?"

Did she really need to answer this question? "Okay, show me again." Her cell phone buzzed. Saved by the bell! "Sorry, honey, I have to take this."

"How do you know? You don't know who's calling yet."

"A professional lawyer develops an instinct about these things." She pushed the phone to her ear. "Hello?"

The voice on the other end was the last she expected to hear. "Kenzi? This is Shel Harrington."

The district attorney himself. "To what do I owe this

pleasure?"

"It's a courtesy call." That seemed unlikely. Harrington tended to do whatever he wanted whenever he wanted. Courtesy to divorce lawyers was not high on the list of things he wanted. "You're on record as representing Morgan Moreno."

"How is that in your wheelhouse?"

She could hear him drawing in his breath. "I have a warrant for her arrest. We've issued an APB to pick her up."

Kenzi felt as if someone had dropped an anvil on her head. "For what? Jaywalking?"

Another deep breath. "Murder."

"What? Who?"

"Her...friend. Sally Beaumont. Attacked near her residence. Strangled to death."

Kenzi's lips parted. *Sally?* Who she'd just seen a few hours before? How was that possible? "The Seattle Strangler got Sally?"

Hailee looked up, her eyes widening. She wheeled closer to her mother. Kenzi tilted the phone outward so she could hear.

"I don't think so," Harrington said. "I can't go into the details on the phone, but it's obvious your client killed her."

"Sally is twice Morgan's size."

"But Morgan had the element of surprise. There's no question about it. I've had several witnesses tell me there was bad blood between them. Apparently your client threatened her this very afternoon. True?"

Kenzi thought it best to dodge that question. "Have you contacted Charles Land? He's the most suspicious character in this story. With a history of violence."

"He has an alibi for the time the medical examiner says the murder was committed. And honestly, it wouldn't matter if he didn't. Your client left a trail of clues a child could follow."

"And that doesn't seem suspicious to you?"

"I see no reason to make this more complicated than it is."

While they talked, Hailee tapped her phone, bringing up websites. The press already had wind of the story and its connection to the pending high-stakes divorce trial. This murder was exactly what the cops didn't need right now, with a string of strangulations and disappearances making the police look incompetent and fueling the "defund" movement. Which probably explained why Harrington was moving so fast. "I'll bring Morgan in voluntarily. No need for a big scene. There's been some kind of mistake."

"I don't think so."

"Let me talk to Morgan and see if we can clear this up."

"I don't know..."

"Let me call her. She'll surrender voluntarily. Peacefully. Can you hold off for one hour? Make everyone's life a lot simpler?"

Harrington sighed heavily. "I suppose. One hour. Downtown headquarters. I'll be waiting for you there."

"Thanks, Shel. You're a peach." Was "peach" old enough for him to understand? Too old? Should she have said he was "rad?"

"Let me ring off so I can talk to her. Bye."

She disconnected and immediately dialed Morgan.

While she did, Hailee read from her phone. "Looks like Sally was killed on her way home from the courthouse."

"Strangled?"

"I guess. So far the articles don't give a lot of detail."

"They probably don't know much yet." She heard a click on the line. "Morgan, this is Kenzi. Are you sitting down?"

Her voice was broken, halting. "I—I know about Sally."

"Do you have any idea what happened?"

"All I know is what I read on my phone. I got a notification. Then I turned on the television."

"The police want to arrest you."

She heard a wail on the other end. "Why me? They should talk to Charles."

"I'm sorry but...the police have some reason to believe you had something to do with it."

"I would never hurt Sally. I loved Sally. Even after—after— you know."

"But apparently they have some circumstantial evidence. And of course, many people heard what you said in the courtroom today."

Morgan rambled as if she hadn't heard a word Kenzi said. "I would never hurt Sally. I loved her. Like I've never loved anyone in my entire life."

"Morgan, listen to me. You need to get it together." While she talked, she scurried around the apartment, gathering her satchel and keys. "Like it or not, the police will insist on talking to you. And they may arrest you."

"I didn't do this."

"And I'll do my best to smooth it over. But you should prepare for the worst."

She didn't respond. All Kenzi could hear was incessant, impassioned crying. It was horrifying to hear an intelligent woman reduced to this. "Morgan, I'm on my way to your place. Don't do anything. Don't talk to anyone. And most importantly, don't leave."

"I—I—I—"

"I'll be there as soon as I can." She ended the call. "Hailee—"

"Already on it. I'll find out everything I can about the murder."

"Thank you. Rain check on the crochet lesson." Ten seconds later she was out the door.

———

MORGAN HAD MOVED to a condo she found on Airbnb after the divorce was filed, and it was relatively near, so with aggressive driving and a complete disrespect for traffic laws, Kenzi managed to get there in twenty minutes. She had to knock for almost a minute before Morgan opened the door.

Morgan looked terrible. Her eyes were red, her clothes were rumpled, and her hair looked like she'd been electrocuted. "Thank you for coming."

"No problem. First of all, we need—"

"I didn't do it," Morgan blurted out. "I didn't kill her."

"Good. But the police think you did. They're desperate to arrest someone, and since they have some basis for pinning it on you they're going to run with that."

Morgan started to pace, rubbing her hands together. "My life is falling apart. I'm losing everything. First Charles. Then the company. Then Sally. Now this. What's happening?" She grabbed Kenzi by her lapels. "What is happening?"

"Morgan, are you feeling okay? Are you having any of those...hallucinations?"

"You'll help me, right? You won't betray me? Like the others?"

"I'm not a criminal attorney. I—"

"You represented Maya Breville."

"That was a freaky one-off, not to be repeated under any—"

"I want you to represent me."

Kenzi sighed, trying not to become frustrated. "You'd be better off with someone who has more criminal experience. I'll talk to Emma and—"

"I want you."

Kenzi started to argue, but this was not the main thing they needed to discuss at the moment. "Look, I promised I'd bring you to the police station within the hour, so let's talk about what you're going to tell them. First, you don't answer a question unless I give you the nod. Second, if you don't know the answer, just say so. Don't speculate. Don't argue. Don't accuse. Just say, I don't know. Third—"

She was interrupted by a pounding on the door. "*Police!*"

Morgan cowered, scurrying into a corner.

What the hell? She was supposed to have more time...

"*Open the door!*"

In the split second Kenzi spent deciding what to do, the police burst through the front door. A stream of officers rushed in...with Shel Harrington at the tail end.

Morgan screamed and threw herself down on the sofa. Two officers grabbed her, one at each elbow, and hoisted her to her feet. She continued screaming, thrashing back and forth, kicking into the air. She looked as if she were having a complete mental breakdown.

Kenzi stepped toward her client, but one of the officers extended a hand to stop her.

"Please don't interfere, ma'am. We don't want to have to arrest you too. But we will, if necessary."

Kenzi pursed her lips but stayed put. Getting arrested would not help her client.

Another officer read Morgan her rights, not that Morgan paid the slightest attention. "You have the right to remain silent. Anything you say can and will be used against you in a court of law. You have..."

Kenzi whirled on Harrington. "You gave me an hour. It's not half over yet."

He shrugged. "The situation changed."

"What does that mean?"

"I'm not at liberty to discuss it."

"You lied to me." She glared at him, or tried. He was not making eye contact. "You followed me over here, didn't you? Calling me was your lazy-ass way of learning where she was."

He smiled thinly. "And a more experienced criminal attorney wouldn't have fallen for it."

"Excuse me for thinking the DA might keep his word. I'm going to file an ethics complaint."

"This isn't kindergarten, Kenzi. And frankly, you're in over your head. Again."

"As I recall, last time I was in over my head I kicked your butt."

"You got lucky. It won't happen again." He nodded toward one of the officers. "Search the house."

"Hey! Don't you need a warrant for that?"

"Guess you were paying attention in Criminal Procedure."

He plopped the document into her hand. "Start in the kitchen."

She gave the warrant a preliminary inspection. It appeared legit.

"The rest of you, spread out. Don't leave a square inch of this place unexamined." One of the officers opened a clothes closet, pulled out everything, and threw it on the ground.

Morgan screamed again.

They ignored her. While one officer dumped the kitchen drawers, another pulled the sofa cushions off and, using a small knife, ripped them open.

"Is that really necessary?" Kenzi asked.

"Absolutely." Harrington waved at the arresting officers. "Let's take the perp downtown."

"I'm coming with you," Kenzi said.

Harrington held up his hand. "No, you're not, and don't follow too close behind the cop cars or we'll have you arrested. You can talk to your client later, after we've taken prints and exemplars and booked her. Give it about six hours."

"I can see her at four in the morning?"

"Did you have other plans?" He followed the officers toward the door.

Morgan whipped around and the officers dragged her to the door, her eyes wild and wide, her face red and blotched. "Kenzi, *do something!*"

But there was nothing to do. Or if there was, she didn't know what it would be.

Morgan screamed as they hauled her out the door.

Harrington smiled.

Kenzi knew she should probably keep her mouth shut, but she couldn't. "You know, Shel, you are a complete and total bastard. And a liar."

"I keep my promises to the people," he said, obviously not bothered in the least. "I promised to keep this city safe. And that means apprehending this dangerous murderer with alacrity to make sure she can't hurt anyone else."

23

While Kenzi waited for the jailhouse gatekeeper to admit her, she texted Emma. She expected a response. She did not expect Emma to appear ten minutes later, decked out in her traditional black but looking much more alert than she would've expected.

"Isn't this past your bedtime?"

Emma plopped down on the seedy, splintered bench beside Kenzi. "I hear you have a client in the joint."

"And you came? Even before you saw my text?"

"You think I'm going to abandon you just when the case veers into territory I actually know something about?"

"Are you going to discourage me from handling this case?"

"There's nothing I could say that hasn't already occurred to you."

"There are many lawyers in Seattle with more criminal experience."

"But few with as much heart."

Kenzi looked up. "What?"

"And few who care about their clients like you do. Which is probably more valuable than jaded lawyers jumping through familiar hoops."

"I...well, I...thanks."

Emma glanced out the corner of her eye. "You know, when we were growing up, sometimes I kind of resented you."

"Do tell."

"I thought you were all flash, no substance. I was a better student and I worked harder, but everyone congregated around you. But after we worked on that Breville case...I saw things a little differently. You're not just the flash. You're the heart. I'm the brain, clearly. And it's good to have both brains and heart, especially when you're trying a case in front of a jury. Right now, you're what Morgan needs."

"I don't know...everything."

"I'll fill in the blanks." Emma gave her a gentle nudge. "If we feel like we're getting in over our heads, we can bring in another attorney. Morgan can afford it. May I ask you a question?"

Kenzi didn't wait. "She didn't do it."

"Tell me you didn't ask."

"She volunteered."

"And you believe her?"

"I do. Do you?"

Emma shrugged. "I don't know anything about people. I'll let you be the judge."

"I think the cops are desperate to charge someone. They've been looking incompetent during this entire Seattle Strangler business."

"But they still wouldn't do arrest her if they didn't have some compelling evidence. They don't want a false charge blowing up in their faces. Remember, once the prosecution picks a defendant, they can't change their minds. Win or lose, they have to go down the line unequivocally insisting the person they charged was guilty."

"I suppose that's true. Any way we can find out what they have?"

"Eventually the prosecution will have to share their evidence.

But they'll wait until the last possible moment. Let me see if I can speed up the process. I have some friends."

Kenzi blinked. Emma has friends?

"They won't give up the farm, but I might be able to pry a detail or two out of them."

"That would be great."

Emma pushed to her feet. "I'll check in with you tomorrow morning. Reassure Morgan. Then get some sleep."

"I'll try." She grinned. "Hailee will want to know everything."

"Nah. She already knows all there is to know."

"From the internet?"

"From her aunt."

"You've been texting?"

Emma paused by the door. "Remember what I said about you being the heart and me being the head? Hailee is the heart and the head. She's going to be better than both of us combined."

———

AROUND THREE IN THE MORNING, they finally allowed Kenzi to see her client. Perhaps because of the lateness of the hour, they skipped the usual visitation room and escorted her to a large holding cell, brought Morgan in, and locked the door behind them with a thunderous clang.

She looked even worse than she had at her home only a few hours before. The harsh fluorescent lighting probably didn't help, and neither did the shapeless coveralls she wore. But if Morgan deteriorated this much in a few hours, Kenzi could just imagine what would happen after a few weeks. Or months. Or years.

Or a life sentence for murder.

"How are you holding up?"

"I'm not. You've got to get me out of here."

Kenzi was hardly an expert, but she thought the chances of getting bail were slim to none. If the people of Seattle heard the courts released an accused strangler right now, there would be rioting in the streets. "I'll request bail at the arraignment. But I can't make any promises."

"I can make bail."

"If it's offered."

"I have money. I have a job. I have no record. And I'm innocent. How can they hold me against my will?"

More a rhetorical question than a substantive one. "I'll try to find out what's going on first thing in the morning. I'll file motions and stir up trouble any way I can."

"Charles is behind this. You know he is. He'll win the divorce now. No one will award me anything if I look like a murderer. And Sally—" She choked on the word. "Sally won't get anything."

"Are you suggesting Charles killed her so he wouldn't have to pay her? Or to frame you?"

"Or maybe he hired someone to do it. That's more his style."

But that seemed uncommonly risky. Just to save money on a divorce settlement? When he had millions? "Are there any other possible suspects? Anyone with a grudge against Sally?"

Morgan sat down, but she couldn't remain still. Her hands kept fidgeting, rubbing up against one another. "Of course not. Sally was the sweetest, most generous person who ever lived." She paused. Her voice cracked. "Until Charles got to her."

Of course, Morgan had described Sally very differently in the courtroom. They'd all assumed Sally went turncoat for money, but no one had any evidence of money changing hands. The truth was, they had no idea why Sally turned on Morgan. And Sally was in no position to explain it now. "What about at the office? There must be someone who didn't like her."

Morgan thought for a moment but came up with nothing. "Sally wasn't all that involved at the office. She was the best of us at Final Fantasy, but probably the least interested in running a business. Mostly she came to the office when we were playing Hearts."

"Would Miguel know who she hung with? Or Vasquez?"

"Maybe. I doubt it, though."

"Friends? Hobbies? Outside interests?"

"That would cause someone to murder her? No."

Kenzi racked her brain, trying to think of everything she should ask, but she was tired and had no doubt she was forgetting something. "Morgan, I have to ask you some tough questions."

"I didn't do it. I already told you that."

"But is there anything the prosecution could use against you? Something in your past or present? I can't make bad facts go away, but if I know about them in advance, I can mitigate the damage."

Morgan thought for a long moment. "I can't think of anything. The truth is, I've lived a pretty boring life. Online gaming. Coding. A little Dungeons & Dragons when I have time. I like podcasts and long walks and for the most part try to stay out of other people's way."

She seemed sincere. But there was always something, right? At this very minute, the DA probably had his minions turning over every rock in sight, trying to find ammunition to use against her. "I know you're tired. If you think of something later, let me know. I probably don't need to tell you this, but—don't talk to anyone. Not anyone. Except me. Jailhouse snitches are so commonplace they're practically a cliché. People get rewarded for going on the witness stand to relate something they supposedly heard behind bars. Just don't talk to anyone. Period."

"And you'll get me out of here?"

"I will try. But in any case—mum's the word. I'll check in with you every day." She took a step closer. "As hard as this may be, keep your spirits up. I'll get us a trial date as quickly as possible. And in the meantime, my friends and I will move heaven and earth to make sure you get a fair hearing. I don't know who's behind this, but I know one thing for certain. We will not go down without a fight."

24

Kenzi got home around three in the morning. Emma must have kept Hailee well informed because she was sound asleep. She moved her alarm back a bit, but it didn't matter. She normally slept like a rock the moment her head hit the pillow, but this night was total insomnia. Too much going on in her head. She couldn't stifle the racing thoughts long enough to get any meaningful rest.

If you can't sleep, might as well work, right? Maybe if she got enough done now, she could sleep tomorrow. She would probably have an abnormally high turnout on the KenziKlan stream, so she chose her attire carefully. The Albert Nipon seersucker that made her look like Audrey Hepburn, fancy sneakers, stylish but comfortable, and the all-important SheFit sports bra. She combed out her side shave, added a little color to her eyes, and decided that was enough.

At the office, she was not surprised to find Sharon knew all about the dramatic events of the night before. She was equally unsurprised to see a mountain of message slips pinned to the spindle in front of Sharon's desk. "I appear to be popular."

"In demand, certainly," Sharon replied. "'Popular' might not be the right word."

"Blowback?"

"Because you're representing a strangler? Who some people have already decided is the Seattle Strangler?"

"Not even the DA thinks that. It's just a coincidence."

"Tell it to the conspiracy buffs. These people avoided the COVID vaccine because they thought Bill Gates was putting tracking devices in their bloodstream. You think they're going to let this strangulation case be an isolated incident? No way."

Kenzi thumbed through the phone messages. Media requests, mostly. That could wait. "I'll be in my office. Hold my calls and—"

Sharon raised a finger. "Not quite yet."

Kenzi knew that look. "Don't tell me."

"Daddy Dearest. Wants to see you immediately."

"About what?"

Sharon gave her a "Come on" expression. "He didn't say. But I think we both can guess."

———

KENZI NEVER ENJOYED these recurring trips to the woodshed, but she enjoyed them even less when she had about a million more pressing chores. No doubt her father already knew how she'd spent the night, and she could just imagine what he thought about her being dragged into another criminal case.

Did the other attorneys in the firm get called onto the carpet by the big boss, she wondered, or was this a special privilege reserved for the boss's eldest daughter?

His assistant, Marjorie, sat outside his office, acting as Chief Gatekeeper. Marjorie had never approved of Kenzi and she very much doubted today would be an exception. She brushed past the woman without so much as a nod. She had an invitation. Really, it was a command performance.

She was not surprised to find her brother Gabriel waiting inside.

She was surprised to find Lou Crozier there.

"Hello, Kenzi," her father said. He sat behind his desk, leaning back in his plush leather chair. The other two sat on the other side, leaving no chairs for Kenzi. She stood, like the defendant in a court martial. "I hear you've had a busy night."

She was getting more than a little tired of this routine. Seemed like he was constantly trying to bully her into doing what he wanted—and when had he ever been successful? "That happens when you have actual clients."

Her father was unmoved. "I've had clients for four decades, but never once have I had to visit anyone at the county jail in the dead of night."

Kenzi felt her steam rising. "If you're planning to strong-arm me into dropping the case because it's taken on a criminal aspect, you can—"

Her father waved a hand in the air. "Too soon."

She blinked. Really? No lecture about how she was sullying the firm's reputation by associating with criminal ilk?

"I mean, don't get me wrong. I hope you will get rid of this mess. As soon as possible. Soon enough that we can accept the DigiDynamics retainer. But I understand you can't do it in the first twenty-four hours. Wouldn't look right."

"I'm not planning—"

"Give it a week, then cop a plea. If that isn't possible, toss it to Fred Williams. He thrives on criminal work. And he'll remember we did him a solid when a divorce case comes his way."

"That's not the way I roll."

Her father stared at her, forehead creased. "I don't even know what that means. But I assume you understand that the firm's goal is to make money. Reciprocal arrangements with other firms—"

"Are called referrals, and taking a cut from a referral is forbidden by the Rules of Professional Conduct."

"You don't take a cut. You simply remember who your friends are."

"It's the same thing."

Her father glanced at Crozier, sighed heavily, then continued. "Lou dropped by this morning to talk about the divorce case. I wanted to be present so I can...keep an eye on things."

Of course he did. She turned toward Crozier. "Bit opportunistic, aren't you?"

Crozier spread his hands wide, his face the picture of innocence. "I don't know what you mean."

"You learned Morgan has been arrested for murder. So you decided to stroll over and see if you could use this unfortunate turn of events to your advantage."

He shook his head and made a tutting sound. "Kenzi, I don't know why you have such a negative attitude toward me. I think you're terrific. I've always admired you, so much so that..." He stopped. Apparently he wasn't going to mention the job offer in her father's presence. "Anyway, I don't get it. Is it because we're on opposite sides of the political spectrum?"

"Conspiracy theories and science denial aren't political positions. They're just delusional."

"Kenzi!" her father barked.

Crozier, on the other hand, chuckled. "You crack me up. You really do. Can't we be friends? I'd like that."

"Then stop all the sleazy tactics."

"Like what?"

"Like bribing Sally to turn quisling on Morgan."

"I had nothing to do with that."

Should she believe him? He certainly used it to his advantage. "And now you're going to toss out some horrible settlement offer while Morgan is in a vulnerable position. Exploiting the DA's mistake."

"I've spoken to Shel Harrington."

"The insufferable ass who broke his promise to let me bring

Morgan in voluntarily. And now reporters are acting like she was arrested while on the lam."

"I won't argue with you about Shel's trustworthiness. I've known him since law school and...well. Less said the better. But he assures me they have a rock-solid case against your client. And I believe him."

"Because you want to believe him."

"No. Because I know that ultimately, Shel will always do what's in his own best interests. Given the high profile of this case, it's not in his interests to proffer charges unless he can make them stick. He doesn't need a major-league embarrassment right now. He needs a win. And he clearly thinks this is going to be it."

She kept a dismissive expression on her face, but it wasn't because his words didn't worry her. She'd had the same thoughts herself. "Could you cut to the chase? As you might imagine, I have a thing or two I need to do this morning."

Crozier passed a sheet of paper to her. "As you predicted, I've got a settlement offer. I think a very fair one."

Kenzi gave it a quick once-over. Bottom line, Morgan took a million dollars from the marital estate, no property, no shares in DigiDynamics. One million, when the company was worth a billion. "You must be kidding."

"Stay calm and think about it for a moment. I'll admit, yesterday, this would've been a pitiful offer. But today, everything has changed."

"Not for the divorce."

"He's right, Kenzi." To her surprise, her brother Gabe had found his voice. "We have laws preventing people from profiting from murder."

"So?"

"Morgan can't get one penny of what might otherwise have gone to Sally. And she won't get stock in the company. No one wants a director or board member who's in prison. The court is not going to have any sympathy for a convicted felon. And given that she'll likely spend the rest of her life in custody, she has few financial needs. She'll be lucky if she gets anything. A million bucks is a generous offer."

"You don't know that she'll be convicted."

This time, all three men exchanged a look. No doubt in their minds.

"Look," Gabe continued, "I know I can't force you to do anything. Probably no one can. But just this once, would you look beyond your own immediate interests? Think about what's best for the firm."

"Throwing over clients when they need us most is not going to develop a good firm rep."

"You wouldn't be throwing her over. You'd be making her a million bucks. She'll need cash for legal expenses. She's going to have major cash flow issues. She probably won't be able to access anything that isn't in her personal checking account at this moment. Make her life easier. Accept the offer."

"Then get rid of the murder case," her father grumbled. "I know Shel will make a plea offer, once the heat has died down. Take it."

Kenzi propped one hand on her hip. "Shouldn't we hear Harrington's offer before we decide to accept it?"

Her father made a dismissive gesture. "You're a terrific negotiator. You'll get your client the best deal possible. And then you can get back to your more profitable and less controversial work. I talked to you about this before, Kenzi. Don't let yourself get so...distracted."

"My first loyalty is to my client. And she says she's innocent."

His only reply was a huge heaving sigh.

She turned to Crozier. "Thank you for your offer. I will take it to my client. But I will not recommend that she accept."

"Kenzi—"

"And I will relay any offer the DA makes too. But Morgan won't take it. She's upset now, but in the end, she's too smart and too strong to allow herself to be railroaded. I don't care how much pressure you and your all-male establishment bring to bear. She's not going to cop a plea to a murder she didn't commit."

Her father's head tossed backward. "Kenzi, be reasonable..."

"I think I have been. I've kept my mouth shut and listened to all this self-serving claptrap. And now I'm done. If you people gave a damn about anyone other than yourselves you wouldn't be trying to convict an innocent woman. You'd be trying to find out who committed this crime, because none of us will be safe until we get these predators off the streets."

25

S haron drummed her fingers against her desktop, fretting about what she should do next. Shel Harrington had called and invited Kenzi to view the crime scene. Granted, he'd probably already removed everything important, including the corpse and all discernible forensic evidence.

But still. He did make the call.

Problem was, Kenzi was still in her father's office, and even after this drumhead ended, she knew Kenzi had much to do. Emma was out of her office and wasn't picking up her cell. If they waited too long, the crime scene would be shut down and there would be nothing to see.

Fine. She'd go herself. Why not? Kenzi said she should take a more expansive role. She was making more money now. So that meant she should start showing some initiative, right? And besides, she grew up in LA and had watched every episode of *Law and Order* ever made, so she was totally qualified to handle crime scenes.

She grabbed her bag and headed out the door.

SHARON SPENT ALMOST forty minutes getting to the alleyway where Sally had been strangled to death. Traffic was a bear, and so many roads were blocked she had trouble finding a parking place. By the time she arrived, more than an hour had passed. She hoped she wasn't too late.

Happily, the sergeant on duty waved her right through. The critical area was surrounded with crime scene tape. Inside, though, it was mostly quiet. No lab techs scurrying around in scrubs and masks and little blue booties.

Sharon spotted only one person inside, a woman who appeared to be assiduously studying a brick wall. Tall, white, willowy blonde, in a brown corduroy jacket and dark blue jeans. She was dressed in plainclothes, but Sharon had the distinct impression she was a police officer. Blood splatter expert, maybe. Like Dexter. So she must be a nice person.

The woman glanced over her shoulder. "Can I help you?"

"Maybe. I work with Kenzi Rivera. She's the attorney—"

The woman cut her off. "I know who Kenzi is."

"The DA invited us to examine the crime scene."

"Darn friendly of him. Now that there's almost nothing left to see." She extended a hand. "Kate Corrigan. Homicide detective."

Oh wow. Full-fledged detective. Impressive. "Nice to meet you. Can you give me an idea what you've learned so far?"

Corrigan seemed to be scrutinizing her. What, did she spill coffee on her blouse? "So far, everything is much as it appears. We think the victim left the bus stop and was walking home."

"She had a place right around the corner."

"But she never made it there. Looks like someone grabbed her. Slammed her against this wall. Right here." She pointed. "They've taken photos and removed the body, but you can still see the trace evidence. She was probably dazed when her head hit the wall, which would undermine her ability to resist. The killer probably didn't have to work too hard to strangle her."

"The Seattle Strangler MO?"

"Not entirely. There are differences that...well, I'm not supposed to talk about. And remember, some of those cases are just disappearances. We don't know for certain all the women involved were killed."

"But the likelihood is..."

"I don't deal in likelihoods. I deal in facts."

"So what are the cops not disclosing?"

"We always omit a few key details so when the inevitable bogus confessions descend, we have a means of knowing whether we're talking to the real culprit or a wannabe. We think maybe this murder was committed by someone who hoped it might look like another Strangler murder. But the killer targeted a specific victim. And left the corpse behind so everyone would know she was dead."

"Sounds like this crime was committed by someone big. Strong."

"Not necessarily. If you're suggesting the murder couldn't have been committed by a woman, I respectfully disagree."

"I'm just trying to figure out what happened."

"Sally was taken by surprise. Tackling someone from behind who doesn't know you're there doesn't require all that much strength. Or at any rate, that's the company line, for obvious reasons. Morgan Moreno is a petite woman, so I can't agree that it required massive size. But strength—maybe. If you're hoping I can exclude your client, sorry. I can't."

Sharon nodded. At least Corrigan seemed to be shooting straight with her. "I appreciate your honesty. Can you give me any idea why the cops latched onto Morgan so quickly? She's hardly the only possible suspect."

"Someone heard your client threaten Sally in the courtroom yesterday. And then Sally turns up dead a few hours later? You can see how it looks."

"Is there any forensic evidence pointing to Morgan?"

"Apparently there is, but I haven't heard about it yet. I just came on the scene a few hours ago. I haven't communicated with the DA's people yet. I'll be brought up to date soon." She paused. "If you'd like to give me your number, I'll call you when I know more."

That was uncommonly accommodating of her. "You'd do that?"

"If I can. Sometimes, the DA's office puts a short-term embargo on the evidence. But..." She looked Sharon right in the eye. "If I can, I will."

Wait a minute. The way she looked at her...

Was something going on here?

And did she mind?

Sharon scrawled her cell number on the back of a card. Anything for the team, right? "Please let me know if you learn anything important."

"Sure. Maybe we can talk about it over coffee or something."

Okay, that was suggestive. "Anything else I should know?"

Corrigan pondered a moment. "Not that I can think of. But I've got your number if something occurs to me later, right?" She actually winked.

"Can I ask you a question?"

"Any time. Any time at all."

"When I came in...why were you staring at the wall so intensely? I mean, maybe you're just really into brick—"

Corrigan laughed. "You're funny. I like that." She pointed toward the wall. "No, I spotted something. Maybe it's completely innocent, or maybe it was here before the murder, but it's right about where I think Sally's head landed. You can see a trace of blood, and the forensic team already took hair fragments. But there's more."

Sharon stepped closer. She didn't see anything. "Like what?"

"I can't be certain without chemical analysis. But to me...it kinda looks—and tastes—like popsicle juice."

"Excuse me?"

"Yeah. Not the kind of thing you hear about on *Law and Order*."

Sharon's eyes ballooned. "You watch *Law and Order?*"

"Love that show. Can't get enough of it. I've watched all forty-two spinoffs. But I don't recall anyone mentioning popsicles."

"Is it important?"

Corrigan shook her head. "I don't know. But I would sure like to find out."

26

K enzi slumped over the desk in her office, feeling a wave of despair rush through her like a tidal wave. How did she get into this mess? And what had ever made her think she was competent to handle it?

And this was how she felt on the first day. Imagine how she would feel when she knew what was going on.

She leaned back and drew in long deep breaths. She needed sleep. Her eyelids were fighting to remain open.

She was swimming upstream in the dark. She would like to believe she was competent to handle this case. But at the moment she just felt tired and overwhelmed. Ready to throw in the towel and ashamed of herself for considering it.

She heard someone clearing a throat. She sat up abruptly, eyes wide.

Sharon stood in the hallway holding a zarf-wrapped coffee cup in each hand. "Is it latte time?"

Kenzi slid a hand across her desk. "It's always latte time." Sharon handed her one of the cups.

Kenzi touched her fingertips to her lips. "Chef's kiss. You're a lifesaver."

"It's decaf."

Kenzi stopped swigging and frowned. "Why?"

"Because you need sleep. This is just a temporary pick-me-up. To get you home."

"I'll be fine. I can drive on fumes."

"As if. I'm driving you home."

"You—"

"Don't bother arguing. It's happening, girl. That's why I brought a drink for myself. Which isn't decaf." She smiled. "I know you hate to drink alone."

Kenzi brought herself more or less upright. "Sharon, I think I have officially bitten off more than I can chew."

"Those are words I never thought I'd hear from your mouth."

"I know. Right? But I may have finally discovered my limitations."

"I don't think you have any limitations. Except on the amount of work you can complete in a single day."

"Which reminds me. Where have you been? I noticed you weren't at your desk."

"Investigating." She patted herself on the shoulder. "I visited the crime scene."

"Sure. That tracks. And what did Sherlock Sharon discover?"

"Mock me not, Lawyer Girl." She placed a thin sheet of paper on the desk.

Kenzi's eyes took a moment to adjust. "Is this the medical examiner's report?"

Sharon beamed. "Indeed. Preliminary. But still."

Kenzi scanned the document. Too many long words for this time of night. "And what do we learn from this?"

"For starters, Sally was indeed strangled."

"Anything else of note?"

Sharon pointed to a line near the bottom. "The examiner scraped something out from under Sally's fingernails. Probably skin. Sent for DNA typing."

"And the results?"

"I have to think someone thought it pointed to Morgan, given that they arrested her."

Kenzi frowned. "Anything else?"

Sharon pointed again. Another line on the form indicated the contents of Sally's purse and pockets. "Bank slip. Big withdrawal."

"Wowza. From whose account?"

"Don't know yet. But Sally had the receipt."

"Then it was her."

"Maybe. Maybe not."

"But it gives the DA yet another motive theory to explain why Morgan would murder Sally. Sally ran off with all the readily available cash. And now, due to the asset freeze, no one can get any more." She snapped her fingers. "Or maybe this is how Charles paid off Sally."

"And when Morgan found out, she would be angry. Giving them another possible motive."

Kenzi nodded. "This is great. I mean, it's terrible, but it's great that we know about it. How did you get this?"

Sharon's eyes wandered. "I met a police detective at the crime scene. She agreed to help in an...unofficial way."

Kenzi blinked. "Did she know you work for the defendant?"

"Oh yes. She believes in fair play."

Kenzi's eyes narrowed. "She agreed to help you because of her deep-seated sense of justice?"

"She seemed to take a...personal interest in the case."

"She?"

"Yeah. Kate Corrigan. Homicide detective."

"I sense that I haven't heard the entire explanation yet." She glanced down at the form. "But I'm grateful to have this. Think you can pry anything else out of your new source?"

"I'm going to meet with her again soon."

"Indeed."

"We'll see what develops."

More eye narrowing. "Do let me know."

"I will. I think—"

She was interrupted by a loud noise outside. A second later, Emma appeared in the doorway—with a large man with spiky hair wearing an oversize hockey jersey. She recognized him from the courtroom. Miguel Batista.

"Is this where the food is?" Miguel bellowed in a booming voice that practically made the glass walls shudder. "I'm starving. Where's the pizza?"

Emma patted him on the shoulder. "On its way."

"Mr. Pink?"

"Nothing but."

"You know this is going to destroy my diet."

"Skip tonight's allotment of Ben & Jerry's," Emma suggested. "You'll be fine."

Kenzi turned to Miguel. "I hear you want to help us?"

"Emma bribed me with Mr. Pink."

"We've become friends," Emma added. "Learned to trust one another."

"Which is no small thing," he said. "Given that you were totally lying and using a fake name when we first met."

"In the line of duty."

"So you could hack DigiDynamics' files."

Emma drew a finger across her lips. *Shh!*

"Your sister doesn't know you're a cyberstalker?"

Kenzi smiled. "Her sister prefers to remain as ignorant as possible about her activities. You are aware that we're attorneys and we represent Morgan Moreno not only in the divorce but now on the pending murder charge, right?"

Miguel grinned. "Is it just me, or did this case just get a lot sexier?"

That was one word for it. "If you help us, you're helping the defense and possibly not acting in the best interests of your boss. Which is fine with me. I just want to make sure you're apprised of the circumstances."

"I get it. But this is exciting."

"Some people will say you're biting the hand that feeds you."

"Point 'em out. I'll launch a dictionary at their heads."

Emma waved him down. "Okay, we don't need any of that."

"Right, right. What was it I was supposed to tell your sister?"

"The backdoor."

Miguel leaned across the desk till he was practically nose-to-nose with Kenzi. "Right. I just have a minute. But do you know what a backdoor is?"

"You mean...in a house?"

"No. In a computer program. Like Face2Face."

"It has a backdoor?"

"That's the rumor. I mean, don't ask me. I'm not a coder. But Morgan is. And so are a lot of other people at the company. Have you heard of an Easter egg?"

Kenzi felt dumber by the second. "Colored foodstuffs people hide and kids try to find even though they have no intention of eating them..."

"No. In computer jargon, an Easter egg is a bonus inside a program or show. Something unadvertised that adds value, at least for a sliver of the audience. I don't know if this is true, but there's a major-league rumor running around the office that Charles had an Easter egg built into Face2Face. While cops are observing criminals, people with access to the backdoor can watch the cops. See what they're planning. Tip off their friends. Maybe even hack into the files on law enforcement computers."

"Why would Charles do such a thing?"

"The same reason he does everything else. Money."

"I thought he made almost a billion bucks selling Face2Face to law enforcement."

"He did. But if this is true, he could make billions—note the plural—selling access codes to criminals. Imagine if you're running some big cartel or syndicate and someone gives you the ability to watch state and federal law enforcement's every move. To know about their plans before they're put into action. That would be worth more than a few paltry billions."

If this was true, it was a complete gamechanger. "How do we find out if this exists?"

"Already on it," Emma said. "I've downloaded a huge number of files. Going through them is slow work. But if there's anything relevant in there, I'll find it."

"I have every confidence in you," Miguel said. "But I need to eat and you don't have any food and I need to get to work on finding that backdoor. Emma, I'll catch you in the morn." He left the room.

Kenzi thumbed through files for a few minutes. Her stomach growled. "Hunger must be contagious. Where's the—?"

"*Make waaaaaay!*

Kenzi heard a shout outside her office. A second later, Hailee wheeled past the glass wall, several flat square boxes resting across the arms of her chair.

"Have no fear! Nourishment is here!"

Kenzi didn't know where to begin. "What—is going on? How did you get in here? And why are you up past bedtime?"

"I might ask you the same question, Mom."

"I sent an Uber for her," Emma explained. "And I told the security guy in the lobby to bring her up."

Hailee wheeled up to the desk and tossed the pizza boxes on top. "OMG, Mom. Have you seen the medical examiner's report?"

"I have. Have you?"

"Yeah. Sharon texted it to Aunt Emma and she sent it to me. I think we need to hire our own DNA expert, Mom. You know the cops won't play straight with us. They'll find some toady who'll say whatever they want him to say. We need someone we can trust."

"I don't think I know any—"

"I've got a list of names." She planted a file on the desk. "I did the research online. These people are local and have good reps."

"I see. So first my sister sent my child out on a school night. Then she exposed her to dubiously obtained evidence?"

"Chill," Emma said. "Hailee wanted to come. And you did say she could help."

"But it's late and—"

Hailee practically exploded. "I couldn't miss a team meeting!"

"Is this a team meeting?"

"Of course it is!" they said, almost in unison.

"I see." A trace of a grin crept out. "I have a team?"

"I would've thought that was obvious by now," Sharon said. "Online, you've got a clan. But in real life, you've got a team. And we've got your six. We're going to make sure Morgan gets a fair shake. With you at the helm and us in the wings, I don't see how this could possibly go wrong."

Kenzi did. But she wasn't going to spoil the mood. "I really appreciate this. Team. To be honest, I was feeling a little down before. But this helps."

Sharon gave her shoulder a squeeze. "No worries, girl. Now. What should we do first?"

Kenzi smiled. She knew they had many days of work ahead before trial. But now she felt certain they could do it. And do it well.

Which guaranteed nothing. But it was much better than doing it alone.

PART II

COURT OF NO RETURN

27

K enzi had worked for weeks to get to this point, but she felt ready. Ready as she was ever going to be. Ready, because she had no choice but to be ready. The trial began today.

She and Harrington had exchanged words on occasion, and he'd made a few tentative steps toward offering a plea bargain, but it never went anywhere. He needed at least twenty years and Morgan wouldn't agree to it. She insisted she hadn't committed this crime and she wasn't going to be bullied into pretending she did.

Kenzi had done her best to get Morgan ready to sit before a jury. A nice new suit, not fancy, but attractive and practical. The jurors were unlikely to be millionaires, so Morgan didn't need to appear to be flaunting her wealth—and couldn't anyway, since most of the money was embargoed. Of course, she also didn't want to appear to be playing poor and irritate the jury that way. Kenzi tried to find a middle road.

Kenzi gave her a light dollop of makeup, too. Morgan complained, insisting she didn't go in for girly-stuff, but Kenzi insisted. Not enough to draw attention. But enough to make up for being stuck behind bars and away from the sun for too long.

She would like to think the jurors would be able to set aside appearances and make evaluations for more profound reasons... but appearances mattered, and jurors were simply not as likely to warm up to a sickly pasty-faced defendant.

Kenzi even gave her a small, barely noticeable (but still noticeable) necklace with a cross pendant.

"I'm not religious," Morgan insisted.

"Do you want to be acquitted?"

"Obviously."

Kenzi slipped it over her neck. "That's your new religion."

She knew Morgan's hallucinations had intensified since she'd been incarcerated. At one point, her behavior was so extreme the jailhouse authorities kept her in the infirmary for days, then transferred her to a solitary cell. That was probably for the best, but Kenzi knew it was hard to live in complete isolation. They allowed her to take her medication, but that didn't stop the flying cheese toast from appearing.

The judge for the case, the Honorable Harvey Odom, had yet to reveal any predisposition or bias. Kenzi knew he was said to lean conservative, but so far it hadn't shown much. He was around fifty, fit, apparently given to camping and backpacking, and had a weekend place on Bainbridge Island. He handled jury selection in an efficient, no-nonsense manner, though it was still painfully slow. Kenzi found it almost unbearable, but she rode it out. Only on television did trials pass quickly, with every minute bringing new, exciting revelations. In reality, even high-stakes trials were rife with dullness, endless procedural snafus, yakking about nothing, and constant interruptions.

Emma handled most of the jury selection, ironically. Sure, let the attorney who never went out, had poor social skills, and might be somewhere on the autistic spectrum handle these critical decisions about personalities. But in a way, Emma's detachment made her better at the job. Other people came to court with biases based upon past experiences, physical appearances, race, economic or educational background, and a host of other factors unconsciously influencing decision-making. Emma had none of that. She did her demographic research, figured out who she wanted on the jury, and made cold, logical decisions. One huge hurdle they had to deal with was race. Morgan was Latinx, as were her two attorneys. Two of the jurors were also Latinx, two were Black, and one was Asian. Normally lawyers had peremptory challenges that allowed them to remove jurors for any reason, indeed, without even stating a reason. But everything changed when race was involved. In *Kittle v. US*, in which a juror was heard to say "all blacks are guilty regardless," the Court of Appeals held that although juror impeachment was disfavored, trial judges could consider testimony "in rare and exceptional circumstances" when racial bias claims might impact a defendant's right to a fair trial. Now lawyers were allowed to inquire into possible race prejudice, and opposing counsel could ask for a legitimate basis for the removal of any juror of color.

Emma took that in stride, too. She did a fine job of rooting out potential prejudice and preventing the DA from removing Latinx jurors without cause.

"If you keep this up," Kenzi whispered to Emma, after the jury was finally selected, "we're going to start calling you a people person."

"That will never happen," Emma replied, with the same amount of emotion one might expect from Wednesday Addams. "People are horrible."

"And yet, here you are, sticking your neck out to help a woman in distress."

She made a sniffing sound but didn't reply.

By the time they were ready to start the trial, the courtroom was packed. Part of that was due to the enormous media attention. Kenzi had noticed that her livestream numbers were climbing, perhaps because her name was prominently featured in every article about the case. Some internet trolls accused her of "aiding and abetting the Seattle Strangler," but most people seemed more level-headed about it, so no major Twitterstorm erupted. She sensed that many of the newcomers to her stream were women who understood her client had not been treated fairly.

Some of the courtroom faces were familiar. All the members of her team were there, including Hailee, who insisted she could keep up with her classes while also rubbernecking the trial. Kenzi was flattered that a teenage daughter was interested in her mother's work. She didn't want her slipping behind in her schoolwork. But she was such a good student there was probably little danger of that.

Miguel Batista was in the courtroom, too, sitting behind Emma. Even though he had not found the mythical "backdoor" yet, he had become an invaluable resource, and he and Emma had become friends. Kenzi was hesitant about adding a new member to the team, but they needed more info about DigiDynamics. He was obviously biased against Charles, but she supposed that was understandable. If they condemned everyone who disliked their boss, few would remain unscathed. She just hoped he didn't lose his job because of this.

Charles was present, of course, sitting behind the prosecution team. She supposed that was to be expected, but his presence rattled Morgan. Must be hard to see someone with whom you've been intimate sitting on the opposite side of the courtroom. He looked angry and unhappy.

Harcourt Quinn, the physician who treated Morgan for Todd's syndrome, was also present. She'd asked him to be available, thinking there was a good chance they might call him to the stand if the prosecution suggested that Morgan was insane, or that she'd committed the murder in a delusional rage. That was unlikely to occur until the defense started putting on its case, though, and that would be several days in the future. So why was he here now?

An even more surprising face in the courtroom—Morgan's ex-boyfriend, the one who snapped the explicit photos. Everything Sharon had told her about Brent Coleman—unkempt hair, lazy posture, sleazy demeanor—fit. Hard as she tried, she couldn't think of a single legit reason why he needed to be in the courtroom. Morgan was disturbed by the presence of Charles, but having her porn photographer lurking about was even worse.

Kenzi decided to see if she could get a feel for why he was here. "Hey. I'm Kenzi Rivera. I'm representing your ex."

He extended his hand.

"May I ask what brings you to the courtroom today?"

"Charles Land asked me to be here."

"Why?"

"I'm afraid I'm not at liberty to discuss it."

"Big secret, huh?"

"Not my place to say. The boss asks you to do something and you do it. End of story."

"Must be hard for you. Seeing Morgan like this. I heard you're still attached to her."

"I'll always have a soft spot for her. But she's not interested. I've moved on."

"Tell me the truth. Were you the one who leaked those photos?"

"Absolutely not. I put that part of my life behind me a long time ago."

"You're not planning to testify, are you?"

A big smile crossed his face. "Again, not supposed to talk. I really know very little about this case."

"Got it. All you know is sexting and strangulation."

He raised a finger. "Morgan and I played those games for fun. I never hurt anybody. I never would hurt anybody."

So he said. But something about the man bothered her.

Just as she settled into her seat at the defendant's table, the bailiff opened the door from chambers and the judge followed close behind. "All rise."

In a matter of moments, Judge Odom took command of his courtroom. He briskly whisked through the preliminaries. Part of Kenzi wished he'd slow down. She wasn't anxious to address the jury. But the smarter part of her realized it was best to get it done.

In no time at all, the judge was ready to begin. "Mr. Prosecutor. Would you care to address the jury?"

What followed would only take a few days. But it would determine the course of the rest of Morgan's life. And maybe hers as well.

28

Kenzi watched as Harrington approached the jury. So much grace and confidence. His charisma started to show before he opened his mouth. No wonder he'd won so many elections. He would soon have this jury eating out of the palm of his hand. What could she possibly do to counteract that charm?

Harrington planted himself behind the rail separating him from the jury box. "Ladies and gentlemen of the jury. First of all, thank you for your service. I know this is taking a bite out of your life. You have other things you could be doing with your time. And you could get out of jury duty if you really wanted to, but you didn't, so I thank you for that. Committed, dedicated citizens like you make this democracy work."

What a suck-up. Did that smarmy crap really impress anyone? She wanted to be cynical, but she reminded herself that Harrington had logged far more courtroom hours than she had, so maybe instead of criticizing she should be taking notes.

"Sorry about the weather this morning," he added with a small smile, "but if you've lived in Seattle long, you're used to it. Settle in, get comfortable, and let me tell you about this case. You're about to be charged with an awesome duty, the duty of determining guilt or innocence. At least this case is not boring. Horrifying, yes. Tragic, certainly. But by no means boring. In fact, this may be the most unusual case I've encountered in my long career as a defender of law and order."

He pivoted slightly and raised his hands, presumably trying to add a degree of visual interest to a long speech. "Some of the details you may already know, or you may have gleaned from the questions we asked during jury selection. Here's the straight skinny. At its core, this case is about three people who considered themselves a 'throuple.' Yes, you heard me right. Not a couple. A throuple. A relationship with three people in it. They like to call themselves polyamorous, as if that's perfectly normal, or the next hot thing the Supreme Court tells us is perfectly normal. Maybe I'm old-fashioned, but it doesn't seem normal to me. And here's something I know for certain. This throuple ended in divorce, disaster—and murder.

"Were there moments of happiness? Apparently so. As the evidence will show, these three people worked together to build a company that is now valued at around a billion dollars. Charles Land, the male in this three-way, led the business, but he has always generously acknowledged that his two companions made notable contributions. For a time, the relationship existed peacefully. But with so much money involved, and such an unusual, unstable living arrangement, it was bound to sour. And it did. Big time."

He leaned forward against the rail, and his facial expression, as best Kenzi could tell from her seat, turned deadly serious. "The first blow came when Charles filed for divorce against the defendant, the woman to whom he was legally married. He said the relationship had become toxic due to the defendant's erratic, unstable, and dangerous behavior. Once the parties were in divorce court, the situation worsened. Horrible photographs surfaced demonstrating what kind of woman the defendant truly is. After the first court hearing, the defendant publicly threatened the other woman in the throuple, Sally Beaumont. And a few hours later, Sally was strangled to death by someone who knew where she was staying, someone the evidence will show she recognized..." He paused. "...someone who wanted her dead. Someone who dispatched her with ruthless efficiency. That person was the defendant. There is so much evidence, all of it pointing in a single direction, that there is simply no serious question about what happened. Morgan Moreno strangled Sally Beaumont to death. Out of vengeance. Sexual jealousy. Passion. And she also stood to gain millions once Sally, who has no heirs, was eliminated."

Harrington took a few steps back, the grim expression still plastered across his face. "Don't be fooled by the defendant's small, timid appearance. You will be presented with an overwhelming amount of evidence proving her guilt. You'll hear from the medical examiner. You'll hear from a forensic expert about DNA evidence placing her at the scene of the murder. You'll hear from people who heard Morgan threaten Sally. And much more. When the prosecution case is complete, there will be no doubt in your mind about who committed this murder."

He pivoted slightly, looked back at Kenzi. "And then the defense will present their arguments. Make no mistake, the defense case will be about trying to stir up doubt—even where none exists. They will attempt to complicate the simple, obvious truth. They will put on a show, grandstand, play tricks, anything that might distract you from what this case is truly about. Don't be bamboozled. You're smarter than that. Follow the evidence, not the showmanship. We'll give you a trail of crumbs all leading to the same gingerbread house. I'm the district attorney of this county and I would not be standing here if I did not know this woman was guilty. So please pay attention, weigh the evidence carefully—and render the verdict you know is right. Find Morgan Moreno guilty of first-degree murder. Thank you."

Harrington left the arena as gracefully as he'd entered it, gliding back to his chair.

Kenzi felt overwhelmed. What could she possibly do to match this sensational orator?

She glanced back into the gallery. Hailee was on the third row, surreptitiously giving her mother a raised fist. 'Go get 'em, tiger,' she was saying.

At least her daughter believed she could do this. One fan was better than none.

As she approached the jury, she realized she couldn't top Harrington so she wouldn't try. She would just talk to the jurors, straight and direct, like she knew them and trusted them and had confidence in their ability to reach the correct verdict. She would talk to the jury as if she were speaking to her KenziKlan.

"Good morning. I will also offer my thanks to you for serving today, and I'll leave it at that. I know you all want to do what's right. I'm here to help you accomplish that. I'm just a facilitator. I show you the path, but you make the decision. Your job is to determine whether the prosecution proves its case beyond a reasonable doubt. If you think they did, you can convict. But if you think there's room for doubt, you must acquit. That's how the system works."

She smiled, not in an unctuous way, but in a simple, friendly way. "Let's talk about this case, because with all due respect to the district attorney, I think he's emphasized the wrong aspects and grossly misled you about the certainty of the evidence against my friend and client, Morgan Moreno.

"Of course, my esteemed colleague has mentioned that there were three people in the relationship, trying to turn this into some lurid, tabloid drama. Here's the reality. These three people loved each other, and for a time, the relationship was a huge success and the nexus of their lives. Is this common? Perhaps not. But I've talked to an expert who tells me it's not that unusual, either. Frankly, these days, who knows what's normal anymore? As a society, we seem to be more accepting, more tolerant, less judgmental, and I have a hard time seeing how that's a bad thing."

She peered at the jurors. They weren't giving much away, but she didn't see anyone curling their lips when she talked about three people loving one another. Perhaps if she talked about it enough, they would stop perceiving it as weird. "Of course, in time, the relationship soured. That seems to be the way love goes in this modern world, and not just for throuples. For everyone. Maybe some of you are divorced." A safe statement, since she knew it to be true for about half of them. "That doesn't mean there was anything wrong with your relationship. It is simply a fact of modern life that not all relationships last forever."

Okay, point made, move on. "The relationship did become tumultuous recently, but that too is not unusual when a divorce is pending. Yes, my client posed for revealing photos, years ago, in the privacy of her home with a man she loved and trusted. But that does not in any way prove she committed murder. There are many possibilities, many reasons to doubt the story the DA is peddling. This city has been racked by a wave of hideous strangulations and disappearances. I'm not suggesting this murder was necessarily committed by the same person. But it's one more reason to doubt the DA's version of the facts.

"Here's what you need to understand. My client was arrested within hours of the murder. Hours. There was no investigation of any other suspect. In their haste to put on a show of arresting someone, they grabbed the obvious possibility. But the first idea that pops into your head is not always the right one. This time, they pounced too soon. I've been investigating this case, me and my team, and I'm here to tell you—they accused the wrong person."

She took a step back, giving the jurors a moment to absorb what she'd said. "The prosecution does have some evidence, forensic and otherwise, but I've seen it and it is less than conclusive. I'll rebut it when they put it on the stand. I will only make one request of you. Don't make up your mind too soon. The prosecution has a huge advantage in criminal trials. They get to go first. But we will have our turn, so I ask you to please not decide until you've heard from us. I promise I will not waste your time. I promise I will not put on any...what was it? Grandstanding or showmanship? But I will make sure you're not hustled into a decision you might later regret. This is a woeful responsibility you have, literally deciding the course of my client's life. Even as little as I know about you, I know you will take that responsibility seriously. I know you do not want to make a mistake. I'm here to make sure that doesn't happen, to make sure you hear both sides of the story, see the case in a balanced light, so you can render a correct verdict."

She lowered her hands, took another step back, and smiled. "Just remember this. The defendant is innocent until proven guilty. You must find my client guilty beyond a reasonable doubt to convict. If the evidence is anything less, you must acquit." She shrugged. "And that's really all there is to it."

29

Kenzi was not remotely surprised that the first witness Harrington called to the stand was the county medical examiner, Dr. Madison Chang. If they were going to win a murder case, they had to prove someone had died. And having cross-examined Chang before, Kenzi knew she would take every possible opportunity to drop hints and suggestions that helped the prosecution make its case—by making Morgan look guilty.

Harrington took his time, allowing Chang ample opportunity to establish her considerable qualifications. She'd been medical examiner for ten years and had examined more than two hundred corpses, many of them murder victims. Her specialty was forensic autopsy, examinations designed to determine how a murder was accomplished and, if possible, who did it.

"Dr. Chang, what was the cause of death?"

"Strangulation. The assailant completely cut off the airway, applying pressure to the trachea. The hyoid was broken. Probably took no more than two minutes."

"The official cause of death would be...?"

"Lack of air to the brain. Anoxia."

"Was this strangulation consistent with prior cases? Specifically, the ones the press has attributed to the Seattle Strangler?"

"No, this was different. For one thing, we have the corpse. If I may remind you," she said, looking at the jury, "only a few of the victims of the so-called Strangler have been recovered. We believe they were all strangled, but we don't know with certainty. In this case, I've examined the remains. I can tell you that Sally Beaumont was strangled. To death."

"How much strength would be required to accomplish that?"

"Not much. The hard part would be preventing the victim from escaping. One assumes she resisted."

"And how hard would that be?"

"Probably not as hard as you might imagine." There she went, delivering testimony that had nothing to do with her medical examination, but might be enormously helpful to the prosecution. "There is evidence of an injury to the back of the head, and there was blood found on the brick wall in the alley at the right height. The logical conclusion is that the victim's head was slammed back against the brick, which probably dazed or stunned her, thereby diminishing her capacity to resist. Strangulation itself induces weakness, loss of focus. After the first twenty or thirty seconds, the chances that the victim could break free on her own were almost non-existent."

"Did you detect any evidence regarding the identity of the assailant?"

"Yes. There was little sign of struggle or attempt to flee, which suggests the victim knew her assailant."

Kenzi almost snickered. That was supposition at best, gratuitous fiction at worst, but she'd deal with that on cross.

"Did you discover anything else of interest?"

"I managed to scrape out DNA traces underneath the victim's fingernails."

Harrington nodded. "We'll hear from a forensic DNA expert in a moment. Thank you for your testimony, Dr. Chang. Pass the witness."

Kenzi strolled to the witness stand in no particular hurry. She didn't have that much to say, so it was best not to act as if she were about to deliver a bombshell. She couldn't deny that Sally had been killed. But she could poke holes in the rest of Chang's testimony.

"You opined that the victim knew her attacker," she began.

"Certainly looks that way."

"But you don't know for certain."

"I can say with medical certainty that the evidence points in that direction."

"But you don't really know, do you?"

"There was no sign—"

"You're not going to answer my question, are you?"

"My examination produced no evidence indicating that the attacker was a stranger."

"It was dark when the murder occurred, wasn't it?"

Chang frowned. "Yes."

"The assailant could have sneaked up on her?"

"Maybe. But I think she would've heard—"

"But you don't know that."

"Well..."

"It's possible the attacker was waiting for her. So little movement would've been required. Once Sally was close enough, the attacker might've sprung on her."

"I saw no evidence of...springing."

"You said the back of her head was bashed against a brick wall."

"True."

"That could be the result of a sudden attack."

"I still don't think—"

"Dr. Chang, I'm much less interested in what a witness who works for law enforcement thinks and much more interested in what the evidence actually proves. You can't rule out the possibility that Sally was attacked by someone she did not know, can you?"

"I...suppose not."

"As you said, there have been a string of attacks on women in recent months, so it obviously happens."

"True. But—"

"Thank you for your honesty." Kenzi plowed ahead, not giving her a chance to waffle. "You also mentioned DNA traces under the victim's fingernails. Isn't that an indication of struggle?"

"Perhaps, but—"

"What part of the body was scraped by those fingernails?"

"We have no way of knowing that."

"My client was thoroughly examined when she was arrested. There were no abrasions on her anywhere."

"I'm not suggesting there were deep gashes. But even the slightest scratch can retain trace DNA."

"As can a million other common brushes or chance contacts common in everyday life."

"I believe this happened during the murder."

"Based upon what?"

"Common sense."

"Meaning, you believe it because you want to believe it."

Harrington rose. "Objection. This is argumentative and circular."

Kenzi frowned. "Yes, it is argumentative. That's pretty much the point of cross-examination. The witness is making huge leaps of supposition to help his prosecution masters, and I have a problem with that."

She detected a tiny smile on the judge's face. "The objection is overruled. But it may be time to move on, counsel."

"Understood." She turned back to the witness. "Can you eliminate the possibility that the DNA traces were under Sally's fingernails before she was murdered?"

Chang twisted her neck uncomfortably. "I can't completely eliminate the possibility, but—"

"Thank you. You've answered the question. Nothing more."

It wasn't much of a win, but it still felt better to sit down after extracting a concession or two.

———

HARRINGTON'S next witness was Dr. Frederick Bonneville, a DNA expert who frequently appeared in Washington courts, always on the side of the prosecution. Kenzi didn't doubt that he knew his stuff, but the fact that he always spoke for the prosecution made her doubt his objectivity. Kenzi had been over and over his report, usually with a medical thesaurus in hand and Hailee to explain the hard parts.

His testimony could be summarized in a single sentence. He analyzed the DNA and it matched Morgan.

Harrington began. "Just so the jury can appreciate the care and expertise you bring to your work, Dr. Bonneville, would you please describe your procedure?"

"Of course." Bonneville was younger than Chang, perhaps forty, and more casually dressed. He seemed eager to please. "I received the sample from Dr. Chang in a hermetically sealed container. Every possible precaution was taken to avoid contamination. I created a standard DNA, then matched it with the profile produced by the exemplar taken from the defendant after she was arrested. They matched."

"Is there any doubt about the match?"

"Not in my mind. Those DNA scrapings came from Morgan Moreno."

"Thank you. Nothing more from me."

Kenzi approached this witness more cautiously. She knew forensic DNA analysis was a techno-landmine, and if she gave him free rein, he would babble circles around her.

"Dr. Bonneville, I've read your report. You actually found two different DNA patterns in the samples found under the victim's fingernails, correct?"

"That is true."

"How can that be? One person can't contribute two different DNA patterns, can they?"

He chuckled. "Some of the DNA must have come from someone else. But the majority came from the defendant."

"Are you suggesting there were two assailants?"

"No."

"Then some of the DNA found under Sally's fingernails came from someone other than the person who killed her."

"Granted."

"Which proves exactly what Dr. Chang was trying to deny. That the DNA under the fingernails could be unrelated to her murder."

"It's possible that part of the sample was obtained earlier in the day. But the majority of what we found came from the defendant."

"Do you know where the other DNA traces came from?"

"No. Frankly, it didn't seem very important. The evidence points to your client."

"You mean, some of the evidence does, and the rest you're ignoring because it doesn't fit into the story you're manufacturing. For all we know, my client's DNA may be the accident, and the other donor may be the murderer."

Bonneville held up his hands. "I have been reliably informed that there is more evidence pointing irrefutably to your client. But that's not my department. I'm just here to say whether the DNA matches. And it does."

"Let's talk about that for a moment. I don't want the jury to be misled and I'm sure you don't either. When you say the DNA sample matches...you're not saying they were 100% identical, are you?"

"I can see you've done your homework. No, I don't mean that. I'm saying that they were so substantially similar that I have no problem saying that the DNA came from the defendant."

"But they were not a perfect match."

"Well...no."

"Forensic scientists sometimes act as if their work is cut-and-dried, but in fact, DNA analysis is more a matter of interpretation, isn't it?"

He shrugged. "I guess you could say that."

"I could say that because it's true. And interpretation can be influenced by preconceived notions, can't it?"

"Theoretically."

"When people go into an examination hoping for a particular result, they tend to find it."

"If you're suggesting that I—"

"You've been hired by the prosecution to testify, correct?"

"I was hired to analyze the samples. I don't charge for testifying."

"How much are you being paid?"

He answered. Two of the jurors gasped a little.

"No one would pay that kind of money unless they expected to get something useful, would they?"

Again the shrug. "I can't speak for other people."

"And in fact, you always testify for the prosecution."

"I've testified all over the state."

"For the prosecution."

He sighed. "True."

"You have a reputation for being helpful. That's why prosecutors pay you the big bucks."

"I suppose."

"And if word got out that you were not helpful to the prosecution...you might not be able to command those huge fees anymore."

"Look, if you're trying to suggest that I lied because I was being paid, you're completely—"

"I'm not trying to make any suggestions. I'm trying to elicit facts. And the fact is, your DNA analysis is far less certain than you lead juries to believe."

Harrington rose. "I'm sorry, your honor. When did opposing counsel obtain her degree in forensic science?"

The judge again allowed himself a small smile. "Counsel is entitled to question the testimony."

"That may be." Harrington acted as if he were replying to the judge, but he looked straight at the jury. "And anyone can criticize. But the man on the witness stand is an expert. And he says the DNA came from the defendant."

"He says some of the DNA came from the defendant," Kenzi corrected. "And some of it did not."

"You're just nitpicking—"

"No, I'm separating science from supposition, a line you're clearly trying to blur."

The judge lightly rapped his gavel. "One thing is for certain. Listening to lawyers argue will not help the jury in the slightest. So cut it out. Immediately."

Kenzi bowed her head. "Yes, your honor. Sorry."

"Is there anything else?"

"No." She'd made her point. Maybe the jury would even believe some of it.

She could only hope. Because the next prosecution witnesses would be much harder to nitpick.

30

Kenzi mopped her brow. Temperatures in Seattle, and for that matter, most of the Pacific Northwest, had abruptly soared and the courthouse was stifling. She wasn't surprised. This was a city where many people skipped the expense of air conditioning. Who needed it in this climate, where it rained half the year? It didn't get that hot, and even if it did briefly, the eco-friendlier solution would be a box fan blowing over ice. The nighttime breeze off Puget Sound was usually cooling enough.

Except today—and if global warming advocates were correct, many days to come. A heat dome had blanketed the area. Thirteen million people lived under major heat alerts, and temperatures in some locations went as high as 109. The antiquated ventilation and cooling system in this increasingly dated courthouse was not up to the task. Unfortunately. She was uncomfortable and tense enough without perspiration dripping down her face.

She noticed that Harrington looked calm, cool, and collected. What was his secret? Was he lack sweat glands? Did he have a tricked-out cooling fan inside his suit? Did he think he had this case in the bag? She wasn't sure, and she didn't welcome having one more thing to worry about.

"Why doesn't he sweat?" she whispered to Emma. "Is he a robot?"

"That would explain a great deal," her sister commented. "But I doubt it. A robot would be more logical."

"And would probably have better fashion sense," Kenzi added. "How do you think I'm doing so far?"

"Two witnesses, two solid cross-examinations. You're doing fine."

"You think I scored some points with the jury?"

Emma craned her neck a bit. "I think you reminded them that there are two sides to this story. Which is all you can do at this point."

"You don't think I buried the opposition?"

Emma gave her a sturdy look. "We both know the worst witnesses are yet to come. Let's see how you fare when Harrington starts putting on the heat."

"How's Morgan holding up?"

"Probably better than we have any right to expect, given all she's been through."

"You think that was Morgan's DNA under Sally's fingernails?"

Emma took a deep breath, then slowly released it. "I believe the prosecution leaned on their witness hard. All experts are capable of making errors. But I've looked at the readouts myself." She turned and looked her sister straight in the eye. "It was Morgan's DNA."

The next witness Harrington called was the bailiff on duty the day of the divorce hearing, the day Morgan lost it and threatened Sally—at least as he told it. He exaggerated somewhat, but not enough to matter. Kenzi didn't bother crossing. Yes, the testimony made Morgan look guilty, but that was in fact what happened and there was nothing she could do about it.

The next prosecution witness was Tyler Bechtel, who worked for CellSearch, an outfit that specialized in helping law enforcement crack cell phones. He had hacked into Morgan's iPhone, which the police confiscated when they arrested her. Kenzi wondered, in retrospect, if this was another reason Harrington made the fake deal to let Morgan surrender voluntarily. He wanted to take whatever they wanted before she erased it or gave it to her attorney. She noted that both the arrest and search warrants specifically gave them cops the right to take cellphones and computers, as well as any other tech on the premises.

According to Emma, these tactics had become all too common. Apple and other companies refused to cooperate with law enforcement requests for a backdoor into phones in several high-profile investigations. Congress considered legislation requiring tech companies to cooperate with law enforcement, but so far nothing had passed. So the police found other ways to accomplish the same thing. Apple tried to pretend this didn't exist, even orchestrating major publicity campaigns suggesting that iPhone users could block tracking and refuse to share data. But if the police wanted your digital data, they were going to get it.

Bechtel's primary partner in this invasive enterprise was an Atlanta company called Grayshift, co-founded by a former Apple engineer, and Cellbrite, an Israeli operation inside Japan's Sun Corporation. Despite protests from the ACLU and others, tens of millions of taxpayer dollars had been spent and at least 2000 law enforcement agencies had the tools to break into encrypted phones. Even small communities, like nearby Walla Walla, paid thousands for these tools. She read that the police in Merrill, Wisconsin, population 9000, with just ten vehicles and two bicycles, had spent over thirty thousand on phone-hacking software in the past decade. Cellbrite was said to have 7000 customers in 150 countries.

Phone-busting was big business.

Which sent a shiver up Kenzi's spine. Sometimes it seemed as if she spent half her life on her phone, and she knew she wasn't the only one. She hated to think about what someone might be able to find there. Her iPhone was encrypted by a six-digit code, but she'd read that, even without fancy tools or software, a patient person trying all possible six-digit combinations took, on average, only about eleven hours to find the right code.

Any determined soul could manage that.

After establishing who Bechtel was and why he was in the courtroom, Harrington brought him to the gist of the matter. "Were you able to successfully recover data from the defendant's cellphone?"

"I was. Perhaps because she works in a tech company herself, the defendant had several safety features you wouldn't normally find. But Cellbrite offers a phone-specific service. Send them a phone and two thousand bucks and they'll crack it open for you."

"Is that what happened in this case?"

"Yes."

"What did you find?"

"The defendant's contacts list. Phone call records. Email. Many texts. Not that many phone calls. She seems to prefer digital communication to verbal communication."

"Find anything interesting?"

"Lots."

Harrington smiled slightly. "If you'd found a confession, I assume you would've mentioned it by now."

"True enough. But I found something close."

Brilliantly staged. Now the jury was wide awake and anxious to hear everything he had to say.

"What was that?"

"The defendant texted Sally Beaumont. Shortly after the incident in the courtroom. We were not able to track the location of the parties when the texts were sent, but we did recover the content."

Kenzi could see that revelation took the jurors by surprise. They probably wouldn't have expected those two would ever speak again. "What did the texts say?" As he asked, Harrington projected a reproduction of the text on the overhead viewscreen.

Bechtel read the text aloud. "*Can we talk? In private?*"

"What was the response?"

Bechtel continued to read. "*Sure. My place? Will be there in half an hour.*"

"And the reply?"

"*Meet you there.*" Bechtel looked up. "The defendant knew when and where Sally would be at the time of the murder."

Kenzi jumped up. "Objection. There's no evidence that my client knew anything about an impending murder."

The judge nodded. "Sustained." Though he didn't act as if he thought the objection amounted to much.

Harrington continued. "Have you read the coroner's report?"

"Of course. And this is entirely consistent." He raised his hands, as if to hold off Kenzi's objection. "I'm not suggesting I know anything about medical forensics. But the doc thought Sally recognized her assailant. These texts suggest that she not only knew her assailant but expected to see her. So she wouldn't have been surprised."

"Until the visitor slammed her head against a brick wall. No more questions."

Kenzi rose quickly, but it was more a matter of giving the right impression than eagerness to cross. The texts spoke for themselves.

"Are you aware of any evidence indicating that my client went to Sally's apartment?"

Bechtel shrugged. "I read the texts. They paint a clear picture."

"That she was hoping to go there. Sometime. But are there any eyewitnesses who saw my client there?"

"Not to my knowledge. I don't know every—"

"Are you aware of any forensic evidence that conclusively puts my client at the scene of the crime?"

"I believe there were DNA scrapings—"

"That could have been obtained at any time."

"But the attack might have led to a struggle—"

"Actually, the coroner seemed to think a fight was unlikely. But my point is, you have no evidence that proves my client ever went there."

"I guess that's a matter of opinion."

"And you're aware that my client was arrested a few hours later at her home on the other side of town."

"She had plenty of time to get from one place to the other."

"Without being spotted? By anyone?"

"It could happen."

"Does it strike you as likely? I don't know if you've noticed, but there are a lot of people here in Seattle."

"Yes, but it was dark, and no one had any reason to be on the lookout for her."

"Would you agree that these texts do not exclude the possibility that someone else committed the murder?" She didn't expect him to agree with her, but she hoped her insistent repetition would get through to the jury.

"I don't think we need to exclude everyone in the world. All the evidence points to one person."

"Objection."

The judge did not appear impressed. "He's an expert witness. He can express an opinion, given an opening. Which you just gave him."

Kenzi hated to sit down on that note, but she had nothing more. Truth was, those texts looked bad. Morgan wanted to see the woman she'd just threatened. She told Kenzi she wanted to reconcile, but the jury could easily reach a different conclusion.

31

Kenzi and her team gathered around her kitchen table. She felt guilty about dragging everyone back to her place. It seemed self-indulgent, didn't look professional, and it had been weeks since she'd done anything resembling housecleaning. But the office seemed too stiff and boring. Sherman's Ferry would be fun, but Hailee couldn't come, since she was underage, and the presence of alcohol probably wouldn't be conducive to the think tank. So home it was.

Hailee brought out a huge whiteboard bearing photos of the jurors, mostly obtained from social media. She even arranged them in their current courtroom seats.

"Here's your jury," Hailee announced. "Thanks to the internet, we know more about them than was revealed during the jury selection process."

"Which is totally creepy," Miguel said. "I mean, not to criticize or anything. But from a privacy standpoint."

"Given that this case involves cops hacking into people's phones and software that can find your face anywhere, I don't think this is our gravest privacy concern."

Miguel fanned his face. "Call me old-fashioned. But I'd like to think we can still keep some things to ourselves."

"You can still keep secrets," Emma commented. "If you don't tell anyone. Ever. Or take phone pics."

Hailee cleared her throat. "But getting back to the jury board. What's wrong with this picture? Or rather, all twelve pictures?"

"They need me to take them shopping," Kenzi replied. "Is Juror Number Two actually wearing a Hawaiian shirt? Please."

"No doubt true," Hailee replied. "But I was thinking more in terms of this case..."

"Those men look very serious," Miguel said.

"And?"

"I don't know. I always assume men who take themselves too seriously must be Republicans. So they'll vote to convict."

"Not exactly scientific."

"I go with my gut. Those guys probably think we should have the death penalty again. For misdemeanors."

Hailee appeared to be struggling to maintain patience. "I was thinking more of the ratio of men to women."

"Too many women?" Emma chanced.

"Exactly. More specifically, too many older women. You shouldn't judge people according to stereotypes, of course. But demographically speaking, women are harder on other women than anyone else. Especially older women who don't approve of the way the younger generation...whatevers."

Sharon grinned. "And there's a lot of whatevering in this case."

Miguel frowned. "Could someone please define 'whatevering?'"

Kenzi tried to help. "She's saying there's a lot in Morgan's background for older conservative types to disapprove of."

"Like?"

"Like a throuple."

"Oh yeah. There is that."

"And sexy nude photos."

"Right. I keep forgetting."

"I've read at least a year of Facebook posts for every one of those women," Hailee explained. "I'd be willing to bet that at least three of them disapprove of same-sex unions. And everyone disapproves of polygamy."

Kenzi raised a finger. "It wasn't polygamy. Charles only married Morgan. It was polyamory."

"And that's so much better when you're trying to persuade someone's grandmother." Hailee blew air through her hair, making her bangs flip up. "Look, there's no way you can tell this story without acknowledging that Morgan had multiple lovers. And at least one of them was a woman."

Kenzi felt distinctly uncomfortable hearing her daughter talk about 'lovers.' Did she know anything about sex? She wished they could move on to a more comfortable subject.

"Do you have any information about these people's religion?" Sharon asked. "That might be useful."

"Not everyone posts about their religion," Hailee explained. "But many do. I'd be willing to say seven of our jurors consider themselves Christians"—she pointed each one out on the board —"and four are regular churchgoers."

"Does that mean they're down on LGBTQ rights?"

"Not necessarily. Statistically speaking, it's about fifty-fifty. Most LGBTQ prejudice is related to upbringing, not religion."

"But they do cling to that little passage in Leviticus, don't they? The one scant passage that says it's adultery if a man has sex with a man."

"Which does not necessarily mean all sex with men is sinful," Miguel said. "It just means sex outside the marriage is adultery. Period."

"You sell that to the jury."

"I'm just saying."

"In any case," Hailee continued, obviously trying to regain control of the conversation, "this could be a problem for us. Some people won't like the fact that Morgan and Sally were in this throuple. And may well believe that sin leads to violence."

Sharon appeared puzzled. "So for the legit marriage, she could just divorce the guy. But for the sinful same-sex adultery partner, she had to resort to murder?"

"Something like that."

"What do you recommend?" Kenzi asked. "To placate these judgy jurors."

"You can't rewrite the facts," Hailee answered. "But you can, at all possible times, reiterate the non-sexual aspects of the relationship. These two women were business partners. They had a Final Fantasy alliance."

"And that's better than sharing a bed?"

"Definitely. Play it more like they were girlfriends. Every older woman wishes she had more girlfriends. Turn the relationship into something they might envy, not despise."

Kenzi pondered. That was not a bad idea. She didn't know if it was possible. But she liked having a plan for making a bad situation better. "Nice work, Hailee. Have you prepared profiles on each of the jurors?"

"Of course." She passed the spiral-bound notebook to her mother. "Everything you wanted to know about the jury but the judge wouldn't let you ask."

Kenzi thumbed through the pages. Impressive. Her little girl was learning how to be helpful.

Miguel leaned over Kenzi's shoulder. "Damn, Hailee. You're making the rest of us look bad."

Hailee giggled, obviously pleased.

"I will spend a lot of time with this," Kenzi promised. "Anything else?"

Hailee wheeled up to the table like she was one of the gang. "I'm still reviewing the final report from the medical examiner. There's something strange about it."

"Strange how?"

"I can't quite put my finger on it. Still, it's fun reading."

Hailee might be the only person in the world who would consider that fun reading. "Let me know if you figure it out."

"I will. Mom, have you considered using a tracking device?"

Kenzi blinked. "So you can find me when I'm working?"

"Not for you. For someone we think might be the murderer."

"Such as..."

"Well, Charles comes to mind." She opened a catalog in her satchel. "I've been researching these high-tech spy devices. I mean, they aren't even expensive, really. Plant one on Charles and wait to see if he strangles anybody."

Kenzi waved her hands in the air. "Can't do it. It's illegal. I'm an officer of the court."

Hailee nodded. "I agree that you can't do it..." Her eyes drifted around the coffee table.

"Or anyone working for me," Kenzi added.

"I don't work for you. Miguel doesn't work for you."

Sometimes, having a smart daughter was not the best thing in the world. "Nonetheless. I have to say no on this one."

"So if we decide to do it, we won't tell you about it."

"That is not—"

Hailee winked. "Got the message, Mom. Received and understood."

"I was not—"

"On the bright side, the KenziKlan loves this new case. Your numbers are trending up."

"I guess polyamory is popular on the net."

"What cyberspace likes is being left alone. I thought you might be hurt when those photos were released. But it seems to have had almost zero impact. In fact, some people like Morgan more because she posed for them, refusing to be body-shamed, and some sympathize with her because they think her ex released them to get even with her. They see it as a #Time'sUp offense."

Sounded good. But she doubted everyone shared that perspective.

"You're getting strong support from Silicon Valley. The unpopularity of Face2Face does not seem to be rubbing off on

Morgan. And many people admire you for representing someone they assume is bisexual."

"All of which is nice, but my popularity is the last thing we need to worry about at the moment. Sharon, were you able to talk to your new gal pal about the DNA records?"

Sharon seemed a bit uncomfortable. "Yes. Kate's been very helpful."

Emma looked at Sharon sharply. "I've never seen anyone in law enforcement be so cooperative with defense counsel."

"She's the best."

"Any particular reason why?"

Sharon tugged at her collar. "She's just a great person, that's all. Has a real sense of justice. I invited her to join us tonight, but she felt it might not be appropriate."

"Understandable. But I can't help but think there's more to the DNA analysis than we're getting. Remember, there were two different DNA profiles found under those fingernails. Even if some of it came from Morgan—Sally also came into contact with someone else."

"Or maybe," Miguel said, brushing a hand through his spiky hair, "it came from one of those dudes who have two different DNA profiles."

Kenzi stared at him. "What?"

"You didn't know? Some guys have multiple DNA."

"How is that even possible?"

"Bone marrow transplants."

If that was supposed to explain anything—it didn't.

Miguel looked incredulous. "I can't believe I'm the only one who knows about this. There was a whole big thing about it on Discovery+. See, there was this dude in California who had a vasectomy and then developed leukemia. Bone marrow transplants from another donor saved his life. But about four years later, scientists found his donor's DNA in his semen."

Great. Her daughter was going to be present for this discussion too. "How can that be?"

"See, a guy who's had a vasectomy doesn't produce sperm, but does produce seminal fluid. Which, after the sperm is gone, is mostly composed of different types of white blood cells. Four years after the transplant, to their surprise, researchers found both the DNA he was born with and the donor's DNA. Apparently, after a transplant, white blood cells come from the bone-marrow donor, so they carry the donor's DNA. Isn't that awesome?"

Emma appeared nonplussed. "It's called chimerism, and it actually occurs quite a bit in nature. There are some marmoset monkeys that have cells from multiple sources. For instance, the DNA in their egg cells come from a different donor than the rest of their DNA."

Kenzi tried to follow the discussion, but it was a struggle. "This is fascinating, but I don't see how it helps us get—"

Emma snapped her fingers. "Didn't Morgan tell you Charles had been sick? That he had several surgeries?"

"Well...yes." Her eyes widened. "Are you thinking...bone marrow transplant?"

"It would explain a great deal."

Kenzi made a note. "I'll ask Morgan. I very much appreciate your help. All of you. The evidence against Morgan is bad and she's going to be convicted of a crime she didn't commit unless we do something to stop it. We need fresh ideas."

"Tracking device," Hailee murmured.

Miguel stretched. "Semen."

Sharon smirked. "You think Harrington's going to pull some courtroom grandstanding?"

"I think he wants to win." Kenzi gazed at her friends solemnly. "And I think he'd be willing to do almost anything to make sure that happens."

32

Kenzi had learned to make a habit of scanning the courtroom each day before the testimony began. She always found it interesting that people took time out of their day to watch a trial. She expected the press. This was a murder case and it involved prominent figures from a major tech company. But she did not expect all the unrelated looky loos, people who were there out of idle curiosity, or perhaps because there was nothing good on television.

She spotted most of the faces she'd seen before—Charles, of course, Dr. Quinn, and Brent Coleman. Harvey Vasquez. She was almost certain Harrington would call Coleman to the stand. What did the long-lost lover know that could be relevant? None of the exhibits pertained to him. Did he know anything about the murder?

Why did she have the ominous feeling she was missing something?

She noticed a few new faces too—Crozier, for one. What business did that vulture have here? Just hoping to scoop up some tidbit he could use in the divorce case? Just hoping to catch her in a moment of weakness when she might accept his job offer?

Sharon identified the shaggy-haired man in the rear as Pete Taylor, the CEO behind the Taylor Petrie dating app. If "dating" was the right word. The app responsible for leaking the explicit photos from Morgan's past. She noticed he sat close to the prosecution table, as if he sympathized with them.

Harrington called Sergeant Noah Smithson to the witness stand. Smithson worked in the cybercrimes unit of the Seattle police department.

"Since this case involves a murder by strangulation," Harrington asked, "why would the department involve a cybercrimes expert?" He gave special emphasis to the word "expert."

Smithson wore horn-rimmed glasses and had curly hair that flopped around when he spoke. "The department received a tip indicating that the defendant might have engaged in criminal activities online."

"What kind of activities?"

"A large group of sexually explicit photos—"

"Objection," Kenzi said, cutting him off as quickly as possible. She knew those photos would get in eventually. But she could delay it as long as possible. "Lack of personal knowledge. Lack of foundation."

"Sustained," Judge Odom said. "Perhaps counsel could lay the proper foundation and establish a basis for the witness' knowledge."

Harrington smiled. "That's okay, your honor. We'll get that with a different witness." He turned back to the witness. "Can you explain what you found during your investigation?"

"Certainly. I found an advertisement on Craigslist soliciting criminal acts. Specifically, attempting to hire someone to sexually assault the victim. Sally Beaumont."

The jury appeared floored. Shocked. Someone was willing to pay for an attack?

Even though he wasn't surprised, Harrington gaped as if he were. "What?"

"You've probably heard of people hiring hit men over the internet. This appears to be an attempt to hire a rapist."

Harrington clicked a button on a remote, putting a picture of the Craigslist ad on the overhead screen. "Is this the ad you mentioned?"

"Yes. You can read it for yourself. The ad purports to be from Sally Beaumont herself. According to the text, she wanted to indulge her rape fantasies. The ad encourages men to come to her home and have sex with her—even if she screams or resists. According to this ad, that's all part of her fantasy, so men should just ignore it. And as you can see, it offers a sizable amount of money to anyone who accepts the offer."

"By raping Sally Beaumont."

"Exactly. Someone desperate for money could read this ad and assault her believing they were doing exactly what she wanted." He paused. "Never for one moment realizing this was actually a diabolical revenge scheme cooked up by the defendant, Morgan Moreno."

Kenzi felt the eyes of the jurors burning past her to Morgan. She knew what they were thinking. What kind of monster would do such a thing?

"Why do you believe this ad was placed by the defendant?"

"Contrary to popular opinion, there are skid marks on the internet superhighway. We tracked down the IP address of the laptop that placed the ad. It came from the defendant's laptop. What's more, we know how the ad was paid for. With Morgan Moreno's credit card."

Harrington shook his head, a disgusted expression on his face. "The defendant was willing to pay someone to rape Sally Beaumont."

"It would appear so."

"She must've hated Sally in the worst possible way. Hated her enough to—"

"Objection," Kenzi said. "Argumentative."

Harrington looked up innocently. "I was just saying what everyone is thinking."

Judge Odom nodded. "Save it for closing argument. Sustained."

Harrington nodded. "Very well. No more questions."

Kenzi rose, though there was precious little she could say. Morgan denied all knowledge of this Craigslist ad, but it did appear to have come from her laptop, and it was without question paid for with her credit card. This was a major frame, but they had no way to prove it.

"Just to be clear," she asked the witness, "you have no direct proof that my client placed this ad, right? You can't prove she knew anything about it."

Smithson was not deterred. "Her credit card was used to pay the bill."

"Which would be a rather stupid way to pay for an ad soliciting a criminal act."

He shrugged. "Criminals aren't always super-smart. That's why we catch them."

"But my client is super-smart. She's got a Ph.D. She creates computer programs that have made millions."

"The world is full of people who are bright as the sun in their professional life—and dumb as dirt in their personal life."

Could he please stop being so wise? "It's possible someone else got her credit card number. Using that traceable means of payment could be part of the frame."

"How would anyone get the credit card number of such a... super-smart person?"

"Ever heard of a data breach?"

"Well...yes."

"In fact, there have been several high-profile cases of hackers getting into retail websites and obtaining credit card numbers and other sensitive personal data." Not to mention explicit photos. "Right?"

"Yes. But I'm not aware of—"

"Or someone might've taken the card from her wallet. Or peered over her shoulder while she was buying something online."

"The ad placement was traced back to the defendant's laptop."

"Which, again, would be a really stupid way to place an ad soliciting criminal activity."

"She had to get online somehow."

"She could go to the library. Or an internet cafe. There are lots of ways to get online without using your own laptop. You're asking the jury to assume that my client is a stupid person. And she's not a stupid person."

"But she appears to have been driven by hate. Extreme hate. And when people are angry, they don't always think through their actions as carefully as they should."

"Did anyone see my client place this ad?"

"I don't know."

"You don't have any eyewitnesses."

"Of course not."

"Anyone hear her place this ad?"

"No."

"It could've been placed by the person who really did kill Sally." She took a deep breath. "It could even have been placed by Sally herself."

That got the jurors' attention. But if she was going to counteract this shocking accusation, she needed to propose something equally shocking.

Smithson peered at her as if she were insane. "You're suggesting Sally placed ads inviting someone to drop by and rape her?"

"It's possible."

"No one would do that. No one in their right mind."

"Except, as you say, extreme hate impacts people's judgment. And Sally betrayed Morgan, turned against her in the divorce. Turned against her at the hearing. This could be one more effort to destroy Morgan, to get her arrested by framing her. If anyone could get access to Morgan's laptop or credit card, it would be Sally."

"In a different situation," Smithson said, "I might be willing to at least consider this perverse fantasy. But given the mountain of evidence proving Morgan killed Sally—no way. Morgan wanted Sally to suffer. And one way or the other, she was going to make sure she did."

enzi tried not to drum her fingers as she waited for Harrington to call his next witness. Part of her anxiety came from impatience, and part came from fear. More and more she felt this case was getting away from her. Each witness made the story more confusing, more inexplicable. And as she knew all too well, the next witness would intensify that feeling.

Elliott Witherspoon had been a banker with First National for more than two decades, but following three years of reeducation at the bank's expense, he'd spent the last six years heading its online banking division, which handled fraud inquiries relating to online transfers and deposits. He'd worked with the police department during its investigation. Kenzi knew Harrington could've called a cop to deliver this evidence, but opted to go with a banker instead. Perhaps he thought the jury might be ready for a change, but all things considered, she suspected he thought a banker would have more credibility.

Witherspoon was not exactly overweight. Just sort of lumpy, with an embarrassing combover. She wasn't going to judge. She hadn't been working out as often as she should lately either. But she did at least maintain her fashion standards. This man was wearing a cardigan, and unless you were Taylor Swift, that was a courtroom fashion crime.

Harrington established that Witherspoon had been asked to assist the police in their investigation. "The bank upholds its depositors' privacy rights to the utmost degree," he explained. "We don't reveal anything unless we're subpoenaed, and even then, only after the police have demonstrated that lives could be in danger."

"And you helped them investigate the defendant?"

He nodded. "The police believe she killed someone and could not rule out the possibility that she might kill again."

"Could you please describe the bank account you examined?"

"Of course. It's a joint bank account. Checking account."

"And the parties to the account?"

"Charles Land and Morgan Moreno."

"Not Sally Beaumont."

"No. She had a separate account with far less money in it. Her only source of income appeared to be regular transfers from the joint account managed by Charles and Morgan. She was outside the family loop, at least financially. She wasn't a signatory on any of the DigiDynamics corporate accounts either. She didn't own stock. She wasn't a signer on their safe deposit box. As far as I could tell, she only got money if Charles or Morgan gave it to her."

"Sally wasn't legally married to Charles. Would that preclude her from being on the joint account?"

"Absolutely not. We have many joint accounts with people who aren't married. Unmarried partners. Parents and children. Siblings."

"Has there been any...noteworthy activity in the account you examined?"

"Yes. As you know, as soon as a divorce is filed, an automatic temporary restraining order goes into effect precluding the parties from alienating their assets beyond what is necessary for ordinary living expenses. That includes business accounts. The parties could only spend what they had or what the court allowed them to take."

"Did this create a financial hardship?"

"Not for Charles and Morgan. They could live for a good long time on what was in that joint account. But Sally was in an entirely different situation. Her account had less than five thousand dollars in it at the time of the divorce, which is about what she spent in a month. She was going to be begging on street corners if she didn't get money from somewhere fast."

"Did she?"

"Oh yeah. Huge deposit. At first, we all assumed this money came from Charles. We knew Sally had sided with Charles during the divorce and everyone thought that there had been some sort of quid pro quo."

"Did that prove to be true?"

Witherspoon hesitated before answering. "Sally received a transfer of just over a million dollars, and since the funds were electronically transferred from another bank, we did not initially have any means of tracing them."

"What did you do next?"

"The police allowed us—assisted us, actually—in tracing the routing numbers back to the bank, and from there to an individual account. Took a flurry of subpoenas and two trips to court, but we eventually learned where the money came from."

He paused, and anticipation mounted. Some of the jurors leaned forward, anxiously awaiting the revelation.

"And the answer?"

"The cash came from an offshore bank account in the Cayman Islands. Like most tax-haven bank accounts, it was anonymous, so we issued another flurry of legal documents. But I'll cut to the chase." He sat up straight, drawing in his breath. "The payoff to Sally did not come from Charles. Despite her best efforts to hide the trail, we learned that the payment came from Morgan Moreno."

Kenzi watched the jurors stare at one another, obviously

deeply puzzled. Sally was bribed into betraying Morgan—by Morgan?

"Needless to say," Witherspoon continued, "we were surprised. Didn't make any sense. And then we realized that in all respects, from the very beginning of this case, we'd been misled by a clever woman who—"

"Objection," Kenzi cut in. "Speculation."

Harrington protested. "Your honor. He hasn't finished his sentence."

The judge shook his head. "There's no way that sentence wasn't going to be speculative. Sustained."

Harrington tried again. "A huge sum of money was transferred from an offshore account that the defendant controlled to an account at your bank in Sally Beaumont's name."

"Yes. And Sally transferred a large portion of that to a new account she had just opened, which is why she had a bank slip on her when she was killed."

"Is there any indication Charles Land knew about this?"

Witherspoon shook his head. "I see no indication that Charles knew this offshore account existed. The whole point of having offshore accounts is so people don't know about them. Especially the IRS. But they have been used to shield money from partners as well. And as you know, they have been used to pay ransoms. Or blackmail."

Kenzi's fists clenched. This was more speculation, but he had framed it in a way that gave her no opportunity to object.

"Blackmail," Harrington repeated, doing his best to plant that idea in the jurors' heads. "That's when people pay money to keep something secret."

"Right."

"This was a huge payment. It would have to be a significant secret."

"I would think so."

"And if the payoff didn't do the trick—"

Kenzi was rising but Harrington cut off the objection.

"Well, I think we all know what happens when money isn't enough to ensure silence. No more questions."

If Harrington had been any closer to her, she might've become a strangler herself. He had cleverly planted the idea of a blackmail payment that didn't work, forcing Morgan to turn to murder. One more addition to his growing list of possible motives.

She strode to the stand and got right in the banker's face. She wouldn't waste her time trying to intimidate a police officer, but she might get somewhere with a career banker. "You said the Cayman Islands account was controlled by my client. What exactly does that mean?"

Witherspoon appeared puzzled. "I think it's self-explanatory."

"Does it prove she's the one who transferred the money?"

He held up his hands. "It was her account."

"Is it possible to open a bank account in someone else's name?"

"I...suppose it's possible. But why would anyone do that?"

"To cover their tracks. Or to frame someone. Or both. Would the person who opened this account have been required to show ID to prove their identity?"

Witherspoon thought for a moment. "Probably not. The bank usually assigns a unique access code, and that's all you need to distribute the funds."

"Then anyone could do it. Do you have any evidence that my client is the person who directed those funds to be transferred to Sally's account?"

Witherspoon looked directly at the jury. "I think the facts speak for themselves."

"You've already mentioned that Sally sided with Charles during the divorce negotiations and that Morgan believed she'd been bought off by Charles. Wouldn't it be clever if he was able to make the payoff in a way that couldn't be traced back to him? That instead made it look as if the money came from Morgan?"

"You know what I think would be clever? A woman who needed her former partners eliminated, but knew she'd be the first person suspected if anyone turned up dead. So she makes it look as if the other two have joined forces to betray her. She makes herself the sympathetic party."

"Objection," Kenzi said. "He's speculating again."

The judge tilted his head. "He is indeed, but you asked for it. Overruled."

Damn. Not that the judge was wrong. But she hated losing objections.

"You suggest Morgan was clever," Kenzi continued. "But I don't see anything clever about giving away a million bucks."

Witherspoon shrugged. "That's chump change for these people. They're the one percent. They give away millions like you and I give quarters to panhandlers." Another comment certain to inspire the jurors to dislike Morgan. "If that money kept her out of prison, it was a bargain. And if it kept Sally quiet, even for a little while, it was worthwhile."

"You have no proof that this payment was part of a blackmail scheme."

Without missing a beat, Witherspoon replied. "What is clear is that this payment was made for something. And it wasn't enough. And as a result...Sally Beaumont is dead."

34

He wondered how long he could stand to wait before he once more savored the delicious thrill that came from wrapping his hand around a woman's delicate throat.

Answer? Not much longer.

He had learned to love this life. The planning. The stalking. Gaining an innocent's confidence. The splendid moment when his hand stretched across her throat, her eyes flew open, and she realized how foolish she'd been.

The moment when he saw the hideous realization in her eyes. The certain knowledge that they were entirely in his hands, literally and figuratively. That he could spare their life or snuff it out in an instant.

It had been several weeks now since his last score. But his foreign partners insisted that he lay low. Wait for the furor to fade. He understood. What he didn't get, though, was that the furor in question was not the hunt for the so-called Seattle Strangler. That had been going on for months and he saw no evidence that the cops were any closer than they had ever been.

He wasn't hamstrung by the investigation. And it wasn't the hubbub surrounding that soccer player, either. He was paralyzed by the murder trial of Sally Beaumont. The DigiDynamics scandal. The naked photos.

A sexy case, to be sure. But that shouldn't prevent him from doing what needed to be done.

Was this an addiction? He remembered when he started, when the attacks were sketchy and scary and he wasn't very good at it. The thrill had been laced with a frisson of fear. He got a high from it.

Did he still get the buzz? Now it seemed like he did it because he had to. Because he couldn't live without it.

Given the circumstances, he had every right to visit the courthouse and observe the proceedings. He couldn't go back into action until this dog-and-pony show ended. Why not watch it unfold?

How easily the foolish are led. People are effortlessly hoisted on their own petards when they're running scared. Desperate. Worried about reputations. Or worse.

Let them play out their little psychodrama. Let the woman be put away permanently. And then when she was gone, let the Strangler reappear. The chain must not be broken.

His only concern was the lawyer for the defense. She seemed a trifle too smart for his taste. From what he could see, she didn't believe the story the prosecution was peddling. She had a mind of her own—a dangerous commodity.

He was not overly concerned. At the end of the day, he knew how to deal with threats. He was probably better at it than anyone else around. All he had to do was wrap his hand around her skinny little neck...

She could be eliminated in less time than it took to sneeze.

You thought Sally's death was quick and shocking? You ain't seen nothing yet.

Make no mistake, Kenzi Rivera. I've got my eyes on you.

And if necessary, I'll have my hands on you, too.

K enzi made a point of getting to the courtroom early the next morning. She hoped to spend some time talking with her client. She thought Morgan had behaved admirably during the early days of this trial. Not that she'd been perfect. There was no such thing as perfect in the courtroom. Occasionally, she couldn't help but react to what she heard on the witness stand. But there had been no tears and certainly no outbursts—not since she attacked Sally at the conclusion of the divorce hearing.

Perhaps she'd learned her lesson. She'd paid for that outburst in the worst way possible.

While they waited for the judge to return, she sat close to Morgan and whispered, "How you holding up?"

"I'll be fine."

"Must be hard. Hearing people say these things. Accuse you of so much."

"I'm used to it. I've never been good at...making friends. That's one reason why what Charles and Sally and I had was so special. I knew it was a miracle that I tumbled into that relationship. And I know that, regardless of what happens here, I'll never have anything like that again."

Chapter 35

"You don't know that. The future is not written."

Morgan looked up, smiling sadly. "I do know that. But thanks for the optimism." She leaned back into her chair and closed her eyes. "I miss Sally. So much. Every damn day. And now these people want to suggest that...that..." She clamped her eyes tightly shut. She couldn't finish the sentence.

Harrington made no attempt to speak to Kenzi, which was okay by her, except it probably meant he thought he had this case in the bag. If he believed there was the slightest chance he might fail to get a conviction, he'd save face by offering a plea bargain.

Gabriel was in the courtroom today, no doubt to spy on her and gauge how much damage this tasteless foray into the sewers of criminal law would do to the firm. She didn't like it, but it could be worse.

It could be her father sitting out there.

Harrington's first witness of the day would be Charles, Morgan's ex-husband, CEO of DigiDynamics. The press had started calling him The Man in the Middle, because he seemed to be in the middle of everything but in control of nothing. More than one commentator had wondered how it was possible to amass such a huge fortune and remain so clueless. The fact that he'd made a billion-dollar sale without Morgan's knowledge seemed to have escaped their notice.

She laid her hand atop Morgan's. "You ready for this?"

"Ready as I'm ever likely to be."

"It won't be pleasant. Comfort yourself with the knowledge that I'm going to rip him to shreds on cross." Or try, anyway.

"I'll keep that in mind. But mostly I'm going to focus on the fact that he's a lying son of a bitch."

"Whatever works."

Harrington spent half an hour walking Charles through his background, including his education and his business activities. Then he shifted to the personal and described how the three-some came to be. Long nights online. Coffee dates that ran to the wee hours of the morning. And in what seemed like a blink of an eye, three people working together to build a keenly successful tech company.

"Please tell the jury about Face2Face."

"Face2Face is a revolutionary facial recognition program, better than anything else on the market. It emerged from an earlier project called the Love Library. Initially, we saw this program as a cool way to find friends on various social media platforms. But law enforcement saw it as a great way to identify suspects and catch crooks. They wanted it."

"And you made the program available to them?"

"I did."

"Did everyone approve of this decision?"

"No. Morgan—the defendant—disapproved. She thought I was, to use her words, 'selling out.'"

"What was your reaction?"

"To be blunt—I didn't care. Overnight we made close to a billion dollars. That's not selling out. That's being a savvy businessperson."

"But Morgan didn't agree."

"No. And that's when the relationship began to sour. We grew more distant. I saw less and less of her. Sally told me she was unhappy. But there didn't seem to be anything I could do about it."

"You mentioned Sally. Did you consider her part of this family unit?"

"Very much so."

"But you married Morgan."

"This nation doesn't allow polygamous marriages, and at the time we were getting together, Sally was still technically married, so I married Morgan. But Sally was there all the time. She even recited vows at the wedding."

"A previous witness noted that Sally was not on the joint bank account."

"Sally wasn't on the legal documents, the mortgage and utility bills and whatnot, so she didn't need to be on that household account. I thought we should add her anyway, just to be fair, but somehow, it never happened."

"Morgan had stock in the company. Sally did not."

"She didn't want to be what she called, 'a corporate shill.' I just gave her money regularly. In effect, a salary."

"How much was the salary?"

"About five thousand a month. Of course, all her bills were paid. Morgan thought we should be conservative about our ongoing expenses."

"Forgive me for saying so, but for three people in a mutually loving relationship...Sally always seemed to get the short end of the stick."

Charles drew in his breath, then slowly released it, his eyelids closed, an unmistakably sad expression on his face. "There's a reason for that."

"And the reason would be?"

Charles looked across the courtroom. "I'm sorry, Morgan. But I'm under oath. I have to tell the truth."

Kenzi didn't like the sound of that. She glanced at her client. Morgan was returning Charles' gaze, but with a steely, unflinching expression.

"What's the reason for Sally's second-class-citizen treatment?" Harrington asked.

Charles sighed. "Morgan hated her."

While Kenzi did not hear any actual gasping, when she looked into the jurors' eyes, she thought she observed the visual equivalent. It was as if everything they thought they knew about this case suddenly turned out to be false.

"But—you've said the three of you were close. You bonded, first over a computer game and—"

"In the early days, that was true. I never felt such warmth as I did when I was surrounded by those two. But everything changed after we moved to Seattle. Or more precisely, everything changed after Morgan and I were married."

"What happened then?"

"I've heard other couples talk about how everything changes once you make the relationship official with a piece of paper, but I never saw it happen as dramatically as I did in my own home. Once Morgan was the official spouse, the one with her name on the bank account and a fancy office at DigiDynamics...everything changed."

"How exactly did things change?"

"Morgan started treating Sally differently. Less like a partner and more like...a servant."

All eyes shifted to Morgan, who sat impassively as if she didn't know everyone was staring at her. Kenzi almost wished she hadn't told her to remain stoic. This might be the one instance in which a little visual outrage might be desirable.

"Please describe how the defendant treated her now deceased partner."

"Like her personal handmaiden. She'd text Sally from work, telling her what she wanted for dinner and instructing her to start chopping vegetables or boiling the pasta or whatever. She'd leave messes in the kitchen and expect Sally to clean it up. I mean, come on, we could afford a maid. But Morgan wanted Sally to be the maid. She'd tell her to come along when she walked the dogs, just so she could rant at her while they walked. She'd huddle with me in the kitchen, whispering, either talking about Sally or making her believe we were talking about her." He paused. "You know, when I said she treated Sally like a servant, I might've been too kind. What she really did was treat Sally like a pet. Like her dog."

"How did you feel about this?"

"I talked to Morgan about it. More than once. But Morgan is extremely strong-willed. She doesn't like to be told what to do. She'd look me in the eye and say, 'Apparently you've forgotten who you're sleeping with.'"

"What did that mean?"

"It meant if I didn't give her everything she wanted and let her do everything she wanted, I wouldn't be getting sex."

Harrington tugged at his collar. "Of course...you had another partner."

"Yes, but Morgan dominated Sally. If she didn't want Sally sleeping with me, Sally would not be sleeping with me. Morgan's a control freak. She wanted to orchestrate every aspect of our relationship. Including sex. As far as she was concerned, unless she wanted a three-way, Sally wasn't going to be with me."

"So you allowed Morgan to treat Sally in this...degrading way."

"I couldn't stop it. At one point, Morgan came home with a dog collar. One of those supposedly sexy jobs with spikes. She wanted Sally to wear it. Which she did. But I don't think anyone thought this was a turn-on. It was just another visible reminder that Sally didn't have equal status. She wasn't a partner. She was a pet."

Kenzi watched Charles carefully as he told this story. He seemed convincing. And yet, she'd seen Morgan and Sally together the first time she met them, and she didn't get a weird doggie vibe then. Was she really that unperceptive?

"Once you understand how Morgan treated Sally, everything else makes sense. Of course she didn't want Sally on the household bank account. Would you give a dog a bank account? Or company stock? No, just give her a little allowance every now and again, so she remains completely dependent upon you for the rest of her life."

Harrington offered a sorrowful expression. "I'm sorry you had to deal with this. Do you have any idea why Morgan treated Sally in this disgusting manner?"

"I already told you. Because she hated her. I think she began to perceive Sally as the 'other woman.' The interloper. Someone she had to grind under her foot. It became clear to me that Morgan has a mean streak. A part that likes to mistreat, to abuse. That gets pleasure from other people's pain." He paused. "A killing instinct."

He didn't exactly call her a murderer. But he was dancing all around it.

"You've heard a previous witness talk about the money that appeared in Sally's bank account. Do you know anything about that?"

"I wanted Sally to be taken care of, but my lawyers told me I couldn't do anything while the divorce was pending. I can state unequivocally that the money didn't come from me, not as a payoff or blackmail or for any other reason."

"Did Morgan make that transfer?"

"It certainly sounds like she did. And who else would have that kind of money?"

"If she hated Sally, why make her rich?"

"Because—"

Kenzi shot up like a firecracker. "Objection. Speculation."

Judge Odom nodded. "That will be sustained."

Thank goodness. She couldn't imagine what Charles' explanation would be. But she was certain it wouldn't be good for Morgan.

"Why did you file for divorce?"

"Isn't it obvious? This was a bad situation getting worse. Daily. Morgan's hostility to Sally, her mistreatment of Sally. I wasn't sure what she might do to the woman. This started as the greatest relationship of my life, but it turned into a nightmare. I wanted out."

"And what were your plans once you were...out?"

"I was planning to start a healthier relationship. With Sally. Only Sally."

Lips parted in the jury box. All at once, the strongest possible motive for murder had arrived. Morgan was about to be replaced. So she eliminated the competition.

Harrington took a step closer. "Do you know who killed Sally?"

"Objection!" Kenzi said. "Speculation."

The judge pondered for a moment. "That depends on what the witness says, doesn't it?" He glanced down at the witness. "I'll allow you to answer, if you know something that bears on the question posed. I don't want to hear speculation or guessing."

"Understood." Charles looked back at Harrington. "It's obvious to me that Morgan felt threatened. She had a motive to commit this crime. And she had the mean streak necessary to bring it off." He paused, choosing his words carefully. "I wasn't there. I won't pretend I was. I didn't see the murder take place." His eyes drifted to Morgan. "But based upon the years I spent with her, it's obvious to me what happened. I can't believe there's any serious doubt about it in anyone's mind. There's not the slightest shred of a doubt in mine."

36

W hen Harrington finished, Kenzi assumed she would cross-examine. She didn't have much to ask and didn't for one moment think she could shake Charles from his story. But she had to try.

Or so she thought. As she started to rise, Morgan grabbed her arm. "Don't cross," she whispered.

Kenzi stared at her, brow deeply wrinkled. "Just let that stand?"

"You won't get anywhere asking him questions. He won't back down."

"I might poke a hole in his story."

"Did you see any holes?"

"Well...no."

"Charles is too smart for that. You're not going to catch him out."

Because she wasn't as smart as Charles? Kenzi tried not to be offended. "It won't hurt to try."

"It might."

Kenzi felt a queasy feeling in her stomach. "Meaning what?"

"His testimony was a pack of lies. But he could've done

worse. I think he moderated his story so he wouldn't look spiteful."

Kenzi could see the judge staring at her, expecting her to proceed. She had to make a decision. Fast.

She stood. "No questions from the defense, your honor."

She could see he was surprised. But he took her at her word and proceeded.

She slid back into her chair.

Harrington had one more witness to call. And given the amount of damage Charles had done, she hated to think about what Harrington was saving for his grand finale.

———

THE BOYFRIEND, damn it all. Of course it was the ex-boyfriend. Brent Coleman, the creep who took the explicit photos.

Brent took the witness stand. He had obviously been cleaned up for trial, but his basement-hacker roots were still apparent. He slumped in the chair, spoke informally, and looked as if he'd rather be anywhere else.

He explained his educational and employment background, mentioned that he had dated Morgan before she met Charles, and acknowledged that he currently worked directly under Charles' supervision.

"When were you with the defendant?" Harrington asked.

"Before she met Charles and Sally. We got along well at first." He whistled. "She's a firecracker. Tough, but worth it."

"Um...I'm not sure..."

"She's a wildcat. You know? A tiger. Between the sheets."

Kenzi lurched to her feet. "Objection. Relevance."

"Disagree," Harrington said. "The defendant's prior sexual history is unfortunately relevant to understanding what led to the murder."

"Baloney." She stepped closer to the bench, out of the hearing of the jury. "Your honor, this is just an excuse to slut-shame my client. Turn the jury against her by suggesting she might've had a prior life. You allow this and you'll be a #MeToo poster boy."

Harrington stepped beside her. "Is she threatening the Court? Ms. Rivera has a huge internet following. If anyone could organize a Twitterstorm, it would be her."

"I'm not threatening anyone," she clarified. "I'm trying to warn you. This is dangerous territory. And not relevant."

Judge Odom shook his head. "I don't like this at all. But I can't agree with your argument. It could be relevant, especially given what we heard from the last witness. I'm going to allow it."

Harrington smiled and Kenzi trudged back to her table.

"So," Harrington said, "picking up where we left off, I believe you indicated that you and the defendant were sexually active?'

Brent laughed. "Yeah. That would be one way of putting it."

"You were...adventurous?"

"You name it, we did it. Acted out little fantasy scenarios. Wore costumes. Did the handcuffs and the sex shop paraphernalia. Even did the reverse cowgirl."

"The...uh..."

"Supposedly the most dangerous sex position. But she loved it. She liked being on top. Which shouldn't surprise anyone."

"And you took pictures of one another?"

"Yeah. We definitely did that." He stopped for a moment. "Well, not of each other. I never posed. I would never do that."

"But the defendant would?"

"That's where those photos came from. The ones all over the internet."

"Just to be clear," Harrington said, "were those photos taken voluntarily?"

"Absolutely. It was her idea. She wanted me to have something to remember her by, like while I was at work. I had one of those as the desktop photo on my phone. Actually, don't tell my current girlfriend but—I still do."

For the first time, Kenzi spotted a small reaction on

Morgan's face. Apparently the thought of her nude photos being on Brent's phone made her sick to her stomach.

"What happened to the relationship? Why did it end?"

Brent tilted his head. "It was fun at first. I'd never seen anyone like her before. But after a while I got tired of it. Never anything normal, you know? I didn't mention it before, but she was into these strange strangulation games."

Two jurors winced at the word "strangulation."

"You know, we'd choke each other to the point of passing out. Gives you a major high. And there was other weird stuff. Which she demanded, whether I was in the mood or not. She was so pushy. Controlling. Strident. Toward the end, she talked about wanting to bring in another woman. That was too kinky for me. Never thought I'd say it, but after a while I found myself just wanting a normal girl who cooked and cleaned and got her ideas from the Bible. Not *Fifty Shades of Grey*."

"Were there any other reasons for the breakup?"

Brent looked confused for a moment. "Oh, right. The temper. She has a major-league temper. She'd get mad and start ranting, you know? An endless stream of anger. She'd go on and on. I could leave the room and she wouldn't stop ranting. And she could be violent, too."

"How so?"

"She'd pick stuff up. Throw it at me. Dishes and vases. Make a big mess. She'd call me ugly names. I don't know how many times she said she was going to kill me."

Harrington's eyebrow rose. "She threatened to kill you?"

"Yeah. She'd get kitchen knives and swing them at me. She could be mean. Scary mean."

Kenzi watched the jurors carefully. None of this proved Morgan was the murderer. But it certainly made it seem possible.

"I'm surprised you stayed in the relationship as long as you did."

"There were some benefits." He winked at the nearest juror. An older man. Who smiled knowingly in return.

"When did you next see Morgan? After the breakup."

"Not for years. Years and years. Of course I heard about her. Her and her little posse. I worked in the tech sector, so I could hardly miss the phenomenal rise of DigiDynamics. Didn't know about Sally, not at first. But I heard all about Morgan and her new spouse, the CEO."

"When did you move to Seattle?"

"Recently. Charles made me an offer I couldn't refuse. He'd seen some of my work at my previous job and said he wanted me on his team. So I moved."

"And now you work directly under Charles."

Brent appeared proud of his current station. "I'm his right-hand man."

"And there's no...discomfort? I mean, you did have a prior relationship with his wife."

"Barely even mentioned it. I don't think he cared about that. As we became closer, I started to realize he was having problems with Morgan too. Just as I did. I mean, I never had a throuple. But I don't think that woman has changed much over the years."

"So it wasn't awkward? Working with Charles?"

"To the contrary, it was like we had something in common. Something we both shared. I could relate to his stories in a way no one else could. I understood the twisted way Morgan thought. When I heard someone killed her dog—I knew it was her, just like I knew she was lying about being attacked. She was setting Charles up for a big fall. He had no choice but to divorce her."

"And you remained close to Charles...even after the nude photos of his wife hit the internet?"

Brent looked strangely at his questioner. "Wait a minute. Do you think I leaked those photos? I didn't. And I didn't post them on that adultery website."

"But you were the only one who had them."

"No. Morgan had them too."

"Surely you're not suggesting that she leaked those disgusting photos of herself."

"Of course not." He paused, his eyes darting around the courtroom. "Sally's the one who leaked the photos."

Kenzi's lips parted. She shot a look at Morgan, then at Emma. It was clear they were just as surprised as she was.

"How did Sally—"

"She got them from Morgan. I don't know how. Maybe she got her hands on Morgan's phone. Maybe Morgan gave them to her, thinking they'd turn her on. I don't know how it happened. But I know Sally did it. She told me she did it. To my face."

"But—why?"

"Isn't it obvious? The pet dog learned how to bite. She was tired of sleeping in the doghouse. She needed money, so she got the photos and threatened to release them unless Morgan gave her some money. Which of course Morgan did."

"You're saying Sally blackmailed the defendant with the photos."

"Absolutely. And maybe more. I think she knew things about Morgan, things probably said in confidence."

"But the photos were still released."

Brent smiled. "Yeah. After she got the money. She got her revenge." The smile slowly faded. "But I guess Morgan got the last word in that conversation."

"Meaning?"

"Morgan has been saying Sally betrayed her, and I guess she did. But people misunderstood what Morgan was saying. Sally didn't betray her in the divorce. I don't know what happened there. But she definitely betrayed her when it came to those photos—and that can never be taken back. Despite all Morgan's success, most people will never remember anything except how trampy she looked in those pics. And you know what? I wouldn't be surprised if Sally planned to reveal more secrets. Maybe that's why—"

He stopped. His eyes drifted to the defendant's table. "Maybe Morgan had to kill her. Before she released something even worse. And who will be next? Charles? Me? Given how little Morgan can control her temper, I don't think Sally will be her last victim. If she's not put behind bars—no one is safe."

PART III

THE BEST OF BOTH WORLDS

37

Once again, Kenzi gathered around her kitchen table with her team, but the mood was considerably more somber than it was the last time. The conclusion of Harrington's case had been devastating. None of it was good, but the last two witnesses were the worst. They painted a portrait that was believable and consistent. Morgan had a temper. Morgan had a mean streak. And Morgan hated Sally. Hated her enough to kill her. Sally might even have been blackmailing her.

Kenzi tried to dent Brent on cross, but she got nowhere. Yes, Morgan was a former flame. So what? Yes, he worked for Charles, but he acknowledged that. They both seemed like reasonable men who'd been trodden into the dust by Morgan's all-powerful boots. They couldn't stop her—and eventually she murdered the woman she despised.

Morgan had barely spoken a word to Kenzi. She passively allowed the marshals to drag her back to her cell. For all that the witnesses talked about her indomitable fury, she seemed entirely beaten. Like she'd lost this trial and knew it. Like she was going to spend the rest of her life behind bars and had no way to stop it.

"We have to do something," Kenzi insisted. "Morgan is being railroaded. We have to stop this runaway train."

Everyone at the table peered at her with concern—Emma, Hailee, Sharon, and Miguel. She knew what they were thinking. If they hadn't had doubts about Morgan before, they did now. And if Morgan's own defense team was thinking that way, imagine what the jurors, who didn't know her and didn't work for her, must be thinking.

Miguel brought some fajita ingredients that he cooked up in the kitchen. His dinner not only tasted great but gave the whole apartment a mouthwatering aroma.

"These aren't ordinary fajitas," Miguel explained as he placed them on the table. "The corn tortillas are homemade and gluten-free. That stuff that looks like beef is seitan, grilled in lemon coconut oil, spiced with paprika and turmeric. Each bite will make your mouth water—and improve your memory."

"I better have a double helping," Hailee said, filling her plate. "I have a civics test tomorrow."

"And I brought java." Miguel hoisted a cardboard coffee server onto the table. "Pike Place latte no froth almond milk hint of lemon mocha double-whip shaken but not stirred. The best."

Emma poured a cup, smiling. "You know, I never realized that what this team lacked was a culinary expert. But it seems obvious now. If I haven't mentioned it before, Miguel—I'm glad you've joined us."

Hailee raised a large bulletin board. "I've updated my murder graph."

Miguel winced. "She's...what?"

Kenzi explained. "Like on TV. Photos and news clippings relating to the case. With yarn indicating the connections."

"I had to make a lot of adjustments after Charles and Brent testified. I'm not sure it all makes sense anymore."

"Amen to that," Sharon said. "There's so much going on in

this case I can't keep it straight in my head. Every witness has a different story."

Hailee cleared her throat. "I also dug up some information about tracking devices."

Kenzi waved it away. "Stop already. We can't do that. Totally unethical."

Hailee did not appear pleased. Emma made a point of admiring her board.

"Hey, I have more to offer than food," Miguel said, gesticulating with the prongs in his right hand. "Let's talk about this cluster-drama we call a case. I still haven't found that backdoor, but right now, that's the least thing troubling me. Charles is the CEO. He's the boss. Morgan writes code. According to him, she treats Sally like their pet. Despised her and treated her poorly. But she's also the one who quietly gave Sally a bunch of money. I mean—I'm confused."

"You're not the only one," Sharon said. "I mean, I had a dog once and I loved that little pooch. But I wouldn't give him a million bucks."

Emma peered at her. "You don't have a million bucks."

"Details, details. The point is, even if I had it, I wouldn't give it to a dog. Or someone I treated like a dog."

"Brent suggested it was blackmail," Emma noted.

"For what?"

"He didn't get to that."

"When I first met them in the office," Kenzi said, "I detected nothing but love. If Sally was having financial difficulties, maybe Morgan gave her the money out of love."

"That makes more sense," Sharon echoed. "Sally was too smart to be anyone's puppy dog."

Kenzi helped herself to another fajita. "Sadly, I don't think intelligence necessarily guarantees people don't make poor choices." She was thinking about her ex-husband, of course. And she'd rather think about almost anything other than her ex-husband.

"I feel we've wandered off from the point I was trying to make," Miguel said.

Sharon smiled. "Got to be more forceful if you want to stay in this conversation."

"Or maybe I just need to throw a few dictionaries."

Sharon went eye-to-eye with him. "Are you threatening me?"

He glared right back. "Only if necessary."

"I'm supposed to be scared by a guy whose hair looks like he stepped out of *Calvin and Hobbes*?"

A tense moment. And then they both burst out laughing. Sharon tumbled into his arms, laughing. "We bad. We both so bad."

"Yeah." Miguel wiped water from his eyes. "Terrible."

A few moments later, Miguel propped himself up against the table. "As I was saying, I don't buy any of that last-day testimony, but I especially don't buy what Charles was peddling. I know the man. I know how hands-on he is. If there was a control freak in that relationship, it was him, not his little computer-nerd wifey. If anyone was going to have a secret offshore banking account, I'd bet on him. Ever since he sold Face2Face, there have been rumors that he skimmed millions off the top."

"He'd have to put it somewhere," Kenzi said.

"Agreed. I've started digging around in the corporate financial records."

"Have you found anything?"

"Not yet. But if I do, you'll be the first to know. I don't think Charles would be stupid enough to use his office computer for online banking, so the records Emma swiped won't help. But I'll scan the paper records for signs of a suspicious transfer."

Kenzi clutched his arm. "That would break the case wide open."

"I know. I'll keep looking. Every spare moment." He paused. "I mean, after I finish eating. A man has to keep his strength up."

Hailee wheeled beside Miguel. "Speaking of invaluable

assistance, I checked out that stuff you were saying about DNA. Turns out, you were right. I found some scientific articles on chimerism and gave them to Mom." She glanced up. "Are you going to use them?"

"Do I have a choice? You did great work, honey. In fact, I'm going to lead with it." Because I have nothing else...

Hailee beamed. "Do you have a DNA expert?"

"I thought it would be more effective to recall the prosecution expert." Meaning: no, I don't have my own expert.

Hailee leaned into Emma. "My mom is so cool."

Emma smiled. "She's the flash." She looked over at Kenzi. "Have you given any thought about what I said?"

She nodded. "I don't think we have any choice. We have to put Morgan on the stand."

"Virtually every experienced criminal attorney on earth would say otherwise."

"I don't care. The jury wants to hear her story. They'll be disappointed—and perhaps angry—if they don't. She says Charles and Brent's testimony was a tissue of lies. Probably coordinated lies. But how can we prove it? Sally's dead. The only one who can speak about Morgan's relationship with Sally, or her relationship with Brent and Charles, is Morgan herself."

"I don't disagree," Emma said. "But there are major risks."

"I know. Harrington is an excellent cross-examiner. He'll go for the jugular."

"And I don't know how well Morgan will hold up."

"She's strong. Stronger than she looks."

"She's a computer programmer. She's spent half her life staring at her screen. She's socially awkward. And she suffers from a serious neurological disability. What happens if she starts talking about killer clowns? Or when the jurors don't see the tears and remorse they expect? We also have to worry about the media hovering over this case. They get judgy if they don't see stereotypical emotional reactions."

"Dingo ate my baby," Miguel murmured.

"Exactly. The cameras hate a woman who can control her emotions."

Kenzi laid down her fork. She'd thought this through a dozen times. But at the end of the day, she didn't feel she had any choice. "I know this is a suboptimal scenario. But I still think we have to call her."

"Harrington will open his cross with those nude photos."

"Seems like his style. I'll beat him to the punch. Have her explain the situation during direct." She paused. "Everyone has made mistakes. Jurors can relate. Might even make her more sympathetic."

Sharon pulled out her phone. "I got a text from Kate."

Kenzi arched an eyebrow. "Kate?"

"Kate Corrigan. The cop? The one I met at the crime scene."

"And she's...sending you texts?"

"About the case."

"A police officer is sharing information with a member of the defense team."

Sharon shrugged. "We've met a few times. Just to talk about it."

"Over drinks? Dinner?"

Sharon looked up abruptly. "And your point is?"

Kenzi raised her hands. "Stay cool. We need all the help we can get if we hope to lead the jury to a not-guilty verdict."

"There is...one other possibility," Emma said cautiously. "One we haven't discussed yet."

"And that would be?"

"Change her plea. Not guilty by reason of insanity."

Miguel whistled. The rest looked from one end of the table to the other.

"We're not doing that," Kenzi said. "Morgan may be atypical but she's not insane. And she's not guilty."

"But it might be the strategic play."

"Morgan would never go along."

"She might. If you told her she should."

"I don't want to throw those dice." She didn't have to be a criminal law expert to know how thorny and complicated the insanity defense could be. The M'Naghten rule dated back to 1840s England. The initial idea was a good one—don't punish people who are mentally incapable of controlling their actions. It allowed defendants to plead insanity if their mental state was so impaired that they either didn't understand the nature of the criminal act or didn't understand that what they were doing was morally wrong. But making those determinations was problematic. And even if defendants suffered from mental illnesses, they couldn't use the defense if they understood their acts were against the law. Modern behavioral science suggested that many defendants cannot control their impulses to commit certain acts even though they know they're illegal.

"To make that work," Kenzi continued, "we'd have to prove Morgan was insane when she committed the murder. That she didn't actually commit. And even then, what would she gain?"

"A ticket to a state mental hospital," Emma replied. "Horrible, but probably better than prison."

"Except a prison sentence has an end date. There's no predetermined end to hospital commitment. In this state, getting out requires a determination that the inmate is cured. And the prosecution can demand a jury trial on the subject. So having first proved she's crazy, we'd later have to prove she's sane. No longer a threat to society."

Emma shrugged. "I'd rather be in the nuthouse than in prison."

"I think Morgan would disagree. She won't go for it. And I'm not going to recommend it."

Emma drew in a deep breath. "Kenzi, you need to give this more thought. You can't bear the thought of an insanity plea because you believe that Morgan is innocent. But everyone else is...not entirely sure."

"Are you saying you think Morgan is guilty?"

"I don't know what happened. But I'm not so naïve as to

believe that if I like someone they're not capable of doing horrible things. We're all capable of doing horrible things, given the right circumstances."

"Morgan did not murder Sally."

Emma's face hardened. "Kenzi, please forgive me, but—grow up. This is not a matter of honor. It's not a search for the truth. It's a battle against government forces with incredible advantages. Whether you like it or not, you must do what's best for your client. And at this moment, the best strategy might be to cop an insanity plea."

"Because you think Morgan is guilty."

Emma dodged the question. "Because the jury does. And I'm not sure we can turn that around. Harrington has put on a good case. And you yourself have said we don't have much defense. Maybe we have to suck it up and do something we don't want to do—for Morgan's sake."

Kenzi slowly rose to her feet, peering down at everyone. "Let me make one thing perfectly clear. We are not going to throw in the towel. And we are not going to throw Morgan under the bus."

"Kenzi...you have to be realistic."

"What I have to be is a good lawyer. And a good friend, which should be the same thing. Morgan is not guilty and I'm not going to ask her to pretend to be crazy."

"Kenzi..."

"This is what always happens to women. First men take credit for their ideas. Like Charles did. Then they take most of the money. Like Charles did. Then once the men have taken everything they can, they get rid of her. I refuse to give into it. Pleading guilty would be another way of perpetuating an ugly pattern that has gone on far too long."

"Kenzi, listen—"

"No, you listen to me. We have a responsibility to Morgan. We're going to honor our commitment. We will not allow men to push her into oblivion. The line must be drawn. And I'm drawing it right here and now."

She leaned in, looking at each of them in turn. "We will fight for Morgan. We will defend her to our last breath. And somehow, we will find a way to win."

38

Kenzi decided to livestream during her walk to work. She didn't want her following to think she'd dropped off the grid. She knew many would be eager to hear what she had in store for the first day of the defense case.

"Hello, KenziKlan. This is going to be a busy day for me, but that doesn't mean I can't find time for my Klan. You are the wind beneath my wings, the people I know I can count on for support. I very much appreciate you."

She turned a corner and strode toward the courtroom. "I think most of you already know about my current case, and you probably know that today the defense goes into high gear. I won't talk about the details, because I don't want to appear to be trying to influence the jury. But I will say this much. I believe in my client. Good people need to stick together, especially when times get tough. Don't judge. Don't condemn others because they make a mistake or have a problem. The true mark of a community is how well we take care of one another. When times get tough, that's when people need your love—not your condemnation."

KENZI WAS SURPRISED to see how many familiar faces were still in the courtroom. Dr. Quinn was present. Brent and Charles were lingering about, no big surprise. Harvey Vasquez. And Peter Taylor, the cheaters' app CEO. She had briefly considered calling him to establish that Morgan had not been trolling for a sex partner or uploading nude photos of herself. But the less said about the pics, the better.

And that's the wonderful world I live in now, Kenzi thought. Every witness I might call could potentially do Morgan more harm than good.

Leaving her with next to nothing.

She only spotted one major change in the gallery. Gabriel wasn't here anymore.

But her father had taken his spot.

"Morning, *Papi*. Are you lost? Divorce court is two floors up."

"I think you're the one who's lost." He smiled. "I wanted to see how my little girl is faring."

"You wanted to spy on me."

"Monitoring the firm's lawyers is part of my job."

"I thought Gabe was the managing partner now."

He smiled but didn't take the bait. "Saw Lou Crozier this morning. His settlement offer is still on the table."

That wasn't all Crozier wanted. "My client turned it down."

"I hear this murder case could go to the jury today. If she's convicted, you'll lose your ability to negotiate the divorce settlement. You should take that offer while you can."

She decided to remain polite. Rather than say what she was thinking. "My client says no."

"She would say yes if you explained it to her properly."

She looked straight back at him. "That isn't going to happen."

He frowned but didn't pursue it. "Crozier also seemed to be hinting that you might leave my firm."

Now he was getting to it. "The only thing on my mind right now is this trial."

"Before, you told me you were planning a hostile takeover of my firm."

"Did that worry you?"

"No. I thought it was kind of exciting. That's the Kenzi I've always known and loved."

"Though not enough to make her the managing partner."

"I did what was best for my firm. And my family."

That stung. But she wouldn't let it show. "I haven't made any decisions yet."

"You know, both my firm and Crozier's are essentially divorce shops. If you continue dabbling in criminal law..."

"We might increase our client base?"

He sighed. "You might send the wrong message. Project the wrong image."

"You want to be the ivory tower firm. Only blue-chip clients. No mucking around with real people."

"You can act that way if you want, but the truth is, the so-called 'real people' are exactly what I've worked all my life to avoid. Bigots. Thieves. Losers. I built a successful business so my children could run it after my time passes. So you can live without rubbing shoulders with the worst elements of society."

"I kinda like the real people. And I need to get to work. Good seeing you. Must dash."

Harrington was waiting for her as she strode down the aisle. Had he finally decided she was worthy of a chat?

He flashed ten fingers at her twice. "Twenty years. Cut and dried. Then we can go home and enjoy the weekend."

"Twenty years? That's like your dream verdict. If every single juror buys every single word you say."

"Not true. We could get life."

"Which you and I both know does not actually mean life."

"But it could mean more than twenty years."

"Maybe."

He shrugged. "You want to roll the dice and hope you get boxcars, fine. But I'm giving you a respectable exit strategy. A generous one, honestly, given how well this trial has gone for me."

Kenzi played tough. "This trial hasn't gone nearly as well for you as you think." She didn't believe that, but maybe if she said it loudly enough she could scare him. You can't negotiate if you don't hold any cards. "And twenty years is not generous. It's my worst-case scenario. Give me ten and I'll take it back to my client."

"No can do. And you will take every offer back to your client, because the Code of Professional Conduct requires you to do so."

Yeah, yeah, yeah. "She won't take twenty years."

He lowered his voice "Look, you may not know this, because you're really a divorce lawyer, but with a twenty-year sentence... she could be out in fewer than fourteen."

Thank you, Almighty Criminal Law Expert. "I was aware—"

"And for that matter, she could be sent to the most comfortable, high-society, country-club prison in the country. She fits the profile."

Kenzi arched an eyebrow. "Meaning?"

"She's wealthy. Money to burn, apparently. And she's..." He shrugged. "You know."

"I don't."

He lowered his voice. "White. Or whitish."

"She's Latinx. Like me."

"Light brown. Close enough."

She felt her stomach churn. "I'll take the offer to my client."

"You know," Harrington added, "there's a benefit bar association golf tournament this weekend. Are you playing?"

Was he kidding? "No. I never understood the appeal of knocking a little ball around a field."

"Then spend the weekend with your daughter. Point is, the weekend would be a lot more fun if we put this trial to bed first."

"Fear not. I'm only calling a few witnesses."

He grinned. "Don't have much to say?"

She maintained a stony demeanor. "I prioritize quality over quantity. You don't need a bucket-load of witnesses when each one is devastating."

She pivoted on one heel and headed for her table. Okay, she may have overstated the quality of her defense. But she wanted him to have something to worry about other than his golf handicap.

She leaned in close to Morgan. "The DA has offered—"

"Rejected."

That didn't require much deliberation. "Do you want to hear the offer first?"

"Does it involve me pleading guilty?"

"Of course."

"Then I don't need to hear it. Rejected."

———

FOR HER FIRST WITNESS, Kenzi recalled Dr. Frederick Bonneville back to the witness stand. The jury already knew who this guy was, so she didn't waste any time. "You testified that you found two sets of DNA beneath the victim's fingernails, correct?"

"That is true."

"And you haven't identified the second set of DNA. The one that isn't attributable to my client."

"Also true. The source of that DNA apparently does not have a criminal record. I haven't been able to match it."

"Maybe you should be looking closer to home." She paused. "How do you account for the differing DNA donors?"

"Apparently the victim came into contact with two different people."

"Are there any other possibilities?"

Now he was wary. "I don't know what you mean."

"Would you please explain the concept of chimerism?"

A suspicious smile crossed his face. Before, he must've

wondered why he'd been dragged back to court. Now he knew. "Is that what you're going for?" He chuckled softly. "Chimerism refers to the extremely rare situation in which a living creature possesses more than one set of DNA."

"Which, just to be clear, actually happens."

"In extremely rare circumstances."

"Such as when a bone marrow transplant has occurred."

"That is correct. But this has only been seen in humans in a few extremely—"

"Are you aware that one of the principals in this case has received a bone marrow transplant?"

He stopped short. "Umm...no. Why?"

"The person in question had leukemia. Which, thanks to the transplant, is now completely in remission."

"I'm glad to hear it. Who would that be?"

"Charles Land. My client's husband. The man who should be one of the primary suspects in this case, and would've been if the police hadn't immediately decided to go after the wife before they'd even begun to investigate."

"Objection," Harrington said. "This is an obvious attempt to divert suspicion from the defendant to a third party."

The judge tilted his head. "And that's an objection? That's more like a description of cross-examination. Overruled."

Bonneville looked embarrassed. "I did not know Land received a transplant. I was never asked to review his files."

"Then you also don't know who he got the bone marrow from, right?"

She could almost see a light bulb forming over his head. "It... usually comes from a close family member..."

"It came from his wife. My client. Morgan Moreno."

Bonneville said nothing.

"It is entirely possible, given the facts of forensic science, that Charles Land could be carrying two sets of DNA. The DNA he was born with, and the DNA of his wife. Right?"

Harrington looked supremely uncomfortable. "I have no reason to believe or suspect—"

"Is it possible?"

He blew out a lungful of air. "It is possible."

"And that means the DNA sample you found under Sally's fingernails didn't necessarily come from my client. It could have come from Charles Land. All of it."

"I don't—"

"Is it possible?"

Bonneville's shoulders sagged. "It is...remotely possible."

"Thank you. No more questions."

39

During the break, Kenzi met Sharon in the back of the courtroom. She was standing beside a tall woman with long blonde hair and a corduroy jacket. Something about her screamed cop.

"You must be Kate Corrigan."

Kate took her hand. "Guilty as charged."

"Sharon has told me all about you."

"All?" She arched an eyebrow, then glanced at Sharon. "Interesting."

Sharon seemed a bit nervous. "We kinda bonded over *Law and Order*. And popsicle juice."

Kenzi blinked. "Did I...miss something?"

Kate answered. "I found something at the crime scene that looked and tasted like popsicle juice. But I had a hard time imagining someone walking around with a popsicle on a cold Seattle night. Turned out it was fruit juice. Pineapple, to be specific."

"Okay. So?"

"The next morning when I went to work, I saw Charles Land in the chief's office. Holding a plastic bottle of Naked fruit juice. You know, that supposedly healthy stuff that tastes like what juice would taste like if you took out everything that makes it good? He apparently drinks Naked every day. Morning and evening. And his favorite flavor? Pineapple."

"And you thought that might be what you found in the alley?"

"There's no way of proving it. But those bottles do tend to perspire, and it's easy to spill a little on your hands. It could end up on anything you touch. I certainly thought it deserved more investigation. But the chief wouldn't let me. Transferred me to another case." She paused. "So of course, I continued looking into it during my free time."

"I appreciate your willingness to help the defense. However... strange that seems."

"I just want to see the case solved," Kate explained. "Correctly."

"Aren't you concerned about Harrington seeing you talking to us?"

"Nah. He knows I'm a renegade. And I don't work for him."

"He talks to your boss like, every day."

"As long as I keep solving cases, the chief will leave me alone. Harrington needs us. Especially if he ever wants to be more than the district attorney."

Kenzi couldn't help but admire the woman's independent spirit. "You're helping us to make sure justice is done?"

Kate nodded. "And to help Sharon, of course."

Sharon laughed again, loud and unnecessarily. "We've become good friends during the past few weeks."

Kenzi's eyes narrowed. "Indeed."

"Isn't that wild?"

Kate jumped in, her voice as calm as ever. "We're dating."

"So I gathered." Kenzi looked at Sharon. "You didn't mention that part."

"Sometimes I surprise myself."

This was definitely something she wanted to explore. But not now. Back to Kate. "Would you be willing to testify?"

"Issue a subpoena. I have no choice, right?" Kate winked. For such an imposing woman, she had a super-cute wink.

"I don't want to deal with a hostile witness."

"You won't have to. Just get me on the stand and let me go to town. You won't be sorry."

———

KENZI COULD SEE Harrington was both confused and concerned when she called Kate Corrigan to the witness stand. Of course, that made it all the sweeter.

She fed the jury Kate's background, her years of experience, her success solving difficult cases, and her devotion to law and order. The concept, not the television program. She thought the jury was impressed. They were probably just as surprised to see a cop testifying for the defense as Harrington was.

She quickly covered the popsicle theory. Though interesting, she wasn't sure how convincing it was. The fact that Charles drank juice hardly proved he committed murder. She wanted the jury to think of him as a potential suspect, but if she over-reached, they might write off the whole theory as a desperate attempt to divert blame.

"Just to be clear, Detective Corrigan, have you been working on the Seattle Strangler case?"

"Yes, though of course, that's a name the press uses, not the police department. Only a few of the victims are known to have been strangled. We try to base our investigation on facts, not assumptions."

"Do you think Sally Beaumont was killed by the Strangler?"

"I can't rule out the possibility. But there were several differences between this murder and the others, enough to warrant investigation."

"Were you asked to conduct any such investigation?'

"No. I was removed from the case. There's a Canadian syndicate operating a sex trafficking ring in the Pacific Northwest and that has demanded a great deal of our attention. Apparently they were chased out of Florida and they're trying to establish roots here. And we have the usual homegrown crimes. Suffice to say, I haven't had trouble finding something to do."

"Were you happy about this reassignment?"

"Frankly, no. I thought the Beaumont case deserved more investigation than it received." Across the aisle, Harrington frowned. "There's no secret about this. I've said the same thing to my boss."

"Based upon your years of experience and expertise, what investigation do you believe needs to be conducted?"

"In any case of this nature, the first possible suspect the police consider is the spouse. I'm sure you already knew that. Especially true when the parties are in divorce court. What person trapped in that nightmare hasn't thought about killing their ex?" She laughed a bit. "But in this case, it's more complicated. Because the victim had two spouses."

Kenzi nodded. "But only my client was charged."

"Right. And that's what I didn't get. As far as I could tell, we had two primary suspects, both equally viable. I didn't find any evidence that clearly pointed one way or the other. Two women had a spat in court earlier that day—so what? Doesn't prove anything. But the district attorney sought an arrest warrant against Morgan Moreno almost immediately and had her arrested."

"The arrest warrant wasn't your idea?"

"Absolutely not. I asked my boss about it. The Chief of Police."

"What did he say?"

"He didn't say anything. But he handed me a file."

Kenzi lifted a folder containing photocopies of the documents in question. "What was in the file?"

"Receipts. Specifically, a record of the history of large donations made by Charles Land to various law enforcement funds. Police Officer's Retirement Fund. That sort of thing. And large donations made to Shel Harrington's election campaign."

Harrington looked supremely unhappy. But he kept his mouth closed.

"Anything more?"

"No. But that file spoke volumes. Charles had bought the favor of the powers that be. Morgan hadn't. So big surprise, Morgan was charged and Charles was never investigated. Even though..." She paused, as if choosing her words carefully. "Many people thought he should be."

Perfect. Kate had given the jury more reason to doubt Morgan's guilt, more reason to blame the prosecution for a biased investigation, and more reason to point the finger at Charles. "Thank you. No more questions."

40

During the break, Kenzi and her team huddled in the hallway outside the courtroom. Miguel paced around Hailee's chair, unable to stand still.

"Oh my God. Oh my God." He seemed beside himself. "I can't believe it. Charles is the guy. He did it. He *did* it!"

"We don't know that for sure..." Kenzi said.

"It's obvious! He bought the cops off!"

"I hope the jury agrees. What do you think, Emma?"

"I think you've definitely created room for suspicion. But I'm not sure there's more evidence against him than there is against Morgan."

"Are you kidding?" Miguel said. "Do I need to throw something at your head?"

Kenzi stepped between them. "That will not be necessary."

"Holy moley!" Miguel pressed his hands against his face. "I worked with the guy. I saw him every day. And he's a killer! Harrington should arrest him right now."

"He won't do that," Hailee said, like the all-knowing teenager she was. "That would be admitting a mistake. Admitting he tried to put the wrong person behind bars. His ego is too big to go there."

"I don't care how big his ego is. The facts are the facts. How else did that pineapple juice get in the alley? Do we think a Hawaiian tourist happened to stroll by that night? Charles is a killer."

"We don't know—"

"Some mornings, I brought Charles his daily Naked fix. And pineapple is his favorite flavor. I'm telling you, this is not a coincidence."

Hailee leaned sideways, a conspiratorial expression on her face. "You know, Mom, even if Harrington won't listen to reason..." She tossed her head to the left, where several reporters were gathered around a water fountain. "...there's always the court of public opinion."

"You're suggesting...?"

"Maybe a well-timed press conference?"

Kenzi deliberated for a moment. "No. If I start trying my case to the press, the judge will get angry. Odom has been mostly fair so far. I don't want to turn him against us."

"Kenzi." Miguel grabbed her by the arms. He was roughly three times her size so she felt as if she were being enveloped in a big bear blanket. "You have to do something. Charles is dangerous. Protect your client."

"I will, by putting on the best possible defense."

He appeared incredulous. "You're going to trust the jury to do the right thing?"

"That is how the system is supposed to work."

"Yeah, and tofu is supposed to be better than beef. But it isn't!"

"Hey," Hailee said. "I like tofu. What's—"

Kenzi spotted people returning to the courtroom. The judge's bailiff must have appeared. "Let's table this discussion for later."

At the defendant's table, she laid a hand gently on Morgan's shoulder. "You ready for this?"

She smiled slightly. "I know the drill. Emma is very thorough."

"But how do you feel?"

"Like some burrowing creature has eaten out my insides. Like I'm so sick I can't even be sick."

Kenzi nodded. At least she was honest. "It won't last forever."

Morgan gazed at the courtroom door. "But if I botch it—the prison sentence will last forever."

———

AS MORGAN TOOK THE STAND, Kenzi couldn't help but notice how eager the jury seemed, how carefully they watched Morgan's every move. Even though the conventional wisdom was that you didn't put your client on the stand if you could avoid it, she wondered if the legal community needed to rethink that tenet. This jury wanted to hear her explain away what they'd heard, convince them she hadn't perpetrated this horrible crime. If she didn't take the stand, there would be a gigantic hole in the story. They would have to make their best guess while feeling they didn't have all the pieces in the jigsaw puzzle.

Morgan settled into the witness chair. Her nervousness showed. Maybe that would humanize her. She seemed fragile, a far cry from the horrible human Charles portrayed. It was hard to imagine the woman currently sitting on the stand yelling at or dominating anyone. She hoped that would work in their favor.

She started by asking Morgan to describe Todd's syndrome in detail, emphasizing that though it was horrible, it did not affect Morgan's judgment, memory, or decision-making ability. Then she established Morgan's throuple without wasting time on aspects the jury already understood. "How long were the three of you in this relationship?"

"Just over twelve years, from the date we first moved in

together, me and Sally and Charles, to the date Charles filed for divorce."

"How would you describe those years?"

"Insanely happy? Deliriously joyful? They were the best years of my life, particularly the early ones. I tend to be a loner. Not the world's greatest social skills. Common in the computer world, I guess. I'd had some problems with relationships before. I mean, why else would I have dated Brent? Isn't he exactly the stereotype of every hideous ex-boyfriend on earth?"

Morgan glanced into the jury box. A couple of the women smiled.

"I mean," Morgan continued, "I just look at him and think, how could I ever have liked him? How did he con me into thinking he was a loving person? But I guess that's what courtship is. We spend a year pretending to be someone we're not. Because we're afraid of being alone."

More head-nodding from jurors. Maybe Kenzi was making too much of it, but she thought Morgan was connecting with some of them. And it only took one strong-willed advocate in the deliberation room to hang a jury.

"Speaking of Brent, he testified that you liked strangulation games. True?"

"Talk about kissing and telling. Like I said, worst ex ever." Someone somewhere laughed. "Here's the reality. He was into it, not me. Like I said, I'm on the shy side. I wasn't pushing or controlling. I just wanted to be with him. I didn't need complications. We did that strangulation thing exactly once."

"And the photos?"

"Also his idea. Granted, I went along with it. I wanted him to like me. And he promised he would never send them anywhere. They were just for him, just to remind himself how lucky he was to have me. That's what he said. I gave it my best effort. But it wasn't something I enjoyed."

She looked up abruptly, staring into the jury box. "But you know what? I did it. I'll own my own actions. I had a choice and

I made it. Not my best move, but I'll take responsibility for it. I'm an adult female sexual human being, and if I want to pose for erotic pics for private use, I have that right."

That was an unexpected turn. Kenzi wondered if that was something Emma cooked up in prep. Didn't matter. It seemed to play well.

"Brent also claimed he wasn't the one who released the photos to Taylor Petrie. Or hacked their computer records. Do you believe him?"

Morgan took a deep breath. "Look. I wasn't there. But I know this. Only two people had the photos. Him and me. I certainly didn't release them. And for the record, I never showed those pics to Sally. Why would I? They're so embarrassing. That was a part of my life I wanted to remain buried. Even if I had shown them to her, she wouldn't have had access to them. Sally didn't release them. Brent either did it himself or he gave them to someone who did." She paused. "Like maybe his new boss. Who actually had a motive for releasing them."

"Brent also suggested that there were some aspects of your past that you wanted buried. And that Sally might be blackmailing you."

Her eyes went into soft focus. "I've made mistakes. Who hasn't? But it sounded to me like he was implying I used to be a prostitute. That's a lie, another attempt to make me look like a tramp so people will find it easier to believe I'm a murderer. Slut-shame a woman and then you can blame her for anything. Everything." She leaned forward. "Yes, I've slept with some losers. Lots of nights I wish I could take back. But I never took money for it. Why would I? I've been supporting myself since I was sixteen. And I still am."

"Maybe this would be a good time to talk about your husband. Charles. Soon-to-be ex-husband. He made some negative comments about you. He suggested that you committed this murder."

"And he knows better."

"Excuse me?"

"Charles knows better than anyone how close Sally and I were. Did we ever have disagreements? Sure. But our love was the deepest imaginable. Even more profound than the relationship we had with Charles. I think he may have been a little jealous. At any rate, the idea that I would treat Sally poorly is preposterous. Did he identify a single witness? No. Surely someone saw me mistreating Sally, right? Treating her like a dog? Except guess what, no eyewitnesses, because it never happened. I wouldn't kill anyone. I couldn't do it if I wanted to. And I absolutely didn't want to kill Sally."

"Why would Charles lie?"

"He has an obvious interest in helping the cops convict me. He's been aiding them every step of the way."

"But why?"

"Isn't it obvious? We're in divorce court. The estate is huge. How much of that money do you think the divorce judge is going to give me if I'm convicted of murder? I'm not even sure it would be permitted. He stands to make hundreds of millions of dollars if I'm convicted."

"Is that the only explanation you can think of for his testimony?"

"Objection," Harrington said. "Calls for speculation."

"Disagree," Kenzi said. "Calls for her to tell the jury what she knows about one of the witnesses who testified against her. To confront his testimony. Which is her constitutional right."

The judge nodded. "I think this might be useful. Overruled. The witness may answer."

Morgan did. "You heard what Detective Corrigan said. Charles is a suspect. Or should be. The only reason he's not sitting at the defense table is that he spread a lot of money around the law enforcement world. And why did he do that? He's not particularly generous and he doesn't care anything about public service. It's almost as if he were setting the stage. Making sure the cops didn't go after him. When the time came."

She paused. "And Brent's testimony is just as unreliable. He's Charles' toady. If there's a puppy dog in this story, it's Brent."

Kenzi saw some heads nod in the jury box. Perhaps some felt she was finally closing the gaps, making an erratic and contradictory story coherent.

"While we're speaking about Charles, were there any other... unusual circumstances that occurred? Before or after he filed for divorce?"

"He's always been violent. He hit me on several occasions. Badly. Sally too. He blew up anytime I wouldn't give him what he wanted. Before he filed, I wouldn't agree to an unfair trial separation arrangement. And the next day, my dog was killed. With a garden trowel."

The jurors appeared riveted by her words.

"And then some disguised stalker threatened me on the street. Coincidence? I don't think so. Charles keeps trying to convince everyone that I'm an awful person. But he's the ruthless one. He's the one willing to do anything to achieve his ends. He baited me by telling me we were building a program called the Love Library—which would enlist the entire tech sector in a drive to provide laptops to underprivileged children all around the world. But he secretly shuttered that after he got me to work on a facial recognition program that was supposed to help family and friends reunite. Then he sold Face2Face to law enforcement —the last people on earth who need that kind of power. He knew I would fight him, so he sneaked around in secret and acted as if my opinion was of no importance." She took in a deep breath. "It's a continuing pattern for him. He sees women as obstacles. To be eliminated. One way or the other." Her eyes drifted to the jury box. "I wonder if he didn't see Sally the same way."

Kenzi paused, letting the jury drink that in. Even the densest juror would have no trouble understanding what she was implying.

"Let's talk about Sally for a moment. According to a cop, you took out a Craigslist ad encouraging someone to sneak up on Sally and sexually assault her. True?"

"Of course not!" Morgan's voice soared. "I would never—" She shook her head back and forth. Tears sprang to her eyes. "I loved Sally. Rape is the worst, most vile, disgusting thing men can do to women. No woman would ever cause that to happen to another woman. Certainly not one they loved."

"A prosecution witness said the payment came from your account."

"There is obviously something hinky about this bank account business. I don't have any offshore accounts. All my accounts are with First National, checking, savings, and trust. I have an investment account at E*Trade. That's it. I've turned over all my records. That prosecution witness admitted he couldn't prove I established or controlled that offshore account—because I didn't. I'm also not the one who paid all that money to Sally. Someone is framing me."

"You think the police have that ability?"

"I think the police are determined to convict me. But I doubt they have the resources to fake internet trails and disguise bank payments." She looked out into the gallery. "But Charles could. That's the sort of thing he does all the time. He has a huge staff of hackers who reshape the internet to his advantage. This would be duck soup for him."

Kenzi nodded. "We also need to talk about what happened in the courtroom, shortly before Sally's death."

Morgan's head hung lower. "I lost it. I admit it. I was so surprised by what Sally said. I realize now she was just trying to survive. Trying to make it through this impossible divorce. Nothing personal, but the way divorce is handled in this country is...disgusting. Takes a rough situation and makes it a thousand times worse. Sally was scared. At the time, I could only see how her words hurt me. So I exploded. Lost my temper. But that's what divorce court does to people, right?"

"Can you describe what happened in your own words?"

Morgan twisted awkwardly. "I confronted Sally, after the hearing ended. We got into a squabble. We even...slapped each other around a little." She sighed. "Maybe that's how she got my DNA under her fingernails, although your witness' suggestion that it came from Charles is...noteworthy. I still replay that scene in my mind, wishing I could turn back time and do it differently. I didn't know—I—I—" Her voice choked. "I didn't know that was the last time I would ever see Sally." She wiped a tear from her eye. "Yes, I texted her afterward. Like the cop who hacked my phone said. I wanted to see her and apologize. To reconcile." Her head dropped, as did her voice. "But I never got the chance."

Kenzi allowed a respectful silence before she proceeded. "Morgan, did you kill Sally?"

She looked up. "Absolutely not. I would never do that. I loved Sally with all my heart. More than I love myself. Much more."

"Thank you. No more questions."

41

K enzi tried to focus but, despite her best efforts, the afternoon passed in a rapid-fire blur she barely remembered afterward. Harrington cross-examined Morgan and predictably brought up her illness to discredit her. How can we believe anything that comes from a witness who sees flying cheese toast? And of course he brought up the nude photos, making them sound as lurid as possible. But he didn't dent the core story she told.

Kenzi had a vague recollection of Harrington delivering his closing, but all he did was repeat himself. He didn't even mention most of the evidence she put on during the defense case. Did he think it didn't matter? Did he have nothing to say in response? Or did he think it was smarter to continue drilling the same story into the jurors' heads without acknowledging the opposing arguments? Maybe he was right. He had far more experience with criminal work than Kenzi.

She delivered her closing. She had no choice. Emma didn't like to speak in public and, even though she preferred to let the evidence speak for itself, she knew the jury expected a big speech to wrap it all up with a bow. Her theme was consistent, if not relentless. Morgan did not commit this crime. Charles has a lot of explaining to do. And the only reason he's not on trial is that he has the Chief of Police in his pocket.

And then it was over. Judge Odom spent about an hour going over the jury instructions and explaining the deliberation procedure. He suggested that the jurors weren't going home any time before midnight, and this being Friday, if they wanted to enjoy their weekend...they shouldn't mess around.

Then the interminable waiting began. This didn't exist in family courts, where all trials were bench trials. Hanging around the courthouse for an unspecified period of time waiting for the jury to return was entirely different—and completely terrifying.

And if she was scared...she couldn't imagine how Morgan felt. Every second must be an eternity.

"Anything I can get you?" Morgan was hunched over the defense table, looking like a small child who'd been told to stand in the corner.

"A not-guilty verdict," she mumbled.

"I was thinking more like a cup of coffee. Or dinner?"

Morgan shook her head. "I couldn't keep it down."

"I wish I could buy a verdict for you at the snack shop. But it's not on the menu."

"You've done everything you can. Now we wait and see if it worked."

That was the miserable state of affairs, succinctly stated.

Several minutes passed before either spoke. Miguel and Hailee brought them some chips and sat beside them.

"You know what I miss most?" Morgan said, at last breaking the silence.

"You mean, since you've been locked up?"

"Even before. Gaming clubs."

"I'm not sure what you mean."

"I bet your daughter does."

"I do," Hailee said, grinning.

Morgan nodded. "She's super-cool, by the way. Takes after her mom. Lots of spirit. No, I mean shops where gamers get together and play tabletop games. You can do it over the internet these days, by Zoom or at Board Game Arena. But it isn't the same. The whole point of tabletop gaming is inter-acting with other people, looking them in the eye, having a good time. I was never very good at interacting with others. Always felt awkward. Couldn't stand parties. And dancing—" She grimaced. "Forget it. But I like games. I'm comfortable playing games."

"That's how you met Sally, isn't it?" And Charles, but she wasn't going to mention that. "Gaming?"

"Yes. Online gaming. But somehow...we got away from that. Got wrapped up in our adult lives. I suppose that's what happens, isn't it?"

Kenzi nodded. "Growing up sucks."

"Amen to that." She closed her eyes. "That's what I miss most. If I'm not convicted, I'm going downtown. Tonight. I know a place where people play Transforming Mars every Friday night in the back of a comic-book shop. Stays open all night. I don't think they'd recognize me. And I don't care if they do."

"I love that game!" Miguel said. "Do you play Scythe?"

"That's hardcore. And time-consuming. But excellent." Morgan sighed. "I know I should go home first. Pay the bills. Catch up on email. And I will. But..."

"No rush, girl," Miguel said. He looked at her intensely. "Have some fun first."

"Yeah. Transforming Mars it is."

Kenzi searched her memory. "I think Hailee tried to teach me that game. Not my thing."

"Why not?"

"If the game takes an hour to learn, I can imagine how long it takes to play."

"Valid point. You need patience."

"Always a valuable commodity."

"And faith. Faith is critical."

That part surprised her. "Do you have faith?"

"I do. Fortunately." Morgan smiled, then looked away. "At this point, that may be all I have left."

———

THE JURY RETURNED at seven minutes before midnight. Perhaps they didn't want to come back tomorrow? Kenzi wasn't sure if that was a good thing or bad. What would the jurors do if they felt pressed for time? Which direction would it go?

She had no idea. And no need to guess.

The bailiff collected the verdict, then passed it to the judge. He stared at it for a moment, making sure it was technically correct, then returned it to the bailiff. His face revealed nothing.

"The defendant will rise."

Morgan pushed herself out of her chair. Kenzi and Emma rose with her.

Some courts had done away with all this drama. Why not just announce the verdict the moment the jury returns? Why not put it in a text? Issue an email? But in this court, the judge preferred to go through the painful, excruciating motions.

She reached out and clasped Morgan's hand. On the other side, she saw Emma do the same thing.

The foreperson, a middle-aged Black woman they had briefly considered removing from the jury, read it out. "On the count of murder in the first degree, we find the defendant..."

Why did she pause? Why did they always pause?

"...not guilty."

Morgan collapsed into her arms. The courtroom was only half-filled, but the noise following the announcement seemed tumultuous. The judge pounded his gavel, though few noticed.

The jury found her not guilty on all charges. The judge thanked the jury for their service, advised them to avoid the media, and ran through the usual procedural rigmarole, but Kenzi didn't hear any of it until he got to the part where he said: "The defendant is free to go."

Morgan wrapped her arms around her and squeezed tightly. "Does that—does that mean what I think it does?"

"Indeed. You will not be spending the night in the lockup. Guess you can play that game tonight."

"Oh thank God. Oh thank God."

Sharon ran forward to join in the hugging, and Hailee followed close behind. Even Miguel joined in the action. Turned out that big man gave a mean bear hug. Tears streamed from Morgan's eyes.

She detected some emotion on Harrington's face, too. But not the good kind.

Kenzi strolled over and extended her hand.

"Come to gloat?" he asked, ignoring the hand.

"That would be unworthy. You put on a good case. The facts weren't on your side." She paused. "Because the woman you charged didn't commit the crime."

He made a snorting noise. "Bull. You buffaloed the jury into thinking the husband did it. Standard defense lawyer tactic. Has nothing to do with reality."

"I'm sorry you feel that way." She saw no point in arguing. This was probably a tough blow. He was an elected figure, after all, and a high-profile loss was not going to improve his chances of reelection.

"I got a call from Crozier," Harrington said. "He was very interested in this verdict."

No doubt. It was going to cost his client millions. And if it led to Charles being charged with murder, it would cost him everything.

"I can handle Crozier."

"Are you sure? He's a ruthless man."

"I can handle him." Especially since he seemed determined to hire her.

"I guess you have nothing to worry about then." He snorted again, then returned to his table.

That was disturbing.

Though not as disturbing as what awaited her at the defense table.

Charles was trying to talk to Morgan.

Sharon stepped between them, but Morgan nudged her aside. "It's okay."

"I don't see how anything good can come from this conversation," Sharon said.

Charles inched closer. "I just wanted to say...I'm glad it worked out this way." He smiled a little nervously. There was a strange tenderness in it Kenzi had not seen before. "I never thought you did it."

"Really?" Morgan said. "Sure sounded like you did when you were on the witness stand."

He shrugged. "That was what the lawyers wanted me to do. I was never comfortable with it."

Kenzi had to restrain Sharon. Her facial expression could be loosely translated as, Can I explode a nuclear device in this creep's mouth?

"I just wanted to say I'm sorry about all that's happened," Charles said. "And...you know. If you'd like to get together sometime, I'm willing. Maybe for coffee. Talk about business and...whatever."

Morgan leaned forward until she was right in his face. "Let me make this clear to you. We will not be going out for coffee. Because I don't want to ever see you again. You lied. You cheated. You did your best to put me behind bars for a crime I didn't commit. And you know why I think you did it?" She pressed her finger into his chest. "Because you want all the money, because you want all the company, and because you murdered Sally. I will not rest until I prove that. So don't get comfortable, you bastard. I'm coming for you."

42

Kenzi cracked open the champagne bottle, sending the cork rocketing toward the ceiling. She used a towel to mop up the spewing golden liquid. "Cheers!"

Hailee brought noisemakers. Emma threw confetti, though with a self-ironic, poker-faced "Hurrah." Sharon dished out plates and distributed pizza. Turned out everyone was famished. Despite how long they'd had to wait for a verdict, no one had eaten much.

Hailee decided that Sinatra's "I Get a Kick Out of You" was the most celebratory song she knew, so she put it on the record player.

Emma watched. "Vinyl?"

"Absolutely," Hailee enthused. "Vinyl is the best. Digital files are so cold. No edge."

"But they don't skip, scratch, jump, snap, crackle, or pop."

"If you have good equipment and take care of your records, that isn't a problem."

Emma laid a hand on her niece's shoulder. "You know what, Hailee? You are my kind of kid."

Kenzi distributed the champagne glasses.

Hailee cleared her throat. "You forgot someone."

"Yes. Because you're fourteen."

"It's just champagne. That doesn't even count as alcohol. It's more like a soft drink."

"Nonetheless."

"You're going to leave me out? After all I've done for this team? All the contributions I made to this fabulous victory."

"I am. Because I'm your mom." Kenzi settled into a chair. "And because I know Emma will slip you some as soon as my back is turned."

Her phone buzzed. "Excuse me. It's Miguel."

"Why isn't he celebrating with us?" Sharon asked.

"Said he had to get home." She raised the phone to her ear. "Yes?"

Miguel went straight to the point. "Kenzi, I'm worried."

Her brow creased. "About what?"

"Morgan."

"Miguel, she was completely exonerated—"

"I not worried about the law. I'm worried about Charles."

Kenzi waved for the others to come close. "Tell me what's going on."

"You saw that scene in the courtroom, right? Morgan practically threatened Charles. Promised to put him away for Sally's murder. And he knows Morgan well enough to take her threats seriously. I've been working with him for years and I know that look on his face. He's worried."

"So now you're worried."

"I'm worried he might decide to do something to Morgan before she has a chance to do something to him."

"Tonight? Surely he wouldn't—"

"May I remind you that this man murdered his other long-time lover? How hard would it be for him to kill this one too? For that matter, we still don't know who the Seattle Strangler is. Maybe it's Charles."

Kenzi felt her mouth going dry. Miguel sounded almost

hysterical. He might be making too much of too little. But he knew Charles much better than she did.

Miguel continued. "Do you know where Morgan is now?"

"Yeah. Remember, she said as soon as she got free she was going to this place for gamers. A comic-book shop. I guess they stay open late."

"Do you know where the shop is?"

Kenzi thought a moment. "I think she said it was near Columbia Center."

"Damn." He fell silent.

"What? What is it?"

After a few moments, he answered. "When I saw Charles leave the courthouse, I followed him. Saw him get into his car. Saw him headed toward Columbia Center."

Kenzi felt a catch in her throat. "You think he might—"

"Yeah. Exactly."

———

MORGAN SUPPOSED WALKING the dark streets of Seattle this late at night wasn't the smartest thing she'd ever done, but right now, she didn't care. It felt so good to be out, walking around, inhaling fresh—semi-fresh—air, not being hassled or watched.

Being free.

She'd promised herself a game or two and by God she was going to deliver on the promise. She deserved it. She'd earned it.

She was also anxious to be home. To sleep in her own bed. But that could wait. One thing at a time.

She'd never expected to win the trial. She liked Kenzi. She had faith in her. But the odds seemed hopelessly stacked and she knew someone was trying to frame her. Somehow Kenzi had managed to convince the jury of her innocence. Or at least convinced them there was room for doubt.

She turned left on Columbia. Only three more blocks and she'd be there. This was a lonely, deserted part of town, this time of night. But Seattle was reasonably well-lit and she wouldn't be here long. She'd always rather walk than drive. Cars were hassles in this city. Where to park, where to garage, where to find gas, yadda, yadda, yadda.

She stopped at the corner...

And heard footsteps behind her. In the distance. But definitely footsteps.

She whirled around and saw nothing. Except maybe...

Was there a blur in the distance? Like someone ducked into an alley?

Or did she imagine it? In this low lighting, it was difficult to be certain about anything.

She kept walking, but she kept listening, too. She took one step. Then another. Listening for the telltale swish of clothing, the tiniest footfall...

She stopped again. The swish continued.

She whirled again. For a brief moment, she saw the faintest glimmer of a silhouette. One that seemed familiar.

She started walking again. Much faster than before.

No doubt about it. Someone was following her.

———

KENZI PRACTICALLY POUNDED her fingers into the phone, but it made no difference. No one was picking up.

"Damn it, Morgan! Answer!"

Emma's face was stone-cold serious. "Why would she not answer her phone?"

"Who knows? Miguel couldn't get her, either. Maybe she's been behind bars so long she's forgotten that your phone is your most prized possession and you never let it out of your sight. Maybe she left it somewhere."

"Maybe someone took it from her."

Kenzi felt a chill. "Charles got super-close to her when they had their scene in the courtroom." She ran her hand through her side-shave. She was pacing, pointlessly burning energy, but she couldn't stop herself. "It makes sense. Too much sense. We should've seen this coming."

"Stop," Sharon said. "You're not a fortune teller."

"I should've seen this. He's not going to give her a chance to nail him. He's going to nail her first."

"Are you sure you don't know the address of this game shop?"

"I'm such an idiot. I didn't think to ask."

Sharon pivoted. "Hailee, what about you? You know the local gaming scene."

Hailee nodded. "Well enough to know there are a dozen different places she could be headed."

"Think Columbia Center. Any comic-book stores in that neighborhood?"

"Several."

Emma leaned across the table. The creases lining her forehead told the tale, even though she was obviously trying to contain her emotions. "Try harder, Hailee. We need to find her."

"Or Charles," Kenzi added. "One or the other."

Hailee wheeled closer to her mother. "I may have a better approach."

"Better than what? Approach to what?"

Hailee bit down on her lower lip. "You remember when I mentioned tracking devices? Repeatedly?"

"I remember I told you that was completely unacceptable and we weren't doing it."

"Well..." Her eyes darted downward.

Kenzi grabbed her daughter by the arms. "Stop messing around, Hailee. What have you done?"

Hailee rifled through her satchel. "I may have not... completely, utterly...followed your instructions to the letter."

"Spit it out. What are you saying?"

She pulled her hand from the satchel. She held a small black device that looked much like a car's electronic key. A red light on the front blinked. "I may have a way for us to find Morgan."

43

Morgan knew the most important survival skill was not panicking. But she couldn't help herself. She was being followed and she had a good idea who it was and she knew nothing good awaited her when he found her. She was miles from home, no one else was around, and she couldn't find her phone. She had no way to get help. Even if she called 911, the person dogging her footsteps could get to her much faster than the police.

So she ran.

She heard heavy footsteps pounding behind her. Someone was after her, keeping pace. And she knew what would happen when he caught her.

Why had she not seen this coming? She'd survived so much. And just when she thought she was safe—she wasn't.

Even without looking, she knew he was gaining on her. She couldn't outrun him.

Fine. If she couldn't outrace him, at least she could pick the place for the confrontation. She slowed to a halt under a dim streetlamp. She would stand and fight. She wasn't going to let this end with her running like a frightened bunny. Come what may, she would face him like the strong woman she was.

She might end up dead. But by God, she wasn't going to be bullied.

Barely five seconds later, he caught up to her. At first, her pursuer was nothing but a shadow. Perhaps she let her predispositions, her prejudices fool her. Confirmation bias was a dangerous thing when someone was trying to kill you...

Slowly, one small step at a time, he entered the light.

Morgan gaped. "But—but—I thought—"

"What difference does it make?" She tried to dodge, but he was too quick for her. He grabbed her by the throat and yanked her closer to him like a rag doll. "Either way, the result is the same. You're dead."

———

KENZI RODE SHOTGUN, trying to monitor three things at once—the road, Hailee's phone, and the tracking device. She was not a great multi-tasker. Divided attention rarely worked well for her. But she did what she had to do.

Sharon drove. Since she'd driven to Kenzi's apartment and parked on the street, her car was the most readily available means of transportation. Hailee stayed home because she didn't want to slow them down, but Emma sat in the back shouting directions. For a woman who normally remained completely taciturn, she was showing a lot of emotion tonight.

"Can't you drive any faster?" Emma's voice had a shrill edge.

Sharon looked tense. "Not without killing us before we arrive, no."

"Try."

"I'm calling 911," Kenzi said.

"And telling them what?" Sharon asked. "We don't even know where we're going."

"I'm calling anyway."

"I already called Kate," Sharon said. "I left my phone line open. She's tracking us."

"Not bad having a cop for a...what is she exactly?"

"Friend. Special friend."

"She said you were dating. You know, it's okay with me if—"

Sharon frowned. "Could we have this discussion another time?"

"Sure." Hailee had linked her phone to the tracking device so she could follow the target's progress on a map. The handheld device beeped if they took a wrong turn. "We're getting close."

"And what exactly are we going to do when we get there?" Emma asked. "Is anyone armed?"

Kenzi pulled a face. "You think I own a gun?"

"Given the company you keep these days, you should."

"I have a mean left hook."

"I hope so."

Sharon made a hard right. "I'll tear that liar apart limb by limb. Just give me half a chance."

"He might have a weapon."

"Maybe. But strangling has been his MO so far."

"Turn right!" Kenzi screamed. "Hard right!"

Sharon did as she was told, but so hard and fast it lifted her Prius up on two wheels. The rear tire skidded and screeched as she swerved, but she managed to stay off the sidewalk.

"I think I see her," Kenzi screamed. "At the end of the street. Under the lamp."

"On my way," Sharon muttered.

"Fast. If he sees us, he might make a run for it."

Sharon clenched the steering wheel so hard her knuckles turned white. "If he makes a run for it, I'll mow him down like roadkill."

———

MORGAN FOUGHT as hard as she could, but nothing worked. He was too strong for her.

What did she expect? He had done this many times. He was

a professional, if such a thing existed. She worked out and stayed in shape, but she could tell he had more strength in his hands than she had in her entire body. And he outweighed her by a significant margin.

And she was starting to see random geometric shapes swirling around her head. Would that be her last memory? Deadly delusions?

She tried to fight him, but he had her arms pinned. She struggled, but he held her fast.

"Why?" she managed to croak out. She barely had enough breath to speak.

"I think you know the answer. And if you don't yet—you will soon. Or would have."

"I—I—don't—"

"As soon as you got home and opened your inbox. I tried to hack into it, but you're too damn savvy, aren't you? So smart I'm going to have to kill you."

His fists tightened around her throat, literally squeezing the life out of her. She knew she couldn't last much longer. "Maybe we—maybe—"

"Don't waste my time offering a deal. I'm not an idiot. There's only one safe solution. And I'm taking it."

Behind them, she heard a squealing of tires. All at once a Prius—seriously, a Prius?—skidded to a stop on the street beside them.

"What the hell—?"

Kenzi leapt out of the passenger seat. "Give it up, you bastard."

"Not till I've finished my job." He squeezed even tighter.

Sharon came out of nowhere and tackled him. She hit him hard around the waist and knocked him to the pavement.

Morgan tumbled backward, grasping the lamp for support while drinking in huge gulps of air. Emma helped her stay steady.

"You're finished," Kenzi said. "I'm calling the cops."

"I'll be gone long before they arrive." He kicked Sharon away, then started running.

And managed to go about five feet before he ran into a tall blonde homicide detective.

"You're under arrest," Kate said, snapping cuffs around his wrists. "Attempted homicide."

"More than that," Morgan said, gasping for air. "He killed Sally. I'm certain of it. For that matter, I think he's the Seattle Strangler."

Kate's eyes bulged. "Seriously?"

Morgan nodded, leaning against the lamppost. "Don't look now, but you may be on the verge of a big promotion."

Kate shoved her perp against a brick wall. "Just so this man goes to prison. That's all I care about." She paused. "Though I wouldn't turn down a promotion."

Sharon smiled and, a moment later, wrapped her arms around Kate. "Thanks for coming."

"Anything for you, sweetheart."

Kenzi and Emma exchanged a look. "Yup. Definitely friends."

Kenzi hovered over the handcuffed assailant, now crouched on the pavement. He cowered, shielding his face. She knocked his hands away. "And you're going somewhere you will have no friends. Probably for the rest of your life."

He turned away, not answering.

"Bad enough you killed Sally. And pretended to be our friend. But you were just spying on us the whole time. I hope you rot behind bars." She grabbed his spiky hair and jerked his head up, forcing him to look at her. "You know what? You're a real bastard, Miguel."

44

Kenzi took a solid week off before she returned to the office. She spent lots of time with Hailee—who definitely deserved it. That meant Sharon got some time off too, which she apparently spent on a beach with her new paramour. And Emma took some time to... do whatever it was she did in her spare time. Honestly, even though Emma was her sister, she had no idea.

Of course, it was one thing to take a vacation from work. But if you took a vacation from social media, in the blink of an eye your following went from thirty thousand to zipporino. So she pulled out her phone and started streaming. It was a bit awkward at first. Had so much time passed that she'd forgotten how to do this? Surely not. After the first few minutes, she found herself falling back into the stream of things.

"...but fear not, KenziKlan. In time, everything settled down and worked out as it should. My innocent client was freed. The true murderer was apprehended. I'm sorry, I guess I'm supposed to say 'alleged murderer,' since he hasn't been convicted yet. But take my word for it, he's guilty, and he's not going to be in a position to sue me any time soon. Best of all, I think we've apprehended the Seattle Strangler, so that reign of terror can end as well. Stay calm and maybe even try going out again. The Kenzi-Klan has triumphed. And our city is a better place because of it."

She paused, put on a more serious expression, then continued. Maybe she could do more than just pat herself on the back. "I hope you're getting the same message out of this that I'm getting. It's time we all started being more tolerant. Of others. Of our differences. And it's time we stopped letting our preconceived prejudices prevent us from seeing clearly. This whole mess began, at least for me, when a client came into my office with a difficult divorce. Difficult because her marriage didn't look like other people's marriages. In its prime, it was strong and good and loving and brought them a lot of joy. But that didn't stop some from hurling shame on them. And it didn't stop lawyers from using that to their advantage."

She paused, thought for a moment, then continued. "My own prejudices, my blindness, prevented me from seeing who the true killer was even though it should have been completely obvious. But he didn't look the way we expect the bad guy to look. We suspect the spouse first, for any domestic crime. Or we hear about a string of murders and expect a brute, or a drug addict, or someone who's just craaaaaaaaaazy." She rolled her eyes dramatically. "So I missed what was right before my eyes. Sometimes even those who appear normal turn bad. Very bad. Desperation, does ugly things to people. I should've seen that."

She stopped walking, turned, and pointed directly toward her phone. "Don't let that happen to you. Don't go through life with blinders on. Don't hate people because of who they are or how they were born. And watch for telltale signs that the people around you are not what they seem. The signs are always there. But sometimes we get too busy to notice."

———

KENZI RESERVED one of the smaller conference rooms so they could all sit at a big table and thrash everything out. Morgan came, and Sharon and Emma followed. She even brought Hailee. She'd earned a spot at this table.

"The police are still gathering evidence against Miguel," she said, "but I know what they've learned so far, thanks to my connections with the district attorney and Sharon's...umm..."

"Law enforcement liaison," Sharon offered.

"Right. Her connections with law enforcement, especially the homicide detective she's shacking up with."

"Would you stop already?"

Kenzi grinned. "We know a fair amount about what happened. Here's a for-sure fact. Miguel was deep in debt. Mountains of debt. Millions."

"How did that happen? He didn't make that much at Digi-Dynamics."

"Which was the problem. He borrowed to invest—through an anonymous shell corporation—in the Love Library, which as you know Charles shuttered once Face2Face was marketable. The Love Library wasn't as charitable as Charles made it sound. He planned to sell laptops to the program at a significant profit. But when Face2Face took off, he let that outfit go bankrupt, sold the program for a huge sum, then used the defunct Love Library as a tax write-off. Morgan was unhappy, but she wasn't the only one. Miguel lost his shirt. He was not only in debt, he was in debt to the kind of people you don't want to be in debt to. If you know what I mean."

"Loan sharks?" Hailee asked.

"The mob," Sharon replied. "And each time he missed a payment the debt got larger. Until they started demanding immediate payment. Or else."

"With usurious interest spiraling daily and people threatening to rub him out if he didn't pay up, he needed money fast. That's how the whole Seattle Strangler bit began. He didn't do it because he was psychotic or misogynistic. At least not entirely because of that. He needed cash. He killed his first victim and a few others to throw the cops off the track, so they would assume they were dealing with a serial killer. But he wasn't killing all of them. He was strangling them into unconsciousness, then abducting them, then arranging to sell them to a Canadian sex-trafficking syndicate."

"I didn't think that sort of thing happened in Seattle," Sharon said.

"Sadly, it does. Kate mentioned it when she was on the witness stand, remember? Grab the girl, carry her across the border. They might stay there or get smuggled to the Middle East or Asia. Cartels adapt to survive in the modern world. Some now specialize in bank fraud, mostly online. Or credit card fraud. Which probably explains that incriminating payment from an offshore account that looked like it came from Morgan, even though it didn't."

"They were helping Miguel just enough to keep the money flowing..."

"But not enough to pay it off. Miguel had to keep supplying them with women." She paused. "And Sally found out."

"How?"

"We're not sure. Maybe she walked in on a meeting. Maybe she read an email that was meant for someone else. I think the divorce triggered it. Sally was scrutinizing financial files for the first time and she tripped onto something that put her on Miguel's trail. One way or the other, she knew, and Miguel knew she knew, and that meant she had to die, before she had a chance to tell someone. He was worried that Morgan might know too, so the sensible solution was to kill them both, but they were never together, and no one would believe the Strangler took both of them at different times by coincidence. So he made it look like Morgan murdered Sally. He dropped all the telltale clues the DA used to frame her. He's the one who planted the so-called rape ad, for instance, but he used his computing skills to make it look like it came from Morgan's computer and his mob allies hacked her credit card account. Charles helped Miguel, unintentionally, when he lied on the witness stand because he stood to make millions if Morgan was convicted. He got his lackey Brent to do the same."

"What about the pineapple juice? Where did that come from?"

"I can't be sure. But given Miguel's obsession with ice cream..."

Emma jumped in. "The first time I met him, he mentioned Dole Whip. Which of course is made with pineapple chunks and pineapple juice."

"And left residue on his fingers." Sharon slapped her hand against her forehead. "I was so close! Not popsicles. Ice cream!"

"Miguel did a good job of misdirection, but Charles and Brent's lies made it worse. They all led the police like dogs on leashes. And the DA is embarrassed."

"No one's apologized to me," Morgan muttered.

"And they never will," Kenzi replied. "What would happen to public trust if they openly admitted the true murderer baited them into accusing the wrong person?"

"Did Sally share what she learned with Morgan?"

"Of course she did. By email. But Morgan never saw it, because she was arrested for murder and I couldn't get bail. Miguel, closely monitoring Sally's internet activity, saw the email. He couldn't erase it—though he tried. He had access to the company mail server, but Morgan had super-protected her email account and he couldn't break in. He knew the email hit Morgan's inbox, so he had to make sure Morgan never saw it. If Morgan was convicted, he had no problem. But when she was set free, he had to act quickly. He stole her phone to prevent her from checking her email that way. And then he tried to kill her."

"How many women did Miguel actually kill?"

"The police are still trying to track down how many were killed and how many were smuggled across the border. But here's some good news—most of Miguel's victims from the last few months were still locked up in his basement. Apparently his mob boss thought the border was too hot and wanted him to wait until the trial ended before moving them. The cops found the women and set them free. Like that college soccer player? The jogger? The mail clerk? All alive and well."

"Thank God," Sharon muttered.

"Exactly. A silver lining to a hideous situation."

"If Miguel was the killer all along," Hailee said, "and he was planning to kill Morgan, why did he tell us Morgan was in danger?"

"So we would blame Charles when she turned up dead. Once again, Miguel was manipulating us. Urging us to draw the wrong conclusion. Remember how hard he tried to convince us Charles was guilty while we waited for the jury? All part of the setup. Why did he befriend us in the first place? He never produced the alleged backdoor to DigiDyanmics' files. He was just using us." She sighed. "And it probably would've worked, if not for my brilliant daughter." She beamed at Hailee. "What put you onto Miguel?"

Hailee leaned in. "When I ordered that tracking device—"

"That I told you not to get under any circumstances," her mother interjected.

"True..."

"But I forgive you."

"I would hope so."

"So you'll only be grounded for a month."

"Mother!"

"Proceed."

"I brought the tracker to the courthouse, thinking I was going to plant it on Charles. But shortly before Morgan took the stand, she made a remark about checking her email, and Miguel got a seriously concerned look on his face. Something about it didn't seem right. I don't know, I couldn't put it all together in my head. But it made me suspicious. And then when he declined to join us after the trial, I was doubly suspicious."

"And that's why you planted the tracker on him?"

"Attached it to his sneakers. I was so sly. I think maybe I

should be a pickpocket."

"Think again," Kenzi growled.

Morgan squeezed Hailee's hand. "I owe you my life."

"We're a team. Everyone contributed."

"True. But let me tell you—when you get to college, if you need help getting into med school—call me. Or if you want a job in the tech sector—call me. We could use a smart spunky thing like you."

Hailee's face lit up. "Really? Wow!"

"And that goes for everyone in this room. I mean, I don't think you should quit practicing law. That's where you're doing the most good. But if you ever need anything...you've got a friend for life. A seriously rich friend. So just call."

Sharon pumped a fist into the air. "Another triumph for Team Kenzi!"

Cheers circled the table. They hugged one another, screamed a little more, and bathed in smiles.

"Well," Morgan said, "I should leave and let you get back to work."

"Before you do," Kenzi said, "could I have a private word with you outside?"

Morgan grinned. "You re-thinking that flat fee?"

"Nah. But still."

The two stepped outside. Kenzi closed the conference room door behind them, then found a quiet corner where they could talk.

"How can I help you?" Morgan asked.

Kenzi gave her a piercing look, then plunged in. "I want you to understand that...I know."

Morgan blinked. "Know how grateful I am? Absolutely."

"No. I know that...you're the one."

"The one whose life you saved?"

"No." She threw back her shoulders, then continued. "I know you leaked those photos. You're as good a hacker as anyone alive. Even better than Miguel and his mob buddies. Brent told Sharon you were genius level. You hacked into Taylor Petrie and uploaded, then leaked, those explicit photos of yourself."

Her voice seemed thin and reedy. "Why would I do that?"

She ignored the question. "Charles wouldn't gain much from it. Most divorce judges would think he was a heel for doing it. Miguel wouldn't gain much from it. But you would. You had the skills and the motive. Making Charles look like the bad guy. If he would do something that low, what else might he do? It implicitly proved all your stories about him killing your dog and hiring a stalker—none of which appear to be true."

"You think I killed my own dog!"

Kenzi stared at her stone-faced.

"And did I stalk myself? Attack myself?"

"I have to point out that there were no witnesses to either event. And although I think Charles is a narcissistic ass...I have a hard time seeing him kill a dog. I don't think he has the strength." She paused. "But you do."

"Are you going to blame me for everything?"

"No. I blame myself. I should've seen it before. I may not have my sister's brains, but I think I have a better understanding of human nature. And you, you and your story, just didn't make sense. You're smart. You're a Ph.D.! And yet, even though you knew Brent had those photos, and you knew he was working for Charles, you did nothing to prevent him from leaking them?"

"How would I—"

"You're rich. You'd find a way. But you didn't." Her eyes narrowed. "You left that door open. So Charles could be your scapegoat."

"You must be—"

"Please don't lie. That's what hurts the most. After all we did for you—you still couldn't trust me with the truth."

A long silence ensued. Kenzi stared bullets into Morgan's brain. And then, all at once, Morgan's eyes widened and the words came tumbling out. "I was desperate. I was about to be cheated out of everything, everyone I loved and the fortune I helped build. And he sold my baby, my program, to the government! So I turned the tables. Made Charles look like the bad guy. I didn't care who saw those pictures. Hell, I like those pictures. I think I look damn hot in them. And if they helped me win the divorce, great." Her voice dropped. "Of course, at that time, I didn't know there was going to be a murder trial. I was just trying to survive. Is that so terrible?"

"I told you I needed the truth, the whole truth, and you promised you'd give it to me. But you didn't. You used me like a pawn and put my whole career on the line. What if the truth emerged and I'd been hauled before the Disciplinary Committee for promoting lies in court? I could lose my license. What would happen to Emma, or Sharon, or Hailee?"

"I—I'm sorry..."

Kenzi waved her hand in the air. "Too little. Too late."

"Are you going to tell the others?"

"What would that accomplish? If you can help Hailee at some point, only a bad mother would stop you. She's going to need friends. But I can't trust you. And I never will."

———

EMMA AND SHARON remained in the conference room.

"What do you think this private tête-à-tête is about?" Sharon asked.

"I don't know," Emma said, "but I saw something going on behind my sister's eyes. She's hiding something."

"Only fair, I suppose," Sharon said. "Because we're hiding something too."

Emma closed her eyes. "Yes. We are."

"She's been too busy to notice. So far. But now that life is quieting down, eventually she'll see it. Or someone will tell her."

"Agreed." Emma let out a long sigh. "Morgan Moreno wasn't the only familiar name on the leaked list of subscribers to Taylor Petrie."

45

Crozier sat in his private office opposite his Canadian business associate, Kingsley. Was that his first name or last? Or neither? Crozier didn't know. And he supposed, it didn't much matter. At least not to him. "Did you read the paper?"

Kingsley nodded. "Another triumph for your favorite attorney, Kenzi Rivera."

"'Favorite' is probably not the word I would use."

"You've offered her a lucrative job. Repeatedly."

"Because I know that if she were in my firm, I could control her. I could keep her so busy she'd never have time to notice... anything else."

"But she will. In time."

Crozier nodded. "Unless we keep her distracted."

Kingsley grimaced. "I can think of a better way to keep her distracted. Permanently."

"Not necessary. At least not yet. This whole mess is about to blow up into something much larger. Once the idiot cops stumble onto the truth. The part we want them to know. There's going to be a purge."

"Sooner would be better."

"Sooner is always better. But 'sometime soon' will be sufficient. We have everything in place. Everything and everyone."

"This is not the first time she's gotten in your way. And each time, she digs a bigger hole into your pocketbook."

"I'm still paying my bills on time, thanks."

"It's dangerous to—"

Crozier held up his hands. "Not yet. Let the process run its course."

"I can be patient. But not infinitely patient."

Crozier lifted his cigar from the ashtray and took a deep drag. "Kenzi Rivera has no idea what she's gotten herself involved in. And she won't. Until it's too late."

SNEAK PREVIEW

Sandy was desperate. He had to get this job done, and he needed her help to do it. But she was not cooperating and he couldn't wait any longer. This was life or death. If he couldn't get her in that chair, he would have to resort to...whatever was necessary. Otherwise, he was a dead man. Or worse than dead. With the people he had breathing down his neck, worse than dead was an all-too-real possibility.

He took a deep breath and wrapped his arms around her, hoping she wouldn't notice his hands were trembling. He leaned in close and nibbled on her neck.

"C'mon, baby, you know you want to."

Her reaction was somewhere between an eye roll and pursed-lip irritation. "I don't know that. I don't know that at all." She had two pots on the stovetop, one cooking the pasta, the other warming the sauce. "I'm busy."

"Dinner can wait."

"It really can't. The sauce will burn."

"Then turn off the heat."

She slapped her hands down on the kitchen counter. "Cool your jets, will you? I'm in the middle of something."

"It can wait." He leaned in closer, pulling her tight against him. His hands started to roam.

"Stop already! Have you not heard a word I've said?"

"My brain isn't working, baby. Another part has taken control."

"Ugh. You need to learn to improve your listening skills."

"Your body is talking. And I hear it loud and clear."

"Really? Are you hearing words of consent? Because there haven't been any." She whirled around and pushed him back. "What is it with you lately, anyway? It's like you want sex constantly. You never get enough."

He grinned. "That's 'cause my sweet-assed babe is such a hottie."

"Is that supposed to flatter me? Because it doesn't."

This was not going the way he wanted. The way he needed. He didn't have the option of playing the sensitive male who puts her desires first. And he didn't have the option of waiting until bedtime. Maybe it was a mistake to come to her apartment, but he assumed she'd be more comfortable on her own home turf. That move may have backfired. Today she had a strength she rarely exhibited at his mancave, at least during the brief time they'd known each other.

"Seems like you don't mind it too much. Once you get started."

She shook her head, eyes closed. "What women do to stroke male egos." She waved a wooden spatula at him. "Just let me finish dinner, okay? Then...maybe."

He grabbed her hand. "I need it now, baby. I can't stay here forever."

"Oh, I get it. Wham, bam, thank you, ma'am, and you're on the road. Maybe to the next woman on your list."

"It isn't like that. I just want you."

She turned back to the kitchen counter. "Fine. Have at it. You can thrust while I cook."

"Tempting. But it's gotta be over there. In the chair."

"And why is that? I thought you liked a little backdoor action."

"It's best that way. You sitting in my lap, straddling me. Totally in control. You're hot as hell."

"I'm plenty hot cooking, too." She started slicing the mushrooms.

"I do love watching that little butt of yours wiggle." He placed his hands on her hips. "You have the tiniest waist. Compact little body. You should be proud. Not an ounce of fat on you. You look way younger than you are. Fantastic package. Especially from behind."

"Especially from behind? Like, you prefer it when you can't see my face?"

Why was this going so wrong? He was saying and doing everything that had worked in the past. But when he really needed it, nothing seemed to please.

He glanced at himself in the mirror in the hallway. Is this what you've turned into? he asked himself. A sex fiend for profit? How did this happen? How did everything go so wrong?

And what would happen next?

"You're using me," she said, her shrill voice pulling him out of his reverie. "I don't believe anything you say any more. You treat me more like your private whore than a girlfriend. And I'm sick of it. Totally, completely sick of it. You're a user, and you—"

"Stop it."

"No, for once, you listen to me. You—"

He clapped his hands over his ears. "I don't have time or desire to hear—"

She dodged his arms and stepped behind him. "Stop blocking me out. You need to treat me like a human being, not a piece of meat. You need to—"

"Shut up! Shut. *Up!*" Without even thinking about it, he thrust his elbows back—and hit something solid. Followed by a sickening crunching sound.

He spun around, horrified. She clutched her nose with both

hands. Blood streamed from her nostrils. She stared at him, unblinking. She was just as stunned as he was.

"Oh my God. Oh my God." He reached out, an apologetic expression on his face. "Honey, I didn't mean—I didn't—"

She removed her hands, backing away. Her nose, still bleeding, looked as if it had been flattened.

"Honey, I'm so sorry. I didn't mean to hurt you. Let me help." He took a tentative step toward her.

Blood trickled from her mouth. She gasped for air. "Stay... away from me." She reached for the phone in her pocket. "I'm calling the police."

"Don't do that." He took a tentative step forward. "You can't do that."

"Watch me." Her mouth filled with blood. Her eyes seemed to have trouble focusing. She pulled out the phone but fumbled with it, unable to unlock the screen.

"Honey? Are you okay?"

Her knees buckled. She reached out to the nearest wall for support, but instead hit an etagere loaded with her insipid Precious Moments figurines. All at once, the shelves and everything on them came crashing down. She frantically flailed around, trying unsuccessfully to catch something. She lost her balance and tumbled backward. The back of her head hit the wall. She cried out in pain.

Did she have a concussion? He wasn't sure. He didn't think he'd hit her that hard, but now she seemed barely conscious. "Honey? You should sit down." Damn, damn, damn. He didn't need this. And he definitely did not need to be hauled off by the police.

She seemed to recover, at least a little. She brought the phone back to eye level. "Be...quiet." She punched the screen, and this time she managed to get to the phone app.

He'd tried to be patient, but this was her fault. First she wouldn't cooperate. Then she wanted to turn an accident into a prison sentence. With his record, even a minor arrest could take him off the streets for a long time. He couldn't afford that. If he failed today, nothing good would be waiting for him when he was released. For that matter, those people could probably eliminate him while he was behind bars.

"Look, just sit down for a moment, okay? I'll get something to stop the bleeding. Sit in the recliner."

She still wobbled a bit, lurching with each step. She made it to the chair, but as soon as she was situated, she dialed 911.

"What's the nature of your emergency?"

"No!" He jerked her up by her hair, pulling away a piece of scalp. Once she was more or less upright, he punched her hard, right in the kidneys. She buckled over, eyes wide, like she'd been hit by a speeding car. The phone clattered to the floor. She raised her hands, obviously trying to fend off the next blow.

"Why wouldn't you listen to me?"

His mind raced. What now? He wasn't going to get what he wanted. Worse, she'd become a liability. But if not her, who? It would take so long to set everything up again...

To his surprise, she started limping toward the kitchen. He didn't know what to do, but he couldn't let that happen. He grabbed her again by the back of her hair, yanking her hard toward him. He swung her around and she slammed into the wall, face first. Her nose bled even more. She was whirling like a renegade top, out of control, barely able to control her motions.

She'd been beaten before. He knew that. She could take a punch. But maybe not like this. He was much bigger and much stronger. She was powerless before him. He could do anything he wanted.

He never wanted this! But he could feel his options draining away...

She clutched her stomach. Had he broken a rib? She started struggling toward the door, so he punched her again, even harder. He felt the crunch. Yes, something bad was definitely happening in there...

She tumbled to her knees. He got down and gazed at her. Her eyes seemed glazed, as if she was barely at home.

You can't leave it like this, he told himself. You have to finish it.

He gripped her forcibly, one hand around her neck. She tried to squirm away, but didn't get anywhere. He pinned her down on her back, still grasping tightly. He leaned in, putting his full weight down on her throat, pinching off the airway. She raised her hands, trying to push him off. He ended that with another punch to the gut. And he kept on pinching.

He closed his eyes and squeezed. In just a few moments, it would be over...

Or so he thought. He was completely unprepared when he felt her fist hammer him between the legs.

The blow electrified him. His eyes ballooned. The pain in his groin burned. He felt sharp daggers of pain racing up and down his body.

Before he fully understood what had happened, she had squirmed out of his grasp.

Apparently she was not as wounded as he thought. Had she been faking? Misleading him into overconfidence?

If she got outside, in the hallway, someone might hear.

He pushed up to his feet, just in time to feel her fingernails scrape his face.

He screamed. His hand went to his cheek. Blood bubbled to the surface. He wiped it away, feeling the stickiness between his fingers.

Damn. This girl could fight.

"You son of a bitch!" she bellowed. "Did you think you were going to knock me unconscious and then have your way with me? You've got another think coming, asshole."

She wasn't going for the door. She was going for the knives. The wood block beside the oven that held five big ones. She grabbed the largest and swung it toward him. Serrated blade. Slightly bent, but that wouldn't make it any less effective.

She crouched like a tiger, knife at the ready, a fierce expression on her blood-streaked face. "You're not the first man to lay a hand on me." There was an unmistakable growl in her voice. "But you're gonna be the last."

Kenzi peered intently at the man on the witness stand. She did not delude herself into thinking her steely gaze would make him come clean...but then again, it never hurt to try.

Kenzi typically practiced in family court, where witnesses tended to be nervous and unaccustomed to being grilled by lawyers. But today she was in civil court representing the plaintiff in a high-dollar suit alleging breach of contract, medical malpractice, and intentional infliction of emotional distress. The man in the chair was Emil Anderson, the CEO of the Washington State Center for Reproductive Wellbeing, which despite the altruistic name, was a large and prosperous for-profit medical corporation.

"Do you know the plaintiff?" Kenzi asked.

Anderson sat up straight, a bit stiff. "I do. She came to my office seeking help conceiving a child."

"Why did she come to you?"

"Apparently she and her husband's efforts had been unsuccessful. They wanted to try in vitro fertilization."

"Could you please explain to the court what that is? Just in case there's some uncertainty about it."

Anderson pivoted around to face Judge Dugoni. The judge's facial expression suggested he already knew everything there was to know about this, but experience had taught Kenzi that it never hurt to make sure. Sometimes judges didn't have time to do as much prep as they would like. "Of course. In vitro fertilization is a complex, lengthy process in which an egg is extracted from a woman, fertilized in the clinic, then implanted in the woman's uterus."

"Does this always result in a pregnancy?"

"Not always. We have an eighty percent success rate. But this process is time-consuming and expensive. Your client had to undergo extensive hormone treatments so she could produce multiple eggs."

"But Julia did get pregnant, right?" Julia Battersby was Jenzi's client, the fair-haired woman sitting at plaintiff's table beside her husband, a stricken expression on her face.

"She did. And she delivered a child. Just as she had dreamed of doing."

"But you're aware of the...subsequent problem?"

"Yes. That's why we're here."

The third book in the Splitsville Legal Thriller series, *Shameless*, will be released March 23, 2022. Order it today!

ABOUT THE AUTHOR

William Bernhardt is the author of over fifty books, including *Splitsville (#1 National Bestseller)*, the historical novels *Challengers of the Dust* and *Nemesis*, two books of poetry, and the Red Sneaker books on writing. In addition, Bernhardt founded the Red Sneaker Writers Center to mentor aspiring authors. The Center hosts an annual conference (WriterCon), small-group seminars, a newsletter, and a bi-weekly podcast.

Bernhardt has received the Southern Writers Guild's Gold Medal Award, the Royden B. Davis Distinguished Author Award (University of Pennsylvania) and the H. Louise Cobb Distinguished Author Award (Oklahoma State), which is given "in recognition of an outstanding body of work that has profoundly influenced the way in which we understand ourselves and American society at large." In 2019, he received the Arrell Gibson Lifetime Achievement Award from the Oklahoma Center for the Book.

In addition Bernhardt has written plays, a musical (book and score), humor, children stories, biography, and puzzles. He has edited two anthologies (*Legal Briefs* and *Natural Suspect*) as fundraisers for The Nature Conservancy and the Children's Legal Defense Fund. In his spare time, he has enjoyed surfing, digging for dinosaurs, trekking through the Himalayas, paragliding, scuba diving, caving, zip-lining over the canopy of the Costa Rican rain forest, and jumping out of an airplane at 10,000 feet.

In 2017, when Bernhardt delivered the keynote address at the San Francisco Writers Conference, chairman Michael Larsen noted that in addition to penning novels, Bernhardt can "write a sonnet, play a sonata, plant a garden, try a lawsuit, teach a class, cook a gourmet meal, beat you at Scrabble, and work the *New York Times* crossword in under five minutes."

ALSO BY WILLIAM BERNHARDT

The Splitsville Legal Thrillers

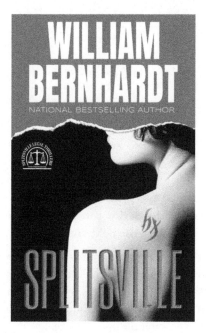

A struggling lawyer. A bitter custody battle. A deadly fire. This case could cost Kenzi her career—and her life.

When a desperate scientist begs for help getting her daughter back, Kenzi can't resist...even though this client is involved in Hexitel, a group she calls her religion but others call a cult. After her client is charged with murder, the ambitious attorney knows there is more at stake than a simple custody dispute.

Exposed (Book 2)

Shameless

The Daniel Pike Novels

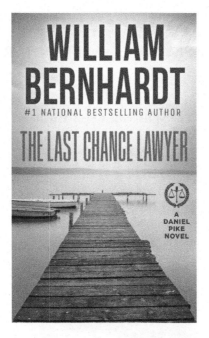

Getting his client off death row could save his career... or make him the next victim.

Daniel Pike would rather fight for justice than follow the rules. But when his courtroom career goes up in smoke, he fears his lifelong purpose is a lost cause. A mysterious job offer from a secretive boss gives him a second chance but lands him an impossible case with multiple lives at stake...

Dan uses every trick he knows in a high-stakes trial filled with unexpected revelations and breathtaking surprises.

Court of Killers (Book 2)

Trial by Blood (Book 3)

Twisted Justice (Book 4)

Judge and Jury (Book 5)

Final Verdict (Book 6)

The Ben Kincaid Novels

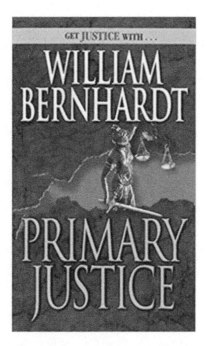

GET JUSTICE WITH . . .

WILLIAM BERNHARDT

PRIMARY JUSTICE

"[William] Bernhardt skillfully combines a cast of richly
drawn characters, multiple plots, a damning portrait of a big
law firm, and a climax that will take most readers by surprise."
—*Chicago Tribune*

Ben Kincaid wants to be a lawyer because he wants to do the right
thing. But once he leaves the D.A.'s office for a hotshot spot in Tulsa's
most prestigious law firm, Ben discovers that doing the right thing and
representing his clients' interests can be mutually exclusive.

Blind Justice (Book 2)

Deadly Justice (Book 3)

Perfect Justice (Book 4)

Cruel Justice (Book 5)

Naked Justice (Book 6)

Extreme Justice (Book 7)

Dark Justice (Book 8)

Silent Justice (Book 9)

Thinking Theme: The Heart of the Matter

What Writers Need to Know: Essential Topics

Dazzling Description: Painting the Perfect Picture

The Fundamentals of Fiction (video series)

Poetry

The White Bird

The Ocean's Edge

For Young Readers

Shine

Princess Alice and the Dreadful Dragon

Equal Justice: The Courage of Ada Sipuel

The Black Sentry

Edited by William Bernhardt

Legal Briefs: Short Stories by Today's Best Thriller Writers

Natural Suspect: A Collaborative Novel of Suspense

Made in the USA
Las Vegas, NV
19 September 2022